HORROR MOVIE

ALSO BY PAUL TREMBLAY

WILLIAM MORROW
An Imprint of HarperCollins*Publishers*

ROR
OVIE

A NOVEL

PAUL TREMBLAY

Grateful acknowledgment is made to Pile for permission to reprint an excerpt from "Away in a Rainbow!" (written by Rick Maguire), courtesy of Pile © 2010.

Andrei Tarkovsky quote from "Andrei Tarkovsky's Advice to Young Filmmakers: Sacrifice Yourself for Cinema," by Colin Marshall, openculture.com.

HarperCollins books may be purchased for educational, business, or sales pro-motional use. For information, please email the Special Markets Department at SPsales@harpercollins.com.

FIRST EDITION

Designed by Elina Cohen

Library of Congress Cataloging-in-Publication Data has been applied for.

ISBN 978-0-06-307001-1 (hardcover)
ISBN 978-0-06-338719-5 (international edition)

24 25 26 27 28 LBC 6 5 4 3 2

FOR LISA, COLE, AND EMMA

In Memoriam, Peter Straub

They should be prepared for the thought that cinema is a very difficult and serious art. It requires sacrificing of yourself. You should belong to it. It shouldn't belong to you.

—Andrei Tarkovsky

Mr. was born
in a cocoon.
He'll come out better.
He'll come out soon.
Or let's hope.

—Pile, "Away in a Rainbow!"

NOW:
THE PRODUCER

1

Our little movie that couldn't had a crew size that has become fluid in the retelling, magically growing in the years since Valentina uploaded the screenplay and three photo stills to various online message boards and three brief scenes to YouTube in 2008. Now that I live in Los Angeles (temporarily; please, I'm not a real monster) I can't tell you how many people tell me they know someone or are friends of a friend of a friend who was on-set. Our set.

Like now. I'm having coffee with one of the producers of the *Horror Movie* remake. Or is it a reboot? I'm not sure of the correct term for what it is they will be doing. Is it a *remake* if the original film, shot more than thirty years ago, was never screened? "Reboot" is probably the proper term but not with how it's applied around Hollywood.

Producer Guy's name is George. Maybe. I'm pretending to forget his name in retribution for our first meeting six months ago, which was over Zoom. While I was holed up in my small, stuffy apartment, he was outdoors, traipsing around a green space. He apologized for the sunglasses and his bouncing, sun-dappled phone image in that I-can-do-whatever-I-want way and explained he *just* had to get outside, get his steps in, because he'd been stuck in his office all morning and he would be there all afternoon. Translation:

I deign to speak to you, however you're not important enough to interrupt a planned walk. A total power play. I was tempted to hang up on him or pretend my computer screen froze, but I didn't. Yeah, I'm talking tougher than I am. I couldn't afford (in all applications of that word) to throw away any chance, as slim as it might be, to get the movie made. Within the winding course of our one-way discussion in which I was nothing but flotsam in the current of his river, he said he'd been looking for horror projects, as "horror is hot," but because everything happening in the real world was so grim, he and the studios wanted horror that was "uplifting and upbeat." His own raging waters were too loud for him to hear my derisive snort-laugh or see my eye-roll. I didn't think anything would ever come from that chat.

In the past five years I've had countless calls with studio executives and sycophantic producers who claimed to be serious about rebooting *Horror Movie* and wanting me on board in a variety of non-decision-making, low-pay capacities, which equated to their hoping I wouldn't shit on them or their overtures publicly, as I and my character inexplicably have a small but vociferous, or voracious, fan base. After being subjected to their performative enthusiasm, elevator pitches (Same movie but a horror-comedy! Same movie but with twentysomethings living in L.A. or San Francisco or Atlanta! Same movie but with an alien! Same movie but with time travel! Same movie but with hope!), and promises to work together, I'd never hear from them again.

But I did hear back from this producer guy. I asked my friend Sarah, an impossibly smart (unlike me) East Coast transplant (like me) screenwriter, what she knew about him and his company. She said he had shit taste, but he got movies made. Two for two.

Today, Producer-Guy George and I are in Culver City comparing the size of our grandes while sitting at an outdoor metal wicker table, the table wobbly because of an uneven leg, which I anchor in place with the toe of one sneakered foot. Now that we're in person, face-to-face, we are on more equal ground, if there is such a thing as equality. He's tan, wide-chested, wearing aviator sunglasses, a polo shirt, and comfortable shoes, and younger than I am by more than a decade. I'm dressed in my usual uniform; faded black jeans, a white T-shirt, and a world weariness that is both affect and age-earned.

He talks about the movie in character arcs and other empty buzzword story terms he gleaned from online listicles. Then we discuss what my role might be offscreen, my upcoming meeting with the director, and other stuff that could've been handled in email or a phone/Zoom call, but I had insisted on the in-person. Not sure why beyond the free coffee and to have something to do while I wait for preproduction to start. Maybe I wanted to show George my teeth.

As we're about to part ways, he says, "Hey, get this, I randomly found out that a friend of my cousin—a close cousin; we'd spent two weeks of every summer on Lake Winnipesaukee together from ages eight to eighteen—anyway, this friend of hers worked on *Horror Movie* with you. Isn't that wild?"

The absurd part is that I'm supposed to go along with his (and everyone else's) faked connection to and remembrance of a movie that has become fabled, become not real, when it was at one time decidedly, quantitatively real, and then the kicker is there's the social expectation that I will acknowledge our new shared bond. I get it. It's all make-believe, the business of make-believe, and it bleeds into the unreality of the entertainment ecosystem. Maybe it should be that way. Who am I to say otherwise? But I refuse to play along. That's my power play.

I ask, "Oh yeah, what's their name?"

I insist people cough up the name of whoever was supposedly on-set with me thirty years ago. I respect the person who at least gives one, putting their cards on the table so I can call their bluff. Unerringly, Industry Person X (now, there's a real monster; *watch out, it's Industry Person X, yargh blorgh!!!*) gets rattled and is affronted that I dare ask for a name they cannot produce.

The umbrella over our heads offers faulty, imperfect shade. Producer-Guy George's tan is suddenly less tan. He asks, "My cousin's name?"

"No." I'm patient. After all, with my ceremonial associate-producer title, he and I are going to be coworkers. "The name of your cousin's friend. The one who was on-set with me."

"Oh, ha, right. You know, she didn't tell me, and I forgot to ask." He waves his hands in the air, a forget-I-said-anything gesture. "Her friend was probably a grip or an extra and you wouldn't remember."

I lean across the tabletop, lifting my foot away from the leg's clawed foot. The table quakes. George's empty coffee cup jumps, then falls onto its side, and circles an imaginary drain, leaking drops of tepid brown liquid. He fumbles for the cup comically, but he's too ham-fisted for real comedy, which must always include pathos. He rights the cup, then leans in, sucked into the gravitational pull of my terrible smile, a smile that never made it on-camera once upon a time.

I say, "Your cousin didn't know anyone who was there, and let's not pretend otherwise."

He blinks behind his sunglasses. Even though I can't see his eyes I know that look. My power play is a form of mesmerism: calling out the liars as liars without having to use the word.

I break the spell by asking him if I can borrow ten bucks for parking because I don't have any cash on me, which may or may not be true. How to win friends and influence people, right?

Listen, I'm a nice person. I am. I'm honest, polite, giving when I can be, commiserative, and I'll give you the white T-shirt off my back if you need it. I can even tolerate being buried in bullshit; it comes with my fucked-up gig. But people lying about being on *Horror Movie*'s set gets to me. I'm sorry, but if you weren't there, you didn't earn the right to say you were. It's less narcissism on my part (though I can't guarantee there's not a piece of that in there; does a narcissist know if they are one?), and more my protecting the honor of everyone else's experience. Since I can't change anything that happened, it's all I can do.

Our movie did not feature a crew of hundreds, never mind tens, as in multiple tens. There weren't many of us then, and, yeah, there are a lot fewer of us still around now.

THEN: THE FIRST DAY

2

The first day of filming was June 9, 1993. I don't remember dates, generally, but I remember that one. Our director, Valentina Rojas, gathered cast and crew. Except for Dan Carroll, our director of photography and cameraman, who was somewhere in the yawning desert of his thirties, the rest of us were stupid young; early or mid-twenties. I mean "stupid" in the best and most envious ways now that I am over fifty. Valentina waited like a teacher for everyone to quiet down and settle into a half circle around her. After a bit of silence and some nervous giggles, Valentina gave a speech.

Valentina liked speeches. She was good at them. She showed off how smart she was, and you were left hoping some of her smartness rubbed off on you. I enjoyed the rhythm and lilt of her Rhode Island accent that slipped out, maybe purposefully. If she sounded full of herself, well, she was. Aggressively, unapologetically so. I admired the ethos—it was okay to be an egomaniac or an asshole or both if you were competent and weren't a fucking sellout. Back then, nothing was worse than a sellout in our book. Compromise was the enemy of integrity and art. She and I kept a running list of musical acts who rated as sellouts, eschewing the obvious U2, Metallica, and Red Hot Chili Peppers, which were givens, for subtler, more nuanced choices, and she'd include our local UMass–Amherst heroes, the Pixies, on her list just to piss off anyone eavesdropping on us.

I mention this now, in the beginning, as our passing collegiate friendship (I'm too superstitious or self-conscious, I can't remember which, to rate it as a full-fledged relationship) was why I was cast as the "Thin Kid." That and my obvious physical attributes, and a thirst for blood.

I know, the blood crack is a fucking awful joke. If that joke bothers you, I get it. Don't you worry, I hate me too. But listen, if I'm going to tell any of this, I must do it my way, otherwise I'd never get out of bed in the morning. No compromise.

With our small army gathered on the shoulder of a wide suburban dead-end road, Valentina reiterated the plan was to shoot the scenes in the film's chronological order, each scene building off the prior one until we made it to the inevitable end. Valentina said we had four weeks to get it all done, when she really meant five. No one corrected her.

I hung out in the back of the circle, vibrating with nervousness and a general sense of doom. Dan whispered to me, not unkindly, that Valentina's mom and dad wouldn't pay for week five. Dan was a short, wiry Black man, exacting but patient with us film newbies and nobodies. He co-owned the small but well-regarded production company that shot and produced commercials as well as the long-running Sunday-morning news magazine for the Providence ABC affiliate. I smiled and nodded at his joke, like I knew anything about the budget.

Valentina ended her spiel with "A movie is a collection of beautiful lies that somehow add up to being the truth, or a truth. In this case an ugly one. But the first spoken line in any movie is not a lie and is always the truest."

Valentina then asked Cleo if she had anything to add. Cleo stood with an armful of mini scripts for the scenes being shot that day. In filmmaking lingo, these mini scripts are referred to as "sides."

Mine was folded in the back pocket of my jeans. The night before had been my first opportunity to read the day's scenes.

Cleo had long red hair and fair skin. She was already in wardrobe and looked like the high schooler she would be playing, preparing to make a presentation in front of the class. Cleo couldn't look at anyone and spoke with her eyes pointed toward the pavement under our feet.

She said, "This movie is going to be a hard thing to do. Thank you for trusting us. Let's be good to each other, okay?"

HORROR MOVIE

Written by

Cleo Picane

EXT. SUBURBAN SIDE STREET - AFTERNOON

The street is a tunnel. Its walls are two-story homes on wooded lots. The interwoven, incestuous tree branches and green leaves hoard the sunlight and form the tunnel's ceiling.

That the houses are well kept and front lawns and shrubs groomed are the only visible signs of human occupancy. This suburban neighborhood is a ghost town -- no, it's a picturesque hell so many desperately strive for, and so few will escape.

Four late-high-school-aged TEENS walk down the middle of the road, one that sees little traffic. There are no yellow lines, no demarcated lanes, which offers the illusion of freedom.

VALENTINA (she's short, thick curly black hair spills out from under a knit beanie, eyeliner rings her downturned eyes, she walks heavily in chunky boots, wears black and gray baggy clothes, the baggiest of baggy clothes, her high school survival camouflage, she imagines the clothes make her if not invisible then ignorable to classmates).

CLEO (dresses like the rest of her classmates, which is a more effective high-school-survival camouflage than Valentina's, she has long red hair pushed off her forehead with a headband, wide-lensed glasses, jeans pegged at the ankles above her white high-top Chuck Taylors, a firetruck-red blazer over a horizontal black-and-white-striped top, Cleo does well in school and struggles with depression and she only leaves her bedroom for school or to hang out with her three friends). Cleo carries a crinkled grocery PAPER BAG.

KARSON (average build and height, slumped shoulders that might one day be broad, he wears overalls because he thinks they make him look taller, overall straps are clipped over a charcoal-gray sweatshirt ripped and frayed around the collar, his dark-brown hair is long in the front and his head is shaved on the sides and back, he has a nervous tic of running his hands through his bangs).

Valentina, Cleo, and Karson walk in a line, a breezy, step-for-step choreography. When no one else is around to see and judge them, they are rock stars.

The three teens don't talk, but they take turns knocking into the person next to them, then passing the hip-bump along while laughing and never breaking the formation. They are, in this moment, unbreakable. Their friendship is beyond language. Their friendship is a perpetual-motion engine. Their friendship is easy and gravid and intense and paranoid and jealous and needy and salvatory.

A fourth teen, the THIN KID, lags, languishes behind their line. He blurs in and out of our vision like a floaty in our eyes.

We do not, cannot, and will not clearly see the Thin Kid's face.

But we *almost* see him, and later, we will have a false memory of having seen his face.

That face will be built by what isn't seen, built from an amalgam of other faces, faces of people we know and people we've seen on television and movies and within crowds. Perhaps we'll imagine a kind face when it is more likely he has a face, to our enduring shame, that does not inspire our kindness.

There will be glimpses of the Thin Kid's jeans, the color too dark, too blue, and his long feet sheathed in sneakers that are cheap, generic, not cool within any subculture.

There will be a clear shot of his pale matchstick arms, slacken ropes spooling out from the billowing sail of a white T-shirt, logo-less, as though he hasn't earned the right to wear a brand.

There will be a blur of shaggy brown hair and his rangy profile in an out-of-focus blink.

The Thin Kid walks behind the three teens, out of step, out of time, working harder than they do, and he's walking faster than they are, but he will not overtake them, nor will he catch them.

Cleo looks over her shoulder, once, at the Thin Kid.

Her easy smile fades, and she clutches the paper bag more tightly.

EXT. DEAD-END STREET/FOREST LINE - MOMENTS LATER

The teens stop walking at the end of the dead-end street, at the mouth of an overgrown path into the WOODS.

A pair of TRAFFIC CONES and a rickety WOODEN HORSE block the entrance.

> KARSON
> (eyes only for the path)
> Are you sure this is the
> right way?

> VALENTINA
> (pushes sleeves over
> her angry hands)
> You're the one who said you
> used to ride your bike there
> and did laps around it until
> you popped a tire.

                         KARSON
                    (stammers)
              Well, yeah, but that was a long
              time ago, and I'm pretty sure
              I got there a different way.

Valentina curls around the cones and horse and onto the
path. Her sleeves accordion back over her hands.

                       VALENTINA
              This is the way we're going.

Karson shrugs, runs his hands through his hair, follows.

Cleo is next onto the path.

She pauses, reaches across the barrier, reaches for the
Thin Kid's hand.

We see him from behind. We do not see his face. We do not
see his expression. We cannot know what he is thinking, but
maybe we can guess.

The Thin Kid stuffs his hands into his pockets petulantly,
or playfully.

                         CLEO
                    (whispers, neither
                    patient nor impatient)
              Come on. Let's go. Trust
              your friends.

The Thin Kid does as she says and steps onto the path.

EXT. FOREST PATH - MOMENTS LATER

The path is overgrown and narrow. They walk single file.
They lift wayward branches or crouch under them.

                KARSON
What if there are other
kids there?

                VALENTINA
There won't be.

                KARSON
How do you know? You don't
know.

Valentina hooks an arm through Karson's arm. With her sleeve-covered hand, she pats the crook of his elbow.

She's being both condescending and a good friend, acknowledging and downplaying his well-founded fears of "other kids."

                VALENTINA
Hey. We'll be all right.

Cleo holds up and shakes the paper bag, like it's a town crier's bell, like it's a warning.

                CLEO
            (uses an exaggerated
            deep voice, her
            father's voice)
We'll just scare those
punks away, and give them
what-for.

Valentina laughs.

Karson shakes his head and mumbles to himself, and when Valentina detangles away from their linked arms, he squeezes the top of her beanie hat, makes a HONK sound, then grabs and pulls the end of her sleeve, stretching it out like taffy.

Valentina mock screams, spins, and slaps him across the chest with the extra cloth.

> THIN KID
>
> Why am I--

> VALENTINA
> (interrupts)
> There's no "why." I'm sorry,
> there never is.

This is important: she isn't mocking the Thin Kid, and she doesn't sound mean or aloof. Quite the opposite. Valentina sounds pained, sounds as sad as the truth she uttered.

She cares about the Thin Kid.

Cleo and Karson care too. They care too much.

The Thin Kid plucks LEAVES from the branches they pass and puts them in his pockets.

In mid-April of 1993 Valentina left a message on my apartment's answering machine. We hadn't talked for almost two years. She got the phone number from my mother, who was awful free with those digits, if you ask me. Valentina said she had a proposition, laughed, apologized for laughing, and then she assured me the proposition was serious. How could I resist?

She and I didn't go to college together, but we'd met as undergrads. I bused tables and worked at Hugo's in Northampton, a bar that was close enough to campus that my shitbox car could survive the drive and far enough away that I wouldn't have to deal with every knucklehead who went to my school. One weeknight when the bar wasn't packed, I was stationed by the door and pretended to read a dog-eared copy of *Naked Lunch* (cut me some slack, Hugo's was that kind of place in that kind of town), and Valentina showed up with two friends. Her dark, curly hair hung over her eyes. She wore a too-big flannel shirt, the sleeves hiding her hands until she wanted to make a point, then she pointed and waved those hands around like they were on fire. She was short, even in her thick-heeled combat boots, but she had physical presence, gravitas; you knew when she entered or left the room. I checked her ID and made a clever quip about the whimsy of her exaggerated height on her government-issued identification card. She retaliated by snatching my book and chucking it into the street, which was fair. Later, she and I ended up playing pool, awkwardly made out in a dark corner, and exchanged phone numbers. We hung out a few times after that, but more often we'd run into each other as regulars at Hugo's. I was happy to be the weird guy ("Weird Guy" was what she called me) from the state school who occasionally entered her orbit. My comet-like appearances made me seem more interesting than I was. I graduated from the University of Massachusetts–Amherst with a communications degree and student loans that I would default on twice. She graduated from Amherst College—much more prestigious and expensive than Zoo Mass. Postgraduation, I'd figured our paths would never cross again.

When I returned Valentina's call, our chat was brief. She wouldn't tell me what the proposition was over the phone, so I agreed to meet her and her friend Cleo at a restaurant on Bridge Street in Providence that weekend. My car (the same beater I'd had in college) barely made the trip down from Quincy, Massachusetts. It had a standard transmission and when on the highway I'd have to hold the gear shift in fifth or it would pop out into neutral. On the ride back, I gave up and drove 70 in fourth gear. I miss that loyal little car.

A restaurant called the Fish Company overlooked the inky Providence River. Too late for lunch, too early for dinner, the place was more than half-empty on a cloudy but warm Sunday midafternoon. I was fifteen minutes late, but I had no problem finding Valentina and Cleo sitting outside, on the wooden dock patio, away from prying ears. They had an open binder on their table, pages filled with rough sketches boxed within long rectangles. I would learn later that Valentina had storyboarded the entire movie, shot by shot. Next to Cleo a paper grocery bag occupied an empty chair. Upon my approach, Cleo slid the chair closer to her, communicating that I wasn't to displace the bag. Valentina closed the binder and stashed it in an army-surplus backpack.

She greeted me with "What's up, Weird Guy?"

Aside from the beanie atop her curly hair, Valentina's appearance hadn't changed much at first blush. After a minute of catch-up chatter, it was clear she'd become an adult, or more adult than me, anyway. The twitchy glances, look-aways, and the we-don't-know-who-we-are-yet-but-I-hope-other-people-like-me half smiles we were all made of in college had hardened and sharpened into confidence of purpose but not yet disappointment. Maybe it was a mask. We all wear them. I got nervous because it appeared that whatever their proposition was must be a serious one. I wasn't prepared for serious.

Cleo was Valentina's friend from high school. She had long, red hair, big glasses, and a boisterous, infectious, at-the-edge-of-control laugh. When she wasn't laughing, there was a blank intensity to her gaze and the memory of her irrepressible laughter seemed an impossible one. Maybe I'm projecting now, all these years later, but she was the kind of person who wore sadness and a type of vulnerability that did not translate into her being a pushover. Far from it. She'd battled and battled hard. But if she wasn't broken yet, she would be, as the world breaks us all.

While we waited for our food Valentina explained that she and Cleo were making a movie; Valentina as director, Cleo as screenwriter, and both would be acting in the film as well. They had funding from a variety of local investors in addition to a modest grant from Rhode Island. It wasn't a lot of money, but they would make it work. They planned to begin production in a few months. They had a tight shooting window because one of their locations, an old, condemned school building, was going to be demolished in midsummer.

I was gobsmacked despite knowing Valentina had completed a film-studies minor as an undergraduate. I don't remember what her major was, but it was a course of study her parents had insisted upon so that she would be, in their eyes, employable. Her mother was a marketing director, and her father owned a local chain of combo car wash/gas stations. Because her parents were footing the entirety of the hefty tuition bill, they had insisted on having a say in what they called their "educational investment." Valentina was an only child, and when she talked about her parents, even in passing, it was with a crackling, bipolar mix of pride and seething resentment. Regardless of the major in which she'd earned her degree, film was her passion. When we were students, I was more obsessed with indie/underground music than film, though I'd spent enough hours as a lonely, brooding teen watching and rewatching movies on cable TV that I could hold on to the threads of her deeper film discourse by my fingertips. She and I had once attended a screening of *The Cabinet of Dr. Caligari*, and later at Hugo's she explained expressionism with the aid of scratchy sketches on bar napkins: the strange, moody, angularly distorted set design represented the interior reality of the story. I remember talking out of my ass, attempting to be smarter than I was by drawing parallels to the performative aspect of punk and art-rock bands from the '70s and '80s. To Valentina's credit, she didn't tell me I was full of shit and helped connect some of those musical dots with me. It was one of those absurd and perfect bar conversations that young, new friends have, portentously vibrating with perceived and real discovery. I can't decide if I'm now incapable of such a discussion because I know too much or because life has proven that none of us knows anything.

In response to their making-a-movie reveal, I said, "Wow" and "Sounds amazing" at least a dozen times because I didn't know what else to say until I worked up the courage to ask the obvious. "So why am I here?"

Valentina said, "Good question. Why is he here, Cleo?" She flailed her arms in the air, overdramatic, hammy. "Are we going to ask him?"

Cleo didn't smile or laugh at what I thought was a joke. That stare of hers. I can still feel it, crawling over, then under, my skin to knock on my bones; the look of a chess master surveying the board and all the possible moves and outcomes, and knowing no matter what she did, she was going to draw or lose.

She said, "Yeah, I guess we should."

"Great." Valentina clapped her hands together once. "So, we want you for one of the roles. One of the most important ones."

After asking them both multiple times if they were fucking with me, they assured me they were not. I told them I'd never acted before, not even in elementary school, which was mostly true, which means it was a lie. I'd taken a drama class my college sophomore year, and our final exam was a group-written and -performed sketch, neither aspect of which is worth detailing here. Suffice it to say, I did not take any more drama classes.

Valentina said, "That's not a problem. We'll get the performance we need out of you."

"That sounds like a threat." I laughed. They did not.

My legs twitched, eyes blinked, heart rate spiked, and I had to fight the urge to run. Instead, I curled into myself, picked at my beer-bottle label, which sloughed off in slashed, wet clumps. I said, "Oh, man, I don't know. You don't want my ugly mug on a screen." At this, Valentina rolled her eyes and waved a dismissive hand at my desperate self-deprecation. "And I'd be so nervous about memorizing lines and fumbling through them or sounding like a robot, unless you want me to play a robot, like the Terminator or something, but I'd have to be the fucked-up, failed prototype. The one Skynet wouldn't send out into the field, and maybe some human or mutant finds me in the trash, turns me on, and all I do is ask them if anyone wants to get a pizza or something. See, I'm already rambling. Is this my audition?"

Cleo laughed. "In a weird way, you're not that far off."

"That's Weird Guy for you," Valentina said. "Relax. It is a big role but it's a nonspeaking role. You'll be on-camera a lot, but you won't have any lines."

Even though there was no way I was doing this, I was disappointed that my role would have no lines. I felt it to be a judgment on my character.

Cleo said, "Well, he has one, maybe two lines in the beginning."

Valentina waved her hands again. "We could even have those read by someone else in post, if you're a complete disaster, but you won't be."

Cleo adjusted her glasses. She looked at me like something terrible was going to happen in my near future. Now I get that look a lot, or maybe I more easily recognize it. But then I'd never felt so watched, so observed, and her scrutiny was a horror initially. By the end of our meeting and meal, having that unvarnished attention paid to me when I'd been so used to hiding, even if it felt uncomfortable and intrusive, was intoxicating. That feeling was why I said yes without saying it. It felt like a chance to create another version of myself, one over which I'd have more control. Which, of course, was ludicrous and wildly wrong. I'd be changed, but would it be by my own hands? Fuck me, I sound like a pretentious actor.

There was something, many somethings, they weren't telling me. I blurted out, "Okay, so why me?"

"We need someone who is your size," Cleo said.

"Oh. So, I really am going to be a robot and I fit the suit?" I sat up straight and robot-chopped my arms up and down. "I hope it's not too heavy or too hot. I wore a full-body pizza slice costume once at a PawSox game. I smelled like a muppet with BO for a full day after."

"You're not playing a robot," Valentina said. "We need someone who is your height and build."

"My height and build?" My face flashed an instant embarrassed red. I noticed Cleo's face mirrored mine. I tried to joke, but I know I sounded hurt. "You mean, my lack of build? It takes a lot of work to maintain this physique." I flexed a nonexistent bicep.

Valentina said, "Oh stop, you look great. It's just the role requires a male who is tall and . . . lanky. Looks like he could still be in high school. And I mean the movie version of high school, which always shades a little older. Not as old as the teens in De Palma's *Carrie*. Fuck, some of those actors had crow's feet wrinkles when they smiled. And Cleo and I will be returning to the hell of high school with you. It'll be fun."

"Yeah, sounds so fun."

Cleo said, "Your name in the script is the Thin Kid." She smiled, winced, and said, "I'm sorry?" like a question.

Valentina lightly backhanded Cleo's shoulder and said, "Don't be sorry."

"Can't his name be the Tall Kid?" I asked.

"Another one, trying to rewrite the screenplay already," Valentina said. "You don't need to go on a diet per se, but if you want to go method, really dig into your character, you could go easy on the pizza and beer for the next two months, maybe even lose five or ten pounds, that would be ideal."

Cleo said, "Jesus, Valentina!"

"What? I'm just saying. Not the rest of his life, just for the shoot. The thinner the better for this role."

I'd had no idea what this meeting with Valentina would have wrought, but I'd not envisioned being asked to lose weight. I was 6'4" and 175 pounds, maybe, and I was self-conscious about how thin I was and always had been. "Self-conscious" isn't strong enough. I hated my body, how stubbornly underdeveloped it was. No need to rehash the bullying I'd endured in middle school and the variety of nicknames that I never had the choice to approve in high school. Seemed I was one of those people destined for nicknames, including Weird Guy. That one I enjoyed, but it was hard not to itemize and take them all personally. My character name wasn't exactly a nickname, but it might as well have been. It's how people knew me then and how they know me now.

I again wanted to get up from the table and run away and ignore any further calls from Valentina, maybe unplug my phone, move away, change my name and identity. I said, "But pizza is a food group."

"Do not listen to her," Cleo said. She sounded more horrified than I was.

"Hey, I'm just kidding," Valentina said in a way that I interpreted, correctly, as she wasn't kidding.

After a few beats of awkward silence, Valentina talked a bit more about the production and how I'd need to be available and on-set for four weeks, at the most six weeks if things didn't go to plan. She asked, "Will you be able to take leave from your job? Um, what are you doing now, anyway? Sorry, I guess I should've asked that earlier."

After graduation I had gone home to Beverly. My parents were separated, and that spring Mom had moved to an apartment on the other side of town. The house in which I grew up was a sad and angry place haunted by the arguments and recriminations that had intensified during my four-year absence. I needed to move out as soon as I could, and to do that I needed a job. I hadn't spent my last college semester writing a résumé and lining up interviews; consequently, I didn't have any leads or any idea what I wanted to do. No one was going to pay me to play Nintendo all day, which was a shame. I signed up with a temp agency, requesting manual-labor jobs, like the Shoe Factory packing and stacking work I'd done the previous four summers. I would've gone back if the factory hadn't closed. The temp agency assigned me to a grocery chain's warehouse, and the first week I unloaded hundred-pound slabs of frozen beef from trailers and stacked them onto pallets. I, or more specifically, my cranky lower back, wasn't up to the task. I got moved to picking orders for individual grocery stores, which was the worst job I've ever had without a close second. Order pickers weren't paid hourly. We were paid by the number of orders fulfilled.

Pickers raced around and between a refrigerated maze of foods and goods riding battery-powered pallet jacks. If that sounds like fun, it wasn't. Like a reverse Jenga game, we hunted then stacked items on a wooden pallet, affixed the order labels, shrink-wrapped the quivering tower, moved the pallet into a delivery queue, and then it was on to the next order. It was ruthlessly competitive. You were allowed breaks, in theory, but you couldn't make money on break. The other pickers were older than I was; or if they weren't, they looked older. They didn't appreciate the skinny college guy bumbling through the stacks. Whenever I got in the way of another picker, which was too often, I could tell by their expression that they imagined my carcass impaled on their pneumatic forks. I lasted two more weeks in the warehouse, averaging less than minimum wage due to a combo of picking deficiency and class guilt, before I went back to the temp agency, took a typing test that I passed, and was assigned to a data-entry job inputting MLS numbers and other real estate info into a company's new database system. At the time of my first meeting with Valentina and Cleo, I had been working that data-entry job for about eighteen months. I was no longer a temp, but I hadn't been an official employee long enough to have earned a two-week vacation, never mind four to six weeks off.

I said, "I can ask for an extended leave. Or quit." This was where I said yes to being in the movie without ever saying yes.

Cleo said, "Are you sure? Oh, please don't quit because of this."

"Don't you want to know how much we'll pay you?" Valentina asked.

"Um, yeah, I would like to know."

"Two thousand five hundred dollars."

Valentina mentioned a percentage of something if/when they signed with a distributor, but I focused on the upfront, real money. That was a lot more than I would make at my data-entry job for four weeks. But was it enough to quit the job and have a financial cushion to pay rent while I searched for another job? Probably not. Back then I measured my future in weeks, and I assumed the far-future me would be a responsible and skilled adult who could figure a way out of any mess the now-me might make.

Valentina and Cleo talked, more to each other than to me, about the various settings they would use for the movie. It was nothing they said, but the oddness of the timing of their offer occurred to me. I said, "Not that it matters to me, but was I the first person you asked to play the Thin Kid?"

Valentina said, "No. You weren't. We held auditions a couple months ago and the guy we hired—let's just say we had a mutual parting of the ways."

"Can I ask why?"

Valentina and Cleo shared a look. That wasn't nice of them to not share with me. Then Valentina said, "It wasn't going to work out. There were—"

Cleo finished for her: "Creative differences."

Valentina said, "That's a polite way of putting it. I know Cleo and I are new at this, and we know the movie won't be for everyone, never mind be perfect. But this is our vision and we're committed to making it our way."

Cleo said, "He wanted to rewrite and change a bunch of his scenes. He wasn't . . . wasn't totally comfortable with the role or story."

Valentina rolled her eyes. "You're giving him too much credit. He wasn't comfortable with us, two women, running the show. He marked up Cleo's screenplay like he was an English teacher, and a shitty one at that."

"Yeah, that was a bit over the top," Cleo said. "I've read a ton of screenplays and I took screenwriting classes too. I'm not saying I'm an expert, only that I'm aware my screenplay is—unorthodox. Very unorthodox." She laughed, and so did I. "But the, um, strangeness of it is purposeful.

"Valentina and I have spent, what, almost two years thinking and talking about why I wrote this the way I did? We're trusting each other's instincts on this." Cleo alternated between holding strict, unwavering eye contact with me and eyeing her straw's balled-up paper wrapper. "I'm not saying every screenplay should be written the way I wrote this one. Definitely not. But for this story and how we want to tell it, it's the right way. Or the best way. Don't get us wrong, we're open to collaboration and ideas, especially when we get on-set. We explained this to the other actor, multiple times. For whatever reason he couldn't get his head around it."

I said, "Well, I don't think I've ever read a screenplay before, so I wouldn't know if it was, um, unorthodox anyway. Unless you wrote it in crayon or something."

Cleo said, "Great idea," and again shared that laugh of hers.

I asked if they were going to give me a copy to take home, and I promised I would read it ASAP.

Valentina said, "I'd prefer not to."

"Yeah, of course. What? No, wait. What does that mean?" I answered my own question, as though I'd been talking to myself, which I sort of was at that point. "You're not sure if you want me for the part and you'll decide after I leave?"

Valentina said, "We want you for the part. It's yours if you want it."

"I'm pretty sure I do. But—shouldn't I read the screenplay first, just in case? To be all official-like?" I sat nodding, my manic bird impression encouraging them to agree with something, anything, I'd said.

"If you insist on reading it before we start filming, of course we'll let you," Cleo said. "But Valentina has a cool idea about when and how you should read the screenplay."

Valentina explained that as a part of her plan to help get the performance they needed from me, an admitted newbie to acting, I would not know the whole story prior to shooting. They would parcel out the screenplay to me scene by scene. I would only read scenes the night before we were to shoot those scenes the follow-ing day. That way, I would be in the same boat, story-wise, as my character. I would be experiencing the story as my character did. As an actor, I wouldn't have the weight of foreknowledge—knowing where the story was going and where it would end—getting in the way of my performance, my relationship to the character. Having almost zero lines to memorize afforded me this opportunity. There wasn't a pressing or practical need for me to have the full screenplay beforehand. Valentina was convinced my performance would be enhanced if I trusted them and went along with their plan.

I said, "Okay, that makes sense. I think." I wasn't lying, and I was excited at the prospect. But this idea of not seeing the scenes until the night before I was to act in them made me uneasy. It was like I would be stumbling into the middle of a dark room I'd never been in before and then turning on the light.

I asked, "What kind of movie is it?"

Valentina said, "Horror movie."

Her concise answer shocked me. I figured she'd go on describing some arty, avant-garde non-genre piece.

"And that's the title," Cleo said. "For now, anyway."

The waiter came by with our food. I asked for another beer. I figured I'd walk it off after driving back to Quincy. With a mouthful of steaming-hot curly fries (I could never wait for food to cool off), I asked Cleo, "Can I ask what's in the paper bag?"

"That I can show you."

EXT. ABANDONED SCHOOL - LATER

The four teens emerge from the woods, through a gap in a mangled CHAIN-LINK FENCE, and onto the cracked pavement of an abandoned SCHOOLYARD confettied with BOTTLE GLASS.

Broken, crooked SWING SETS dangle rusty chains. A metal SLIDE leans askew, and it is warped and missing a middle panel.

There are no visible main roads leading to or away from this place. It's as though the forest swallowed the school grounds.

Lines of IVY slither up the crumbling brick façade of the two-story school building.

The teens walk to the cement STAIRS that lead to a propped-open SIDE DOOR. The door is gray and metal.

                    CLEO
          Don't you wish you went to
          this school?

                    VALENTINA
          We all went here. Don't you
          remember?

Valentina giggles at her obvious lie.

Karson looks confused, with one foot on the stairs and one off. He tilts his head like the little lost puppy he is.

                    KARSON
               (says the statement
               like a question)
          We went here?

Valentina and Cleo talk rapid-fire, finishing each other's sentence/story.

CLEO	VALENTINA
Remember the first-grade teacher, Mrs. Fang?	Oh yeah, her.

CLEO	VALENTINA
Wasn't she so scary?	One yellow tooth hung over her bottom lip when she smiled.

CLEO	VALENTINA
Leered, really.	Or frowned.

CLEO	VALENTINA
She said she could open a can of soup with it.	Maybe she's still here, hiding in her room.

CLEO	VALENTINA
She keeps that tooth clean.	And sharp.

The teens walk up the stairs and into the school, orderly, like children returning to class at the recess bell.

INT. ABANDONED SCHOOL, HALLWAY - MOMENTS LATER

The hallway is dark, dusty, but oddly clear of debris.

The LOCKERS and WALLS are graffitied with threats, odes to new love, sex jokes accompanied by crude anatomic illustrations, and cryptic messages understood only by the message writer.

Doors to the empty classrooms are all propped open. Weak sunlight filters through the classrooms they pass.

As they walk the hall's length, toward a wide STAIRCASE, their footfalls echo, become the ghosts of who they were, who they could've been.

Valentina and Cleo, each filled with nervous energy, restart their two-person routine.

<table>
<tr><td>

CLEO
Remember Mr. Shallow?

</td><td>

VALENTINA
His eyes were sunken
so deep in his head.

</td></tr>
<tr><td>

CLEO
When he blinked his
eyelids made a wet *click*.

</td><td>

VALENTINA
Remember Ms. Boots?

</td></tr>
<tr><td>

CLEO
The scariest ever. She
stomped around class like
Godzilla.

</td><td>

VALENTINA
Squishing little toes.

</td></tr>
</table>

KARSON
I remember Mr. Whalen. Fourth
grade. When he asked how come
I hadn't memorized the poem
"The Crocodile," I told him
it was because my cat had run
away. I cried when I told him.
I was lying, and when he
figured that out --

VALENTINA
Mr. Whalen fed you to a
whale!

KARSON
No. He announced, in front
of everyone, that my parents
had called and said my cat
had come home. Then he asked
me what its name was, and

with everyone staring, I froze,
I couldn't come up with a
name.

                    CLEO
Don't worry. Mr. Whalen isn't
here anymore.

                  VALENTINA
Your cat's name was Snip.
Which is *pins* spelled backward.

INT. ABANDONED SCHOOL, STAIRWAY - CONTINUOUS

The teens stop, pooling at the bottom of the wide staircase. Large, cracked WINDOWS are twin moons hovering over
the landing above.

                  KARSON
I didn't memorize the poem
because it gave me nightmares.
A big, cartoonlike crocodile
would come into my room and
eat me. Bite me right in half.
So stupid, right?

                  THIN KID
            (small, unsure voice)
That's not stupid.

                  KARSON
What if the *crocodile* from
the poem is here? Waiting to
greet us little fishes
with gently smiling jaws?
Fine, so I did memorize the
poem eventually.

Valentina walks up the stairs first.

> VALENTINA
> Okay, no more talking, now.
> This is going to be hard enough
> as it is without us goofing
> around.

> KARSON
> I'm a goof, but I wasn't
> goofing around.

> VALENTINA
> That's not what I meant.
> Shh.

Cleo cradles the paper bag with her left arm. The moment one sneaker contacts the first stair tread, her right hand dives into her front PANTS POCKET, as though her two bodily movements are connected, tethered.

Her hand remains hidden in her pocket as the teens climb the dusty stairs to the second floor.

INT. ABANDONED SCHOOL, SECOND FLOOR, HALLWAY - MOMENTS LATER

The second-floor hallway is in a similar state as the first.

This hallway is another tunnel, one that doesn't have light at its end. Instead, light spills out of the open CLASS-ROOMS. Those doors are portals to another past and an uncertain future.

The teens walk. Their feet shuffle and scuff.

Valentina pushes ahead of the group. She ducks into doorway openings left and then right, until, finally, she finds the correct classroom.

She points at the open door, arm horizontal, her hanging sleeve sagging and drooping.

The teens creep into the room. The Thin Kid is the last to enter.

INT. ABANDONED SCHOOL, CLASSROOM – CONTINUOUS

The floor's linoleum is cracked and curling up in spots.

Missing foam tiles checkerboard the ceiling, exposing the rotting guts of the place.

Mid-wall-to-ceiling WINDOWS are on their left, denuded of shades. The light outside is fading.

The teacher's wooden DESK has been flipped upside down, four legs pointing skyward, a caricature of a dead animal.

A BLACKBOARD covers the wall behind the desk. It is intact, though it is missing the chalk tray. Every inch of the board is covered with WRITING, printed letters and looping script.

> KARSON
> (whispers)
> I think this was Mr.
> Whalen's room.

Cleo pats Karson's arm, then goes to the board and reads, her face inches from the chalk dust. There are messages here, but she can't decipher them. Maybe if she had more time.

The Thin Kid reads over her shoulder, and she hears a whimper, but it's low and soft enough that maybe we don't hear it, we imagine it, and we recognize it as the lost, desperate sound we make in our own heads when we are alone.

To the right of the board and teacher's desk, student DESKS are piled against a door labeled SUPPLY ROOM.

Valentina is the first to pluck a desk from the pile and move it to the middle of the room.

Karson and the Thin Kid (we do not see his face, ever) help Valentina clear away the desks.

Cleo stays at the chalkboard, reading the mess of writing, holding the paper bag. Her eyes widen in recognition and terror, and she covers her mouth with a hand, holding back a scream. Then she wipes her eyes under her glasses.

Once all but one desk are cleared from in front of the supply room, Valentina opens the wooden door. It creaks.

INT. SUPPLY ROOM - CONTINUOUS

Valentina steps inside.

The room is an empty rectangle, with space for perhaps two people to stand an arm's length apart. There are SHELVES on one wall and two COAT HOOKS on another. It is claustrophobically dark.

INT. CLASSROOM - CONTINUOUS

Valentina steps out of the supply room, and with a foot she slides the lone student desk/chair combo so it blocks the supply-room entry.

She points at it.

Cleo, standing by the blackboard, points at it.

Karson, with a shaky, reluctant arm, points at it.

The Thin Kid sidles over, folds himself into a seated position at the tiny chair, one bent knee pressed against the desktop, the other sticking up over the desk.

The three teens encircle the desk and the Thin Kid.

From the Thin Kid's POV, Cleo opens the paper bag and removes a MASK.

It is green, but we do not yet see its features. She hands the mask to Valentina.

Valentina raises the mask over her head and brings it down slowly and over the Thin Kid's head, over *our* heads.

Our vision goes blank, long enough for us to fear that blankness, to fear that not only will the blankness be never-ending but we'll also be aware of its never-endingness.

Then we can see through the mask's two eyeholes. The three teens lean toward us and stare. ~~We see them in black and white. No color.~~

There's the whimpering sound again, this time loud, unmistakable, and at the sound, we switch out of the poor Thin Kid's POV.

Now we see the mask.

It's a gray-green, covered in scales, reptilian, alien, demonic. It reminds us of the *Creature from the Black Lagoon*'s Gill-man, but the more we look and the more we study, it is obviously different.

The mask has a brusque, flattened snout, almost mammalian but not quite. Its large, closed mouth has such great potential for teeth, both in number and in size.

Look.

Look again.

Now the mask reminds us of a gargoyle, something carved from stone, something made as a warning, made to ward off evil spirits, made to ward off all spirits. The visage is otherworldly yet unmistakably sculpted by our hands.

The mask is ugly and grotesque and familiar, and we cannot stop staring at it because all monsters are mirrors.

THEN:
THE PITCH PART 2

4

Cleo held up the mask, the crown of its head pinched between her fingers.

She said, "I know it doesn't look like much." She slid one fist inside, like the mask was a puppet. Her hand fell well short of filling the head, and its features were slack, distorted, a Munch or Dalí painting not quite come to life. "But it photographs well."

I said, "I'm guessing I'll be wearing that."

Valentina said, "Yes."

"For the whole movie?"

"Pretty much."

I knew less about mask-making than moviemaking. Still, I asked if they needed a mold of my head or face to make sure it fit properly.

"You might have to cut your hair shorter. But we can adjust, pad it out, or make a new one if it doesn't fit," Valentina said, and she smiled at Cleo.

Cleo practically screamed her response. "Yeah, right. *Make* a new one."

She passed the mask over to me. The latex was cold and clammy. Or maybe it was my hands that were cold and clammy. Cleo fidgeted as my fingers inspected and explored the mask. Okay, I assumed I would be playing some sort of creature, given that they'd told me

I didn't have many or any lines of dialogue. The mask looked ridiculous and fake, something you might pick up in a department store before Halloween. I wanted to ask if they were joking again, but I didn't want to risk hurting anyone's feelings. I thought about trying it on, but I got the sense Cleo would've stopped me from doing so with her fork. Whereas previously she'd sat in a sunken slouch, now she was curled over the table, ready to strike.

Valentina said, "Yeah, it looks underwhelming now, but it's disturbing as fuck when someone wears it. Tell him the story behind it."

"It's the weirdest thing." Cleo barely got the sentence out before the two of them broke up laughing.

Valentina said, "Be serious."

"I am!"

I laughed even though I wasn't in on the joke and assumed I very much was the joke. I dropped the mask and it flopped onto the tabletop. "You guys *are* fucking with me. You had me going."

They assured me they were not. I asked why they were laughing, which made them laugh harder.

Valentina finally said, "Because what Cleo is going to tell you about the mask will sound bonkers, but it's the truth."

Cleo spun her tale: The Rhode Island town in which they grew up had experienced precipitous population decline after mill closings in the '60s and '70s, so the town had consolidated its three elementary schools into two. The abandoned McKay Elementary School, the same one they would be using as one of the locations for the movie, became a not-so-secret hangout for high school kids on Friday and Saturday nights. Cleo, Valentina, and another friend, Karson, who was also going to be in the movie, explored the place on Sunday mornings or after school, when they could have it to themselves. Cleo went alone sometimes, usually during the summer. She sat in the different classrooms and wrote short stories, nothing more than a paragraph or two, about a student or a teacher she imagined had once been in the room. Upon returning home from college, and knowing Valentina was planning to make short films and possibly a full-length movie, Cleo wanted to write a screenplay that would make use of the school. Last spring, for the first time in years, she returned to the school looking for story inspiration. In one of the classrooms on the second floor, the remaining student desks, most of which had been mangled and smashed, were piled in the center of the room. It was bright outside, but not a lot of light filtered through the milky, cataracted windows. The room was dusky. If she squinted, the desk pile looked like a thicket of denuded branches. Ringed within the rubble, a shadowed lump jutted up from the floor. It looked like a head. She circled the desks, looking closer, trying to convince herself it wasn't a head, but the more she looked the more she was sure it was a head, and there, by herself in an empty room in an abandoned school in a dying town in a dying world, she thought she saw eyes and she thought she saw them blink. At this point in her story, Cleo was laughing, but it was a different kind of laughing. There are so many kinds of laughter, aren't there? She described her panicked flight from the school, the knocks and slaps of her own fleeing footsteps, not daring to breathe until she left the building, and once she was outside, the world appeared changed by what she'd seen. Cleo corrected herself; of course the world wasn't changed—and here for the only time in her tale, she stammered, searching for the right words. The world was the same, but a new part of it had been revealed. Even if what she found wasn't a head, the world was indeed a place in which she might find one. She didn't tell anyone what she saw, at least not until she showed Valentina her first draft of the screenplay a few weeks later. Upon returning to her childhood home, her bedroom, she spent the afternoon and that evening and the next morning convincing herself she didn't see a head, and if it was a head, it wasn't a real head, and by "real" she meant a head that was once atop a living body, and that this not-real head didn't have eyes that blinked. She returned to the school the next day, after work, and instead of her notebook she brought a flashlight, long and heavy enough to be a cudgel. Cleo stood at the base of the cement stairs and looked up at the brick building, at how big it was, and then she stared at the slitted mouth of the propped-open door and remembered the emptiness inside the building and how awful and wonderful it had felt to be alone within the emptiness, so she crept back into the school, listening for sounds that were no longer there, for sounds that would be heard by no one but her. With that kind of reverence in her heart, she walked up the stairs to the second floor and that classroom at the other end of the hall, where everything was where it was, where it had been. She said "Sorry" out loud to no one and turned on the flashlight, which rudely burned away the murkiness and exposed the head as a mask. She supposed there still could be a head under the mask, hiding its true face, but she didn't think that was the case, and she admitted it was weirdly disappointing to no longer believe it was a real head. (I didn't think it was weird, and I told her so.) Cleo pulled apart the desk pile until there was a path to its center. There was no blood on the floor, no neck drippings. We all giggled at her phrase "neck drippings." She tapped the mask with her flashlight and it toppled over, exposing a white neck or base. Later, when she was home, she carefully removed the mask from the featureless Styrofoam head. The foam was mealy under her fingers, sloughing off and disintegrating at her touch. The schoolroom floor within the ring of desks was extra dusty and grainy with foam granules. The tile under the head was all scratched up, and the longer she looked, the more certain she became that the scratches were purposeful. Since she was taking the mask and would write a story using it, Cleo decided to leave some sort of offering, something of herself in its stead. A gift for a gift. She pushed and piled dust over the floor scratches, then she wrote what she thought would be the first line of her screenplay into the dust. When she brought Valentina to the schoolroom a month later, the desks were still there but what she had written in the dust had been smoothed away.

I didn't believe her story about finding the mask and I said so, multiple times. Valentina and Cleo both insisted Cleo was telling the truth. I wondered aloud if what they were telling me was a scene from their movie. Valentina said they contemplated incorporating the discovery of the mask into the screenplay but had decided against it, opting to leave its origin mysterious. I picked up the mask and inspected it some more. I'd never seen anything exactly like it, but it also wasn't wholly unfamiliar. I assumed they'd made it and I said that I thought they were giving me this cursed-mask legend to inform my performance.

Valentina and Cleo spoke at the same time: "Who said anything about a curse?" and "I never used the word 'curse.'"

I said, "Well, assuming this is legit. Any lost object is cursed."

"Isn't the mask a *found* object? And cursed by what?" Valentina asked.

I shrugged, and it was my turn to stammer and stumble through saying not quite what I wanted to say or mean. Maybe some of us make movies because words so often fail us. "I—I don't know, I guess, cursed by, um, whatever happened to it, you know, to make it lost."

Cleo said, "The mask wasn't lost. It was left there on purpose."

"Sounds even more cursed to me," I said, and chuckled. No one laughed. I'd hoped they would.

During the fifteen years after filming and prior to the 2008 leaked images and scenes, I haunted costume shops and made countless deep-dive online searches, but I never found another mask that looked exactly like that one.

NOW:
THE DIRECTOR
PART 1

5

I spent a few months chatting with a flurry of prospective directors on the phone about the most recent iteration of the proposed reboot. They tended to ask me the same questions about the original film, the vibe on-set, and Valentina's process. None of them asked me about the—let's call it "the aftermath." None of them asked about Cleo directly, though they would talk about the screenplay and, in broad terms, what they wanted to change. I never scoffed at the suggested changes. Scoffing wasn't my job as an in-name-only associate producer. I knew my role on Team Reboot was to be enthusiastic, no matter what anyone said, and to play the mascot, the living relic from a time that never was. I like to think I performed my role with nuance.

There was one *big* director briefly interested. He opened the call with, "Hey, brother, it's so great to finally talk to you," as though he'd been waiting his whole life for the opportunity. This strain of faux Hollywood enthusiasm was as common as the fuck-you handshake, and this guy coupled it with unfettered egoism born from undeniable talent grown into a colossus within the hothouse of wealth and power. His artist's ego was not the same as Valentina's. Hers was purer, born from desperation and the will to fight and claw her vision into being. The director detailed what he planned to change, including adding more explication of the how and why of the plot and my character's transformation. Whatever. He told me that buried within all the grim weirdness of *Horror Movie* was a high-concept conceit that could be as big an idea as a "dinosaur on an island," and that concept was too big for the other potential directors to handle. Throughout the call, he made a point of saying, multiple times, "This was a dinosaur-on-an-island idea." I knew he was referencing the *Jurassic Park*(s) franchise (I hate myself for many things, but I'm adding my willing usage of the term "franchise" to describe movies to my list of egregious offenses against humanity). To test his patience, willingness to work with others, and sense of humor, or to simply fuck with him, I said I hadn't seen the movie *Dinosaur Island*, and with my laptop in front of me, I informed him that the IMDb score for the 2014 family adventure box-office bomb was 3.6/10. It would be vain of me to presume I scared that director off the project, but I like to imagine I did.

Today I have my first in-person meeting with our new and contractually obligated director, Marlee Bouton. The Canadian-born Gen-Xer has had a critically successful run of three independently produced and grant-funded supernatural horror films. The latest was an adaptation of the cult classic punk-meets-haunted-house novella *Please Haunt Me*, written by Elizabeth Hand. The movie had a full theatrical release in the United States. Given the complexity of the material, the film was a surprise hit in the context of the pandemic-reduced theatergoing audience, which placed her name in good standing with the studios. Marlee has a reputation for being somewhat of a recluse, which equates to her not actively pursuing the spotlight and not living in Los Angeles full-time.

Marlee and I are to meet at the house she's renting in Laurel Canyon, a famous suburb within the Hollywood Hills. My winding drive into the Hills is anxiety-inducing. The roads are steep, narrow, and follow a logic-defying, varicose vein–like map. The houses are on top of one another, jigsaw-pieced into the mountains in a way that makes me think of mudslides and earthquakes. My little car's four-cylinder engine groans during the near-continuous incline, and I fear everyone is watching, listening, judging from behind curtains and tinted windows. After ten minutes of strangling the steering wheel, I park on the street and pull up the emergency brake as far as it can go. Parked on such a steep incline, I debate whether I should leave my wheels turned toward or away from the curb. I won't admit my solution in case I got it wrong.

Finally, to the house, which is a modest white, one-level stucco bungalow with a garage sheltering under the front deck. Marlee greets me on the stoop with a handshake and tells me that her partner, Cait, a video game writer and developer, is on a hell set of Zoom calls so we'll have to chat in the backyard. I follow her around the house to a tree-and-shrub-enclosed slate patio. We sit at a glass-topped table for four. The umbrella is up, though it isn't necessary this time of day; the entire yard is shaded thanks to the house and trees, and it's at least five degrees cooler here than at the front of the house. Granted, I am overheated, as though I were the car that had driven halfway up a mountain. I sit and Marlee disappears through a slider and returns with two glasses of ice water. Marlee is a white woman with an avid jogger's build, her graying brown hair kept in a short and neat bob. She wears a black T-shirt and high-waisted jeans and flip-flops.

We open with small talk. Marlee tells me she and her partner live in Vancouver, but they rent a house in this area for two to three months at a time, depending on schedules and work assignments. Cait's asthma is serious enough that the air quality at this elevation compared to the surrounding valley makes a difference. That leads to a brief exchange about AQI and the PM2.5 particulate, and my chest tightens at the science.

After a lull, Marlee asks about what I've been doing, aside from the reboot pitch.

I say, "Two weeks ago I signed a contract to write a book about my experience on-set and off, including what's happening now with the reboot pitches and what may happen next. So, consider yourself as being in the book already. It'll be audio only at first. If it does well enough, then maybe a print version."

"Be nice to me, please. And congratulations!"

"Thank you. Yeah, we'll see. I might've bitten off more than I can chew."

"I'm sure it'll be great," she says. "Not that I know anything about writing a book. Can I ask what you were working on before the book deal? Sorry, I don't mean to sound like I'm interviewing you for a job. I'm genuinely curious."

I say, "Nothing worth mentioning. I've been living off the kindness of strangers. Like a parasite. Speaking of parasites, Producer George tells me that you're officially signed on to direct as of last Friday."

She laughs. It's brief, loud, and unhinged, and I'm reminded of Cleo's laugh. "I've already started working on the screenplay, which really doesn't need much work."

I nod, though I wasn't asked a question that required a yes or no answer.

She continues, "In fact, I only plan on adding some scaffolding, connective tissue between some scenes, bits around the margins, and possibly bulking up the ending. 'Bulking up' isn't the right phrase. How about something obnoxious like layering in more texture? We'll see how I feel when I get to the ending. I'm not cutting anything, including the parts that you typically don't include in a screenplay. For this film, I share Valentina and Cleo's opinion that it's important for the actors to access those hidden parts of the story too. That's where story lives sometimes, I think, and that's hard for a filmmaker to admit."

I tell her that I agree. And I do agree. "I'm surprised the financers are on board with your take."

"Come for the Canadian director, stay for the grant money."

I tilt my head. Bemused, charmed, and confused.

"Sorry, a joke I've been saying to Cait all week. Initially, the producers were intrigued, let's say, by my track record with securing Canadian grants. But turns out the studio is footing the entire bill. They're convinced the *Horror Movie* fandom will show and show big for this."

"What do you think?"

"I managed to convince the studio the fans would show but only if we come as close as possible to the movie they never got to see. I insisted on using the original screenplay and, like I said already, any changes would be cosmetic."

"Interesting, and surprising, frankly. I figured if the movie ever got made, it would need all the rough and sharp edges filed off, and bright sunshine and shimmering eyes for the credits roll."

"Not my version of the movie."

"Well, you say that now. Wait until the test screenings, yeah?"

"We'll torch that bridge when we cross it."

"Playing the devil's advocate." I hold up my hands, as though to say *nothing up my sleeve; I have no sleeves.* "Are you worried you could make something too close to the shot-for-shot Gus Van Sant remake of *Psycho*?"

"That's not quite apples to apples. If people had had the opportunity to watch the entire movie you all made, I would approach the reboot differently, if I would do it at all."

"You can't replicate a moment in time, especially a lost one, can you?"

"It's not about replicating a specific time. A movie—any movie, even one that fails—is a conversation with the viewer who chooses to engage. This movie will communicate emotional truths that can only be communicated by the language of film and of horror. If we do it right, the movie will speak to us now as it would've thirty years ago and as it will thirty years from now, if any of us are still around, projecting movies onto the walls of ruined buildings."

During her spiel I lean forward, drawn into her gravity, elbows on the table and fists propping up my chin. What she says is pretentious bullshit and I love it. Just because it's pretentious doesn't mean it's not true, or that I don't want it to be true. I lean back and say, "That's heady stuff for a slasher flick."

Marlee sips her water, then says, "That's exactly what Producer George said."

"Oh fuck, I take it back. I take it back!"

She laughs, says, "You better take it back." Now it's her turn to lean on the table. She presses her palms flat on the glass top, spreads and stretches her spider-leg fingers. "If you don't mind my asking, is any of this difficult for you? It has to be."

I could be a wiseass and pretend I don't understand what she's getting at. But she doesn't deserve that. At least not yet.

"Not as difficult as it once was."

"You say that, but what about when you're on-set?"

"At the moment that's a wholly abstract concept. I don't know if I can answer that until it happens."

"To be totally honest . . ." She pauses and smirks.

"Here it comes," I say.

"I've been obsessed about *Horror Movie* and Valentina Rojas in particular, but I'm finding it difficult to get my head around working with you."

"I get it. I do. Though you're the one who invited me to your house. Let me walk through your door."

"You haven't actually gone through the front door."

"Metaphorically speaking."

"Of course."

"I don't know what to tell you. I find it difficult to work with me too."

Marlee doesn't respond. She slowly slides out from her crouch over the table and into an imperious sitting position. I can't tell what she's thinking. Or maybe I can. She thinks I'm a terrible person and that associating with me might taint her with my terribleness, but making the movie will be worth it, and this exchange, this barter of terribleness, is necessary for the film to be what she wants it to be.

I add, "When shooting begins, I promise I won't be hanging over your shoulder, offering notes on the dailies. How often or how little I'm on-set is up to you."

She says, "Part of my pitch to the studio—and I think it's what sold them, ultimately—is that you'd be in the film."

I blurt out, "What?" As my brain implodes, thirty years melt away. I'm back at that table in Providence with Valentina and Cleo and they're asking me to become the Thin Kid again. I can't say no, don't get to say no, there is no choice, choice is an illusion. I've never left that table and everything that has happened since has been a dream, one that hasn't ended, and the most horrific thing I can imagine is that the dream will never end.

Marlee says, "Sorry to spring this on you, but I wanted to present this to you face-to-face before we let the producers and managers take over."

I blink and I squirm and I run a hand through my hair and rub my wiry beard. "Wow. Okay. Yeah. I guess I get it. I'd be playing Karson's dad, right? I don't know if my voice is gruff enough. As you know, I didn't get to use it much the first go-round."

"No. You'll be reprising your role. Or part of it."

INT. CLASSROOM - CONTINUOUS

The Thin Kid turns his masked head in every direction, twitchy, a trapped bug, a mantis still folded up in the chair. We hear his elevated rate of breathing.

Karson and Valentina crouch in front of the Thin Kid. They untie his sneakers, remove them, and pull off his socks. Then they stand, and each takes one of his arms and gently helps him out of the desk/chair.

The Thin Kid stands, but not at full height. He is hunched over but looks ready to flee.

Cleo pulls SCISSORS out of the paper bag, gives them to Karson.

Karson slowly takes the bottom hem of the Thin Kid's T-shirt and slides the cloth between the beak-like opened scissor blades. He cuts, carving a path up and over the Thin Kid's chest and toward the neck.

Valentina tears the T-shirt away as Karson cuts, but the stubborn collar remains, doesn't give in to the scissors easily.

The Thin Kid cranes his head up toward the ceiling, exposing his throat and the bottom flaps of the mask.

The dulled side of the bottom scissor blade presses against the Thin Kid's neck.

Karson's hands squeeze, shake with the effort of closing the blades, until finally an abrupt SNICK as the scissors bite through the collar.

The Thin Kid presses a hand to his neck and then holds the hand in front of his face, checking for blood. He does it repeatedly, as though not believing what he is not seeing.

The three teens point at and tap the Thin Kid's jeans.

He understands their pantomime. He unbuttons his jeans, lets them fall like a curtain, and steps out of them.

Cleo gathers his clothes and stuffs them into the paper bag.

Karson sheaths the scissors in his back pocket.

Valentina moves the desk/chair away from the supply-room door opening.

The Thin Kid now wears only the mask and threadbare, navy-blue BOXER SHORTS with a button fly. He doesn't know what to do with his arms. He alternates folding his dangling hands in front of his crotch and hugging his arms across his hairless, goosebump-and-acne-dotted chest. Without clothes he appears even thinner, almost emaciated. His ribs and collarbones are hard ridges. His pointy shoulders are loose, unmoored.

The three teens close their circle around the Thin Kid, place their hands on his slumped shoulders, and gently turn him around so he faces the supply room.

He's hunched over in a defensive posture. The knobs and notches of his spine protrude like a dinosaur's back plates.

The teens slowly push him into the supply room. They close the door as he still faces the rear wall.

The teens stand and watch the supply-room door.

The Thin Kid's hands paw, bump, and slide across the wood until the doorknob RATTLES, then twists slowly. The door opens a creaky inch.

Valentina pushes the door shut, violently, with two hands.

They watch the door again. The passing seconds are heavy. The door remains closed.

With the Thin Kid hidden away, the teens walk out of the classroom.

We remain behind in the classroom, with a wide shot of the room and the blackboard.

Valentina and Cleo restart their talking-about-teachers routine, and they continue until we can't hear them anymore.

<table>
<tr><td>

          CLEO (O.S.)
Remember Mrs. Horse?

</td><td>

        VALENTINA (O.S.)
Of course!

</td></tr>
</table>

          CLEO (O.S.)   VALENTINA (O.S.)
How about Mr. Sharp?   His handouts always
                                  gave us papercuts.

          CLEO (O.S.)   VALENTINA (O.S.)
He collected our bloody   Never handed them back.
assignments.

We continue to stare at the blackboard across the room until we no longer hear the teens talking.

We want to read the blackboard, want to read what Cleo read. The words are just out of focus, just out of reach.

The supply-room door clicks open, but only an inch.

The CAMERA slowly zooms toward the door and its sliver of opening, knowing we can't wait to peer inside.

                                     FADE TO:

6

I was the only cast/crew member from the movie banished to a tired Howard Johnson's on the outskirts of Providence. The others, if they weren't simply commuting from home, stayed at the downtown Biltmore, a seventy-year-old high-rise upscale hotel featuring dusty, dimly lit luxury rooms and dreams. Valentina wanted to prevent me from socializing, to keep me mysterious to everyone else working on the movie. As she'd explained it, remaining somewhat isolated would also help me to focus on my character and performance.

The night before our first day of filming I read the sides five times, which ended with the teens gathered outside the abandoned elementary school. Of course, I didn't know then how far we'd go.

I wasn't given any acting instruction with the pages, but it was easy to imagine myself as this Thin Kid, so I did. I gave him my high school background. I briefly itemized my least pleasant experiences, memories flickering in a movie montage; the chaotic flashes of casual cruelties upon which schools and their tween and teen societies are built, the personal failings and longings that had become encoded within my DNA. While those wounds still stung when I prodded at them, I spent more mental energy rebuilding the smoglike indifference and dullness of my prior teenage life. I believed that was where I would find the Thin Kid; the countless hours spent watching television by myself or wordlessly with my siblings, their own struggles and social strata as distant and alien as other galaxies; or listening to music in my room while lying in bed, staring at the yellowed ceiling, Walkman headphones barnacled over my ears; or shooting the basketball alone in the backyard, navigating a craggy, undulating square of blacktop, dreaming basketball dreams despite having tried out for the freshman team and not making it and then never trying out again. While I didn't think Valentina and Cleo were banking on the existential horrors of boredom and angst to inform their movie, with the opening scene of the teens walking down the middle of the street all but ignoring my character, I thought it could help. In this mundane way, I would inhabit the Thin Kid until he could inhabit me.

Between each script reading I paced the hotel room. It was more than probable that this movie wouldn't amount to anything, would be a minor blip in the film world and in my life. Yet I was convinced that the next day would be a personal inflection point. How many of those are we presented with? How often are we aware of an inflection point before it happens? I was both eager and terrified.

Two nights later, Cleo handed me the pages for the classroom scene, the one in which I don the mask and am left behind in the closet. I did not dwell on how uncomfortable the mask would be nor how long I would have to endure wearing it. Instead, the thought of removing my shirt and pants in front of everyone, in front of the camera, shriveled my insides into a Big Crunch particle at the center of my being. Having to take my clothes off in a classroom, abandoned or not, would be one of my worst nightmares come to life.

I called Valentina's hotel room and she didn't answer. I called Cleo next. She answered, and she sounded blurred, distant, like I'd woken her up despite the relatively early hour. She didn't rush me off the phone, though. Anticipating why I was calling she asked if I had a question about the script. I said not exactly, and then I danced around my discomfort at having to disrobe on-camera. "Disrobe" was the word I used, and it sounded ludicrous, but I said it multiple times. Cleo, to her credit, understood what I was and wasn't saying. She was patient and kind, but unreachable in her uniquely Cleo way. That's not to say she was emotionless or didn't care about what I was saying. To the contrary, she cared, perhaps too much. Her unreachableness registered more as resignation; no matter what any of us said or did, the outcome—one that she could clearly see—had been predetermined. Cleo said that she sympathized with my discomfort and assured me that my state of undress was necessary for the story, otherwise the script wouldn't require it. She phrased it as though the *script* were making the exposed-flesh demand, not its author. When I didn't respond, she sounded as uncomfortable as I felt, stammering through promises that no one on-set would be judging or commenting upon my appearance, that we would all be professionals about it, and as an afterthought, she said that my body was beautiful and there was nothing to be ashamed of and that she'd be happy to talk me through it tomorrow in person. I thanked her, although I felt even more panicked. I'd hoped after hearing my poorly worded objection Cleo would allow me to wear more clothing. Shorts and a tank top, perhaps? I knew I had some leverage, at least in theory, as I could've threatened to walk off the movie, and they would've been screwed. But that threat was never a real possibility, and I think Valentina and Cleo realized I wouldn't quit, no matter what, and that was another reason why I had the part. How they knew that about me, I didn't know. Maybe it was written on my face. I think most of us have our personality, our character, plainly etched in a wordless language on the skins of our faces, as obvious as a bleeding heart on a sleeve. I told Cleo that I had already agreed to perform in the film while keeping the remainder of the script secret from me, but I needed assurances that I wouldn't have to *disrobe* beyond the blue boxers. I sighed at myself as I'd given in so quickly, so easily, and was now begging for no further indignities. Cleo promised that the underwear would remain on for the entirety of the movie, although Valentina might want the Thin Kid to wear tighty-whities instead of the boxers because they'd make my character look more pathetic. She didn't pause (and I imagined her on the other end of the phone not blinking either) at the word "pathetic." I didn't agree to the wardrobe change, but I also didn't not agree to it.

With the wardrobe problem solved/not solved, we waded through a few minutes of stilted chitchat with the hope our call would end in a better place. Valentina and I were the ones with a past, as small and compartmentalized as it was; there wasn't any shared experience for Cleo and me to fall back on.

Cleo asked if I liked acting so far. I said "Yeah" in a way that meant not right this second.

I asked her the same question. She said, "I don't know. I haven't started acting yet."

Upon hanging up, I paced the room again, then I took off my clothes. I happened to be wearing tighty-whities, and I imagined the next morning, my beating Valentina to the punch by suggesting I wear these, as they were already worn and saggy; a lot less tighty and whitey.

I stood in front of the hotel bathroom mirror, the bright, cruel yellow lights flashed on my hairless chest, the stubborn clusters of blemishes, underdeveloped musculature, sloped shoulders. I raised and bent my arms randomly, mechanically, twisted and torqued my torso, hoping the body parts might appear like they belonged to some other body and not my own. It didn't work, and I met my own shame-filled eyes in the mirror as I had countless times before. I was seeing who I always saw and who everyone else would see. Though maybe this time, that wasn't quite true.

I stalked into the hotel room proper and read the scene again. The shirt and pants would not come off the Thin Kid until after the mask covered his head. I returned to the bathroom and the un-forgiving mirror, held my hands over my face so my fingers were a mesh over my eyes, and I observed and I breathed, and I imagined.

Well, seeing my body with my face obscured changed everything. With the mask on, people wouldn't see my face as the rest of me was being seen. It wasn't so much altering my identity as covering it, shrouding it, making myself into a blank, but not a blank the observer could fill with their judgments.

With the mask I could be inscrutable, maybe even implacable.

THEN: CLASSROOM SCENE

1

It was approaching the dinner hour and my scenes were finished. I could've gone back to my hotel, but I stayed to watch the last shots of the day. I hadn't put on my clothes yet. I was only wearing my underwear beneath the thick blue robe I'd hidden inside between shots or when we'd had a break. I'd geared up so much psychic energy for what would be the Thin Kid origin scenes, I think I was empty, numb. Stripping down to the well-worn tighty-whities hadn't been as bad as I thought it would be. And at the same time, it was worse. But I wouldn't admit that to myself.

In an uncharacteristic break from the verisimilitude of the filmed story, Valentina had asked Cleo to act as the stand-in Thin Kid hiding from view inside the classroom's supply closet. To her credit, Valentina had observed that I was too keyed-up for even a subtle door creaking.

Valentina shouted her directions: simple, one-word commands. "Quiet. Rolling. Action." Using the handheld Steadicam instead of setting up a dolly track (Valentina's pragmatic decision; she wanted to get the shot now and not go into overtime, which would've meant, by observed union rules even if most of the crew weren't union, starting an hour later than scheduled tomorrow), Dan crept down the gullet of the classroom at an even pace. There wasn't any dialogue to fill the anticipatory silence, and I had the inexplicable urge to shout nonsense, to speak in film tongues because part of the story, a small part, but maybe the most important part, was being created without me. Then, Valentina again, her voice rising above us, "Now, Cleo," and the supply room's latch clicked, the door creaked open a few inches, and I strained to get a glimpse inside, afraid I might somehow see myself in there.

After the third take, Valentina said, "Cut, check the gate. And that's a wrap for today." She clapped her hands and the rest of the crew joined the applause briefly, as was our end-of-day tradition.

Cleo popped out of the closet, posing, flipping her red hair, smiling madly, waving hi, batting her eyes behind her glasses, and Dan pretended to film and shouted, "Work it!" earning appreciative laughter from the crew. As the small crew broke down and packed up, Cleo, now in her role of script supervisor, huddled with Dan, he now wearing his director of photography hat, as she jotted notes into a big green notebook.

I got dressed under the robe (a contortionist would've been impressed). Karson, the eponymous actor and lead makeup/effects artist, gathered the robe and hung it on the *"rolling wardrobe rack from hell,"* which was what someone in the crew had christened it with a handwritten placard. I hadn't got a bead on Karson yet. He had gone to the same high school as Valentina and Cleo, but he was a few years older than them. He had earned a two-year associate's degree in radiology technology and prior to this film had worked as a stagehand for the Providence Performing Arts Center. It was never clear to me if Valentina, Cleo, and Karson had been close friends prior to the filming, though I assumed they had. Karson had one makeup/effects assistant or coworker named Mel, short for Melanie. She was his cousin and did makeup and hair for local weddings. Mel was loud and provided necessary laughter when the mood on-set became too serious, too grim, and she often shared non sequitur gossip about her extended family while working on the actors in her makeup chair. Between scenes, when Valentina and Cleo consulted the script and storyboards with Dan, Karson hung out with Mel. I assumed Valentina had told him he wasn't allowed to buddy around with me to keep me and my character isolated. Upon introductions on our first day on-set, Karson had said that he and I would get to know each other later in the shoot when I would be spending the morning hours sitting for makeup and prosthetics. The prosthetics had been news to me. However, when those mornings came, there wasn't any of the promised get-to-know-each-other banter. Without being able to look me in the eye, hiding his own behind his long, straight bangs, Karson apologized for what had happened the day before. I told him he didn't need to say he was sorry, that he wasn't his character, and then he apologized for what he was about to do to me. We enacted this routine often enough that it should've become a joke, our joke, but it never did. Karson remained sullen and serious, unsettled in my presence. I wondered if he was method acting, being the Karson from the script full-time. Why not, right? Maybe that was his choice. Maybe Valentina had given him a prescriptive directive on how he should play the character of himself. Maybe he was just being who Karson was. Maybe he wasn't acting, like how Cleo had joked she wasn't acting. They were using their real names as the characters' names because they were playing or displaying some real version of themselves, even if it was their worst version.

Valentina tugged my elbow and led me to a quiet corner of the classroom by the blackboard. She and I had decided we would meet at the end of each shooting day to discuss how things were going on my end and afterward she would formally present me with the next day's sides.

Valentina laughed and shook her head.

I said, "What," though I was nervously laughing too.

Her laugh became an all-knowing smirk. "*Weird Guy* is officially the Thin Kid now. I can and can't believe we're doing this."

I said, "It's all your fault. When does the German Expressionism come in?"

"You haven't figured out that you're Cesare yet?"

I blinked and gawped until I figured out she was referring to a character from the film *The Cabinet of Dr. Caligari*. "Oh, right. Does that make you Dr. Caligari, then?"

"I thought you wouldn't remember that movie, and I was gonna punch you. You were great today. Really."

"I took off my clothes and put on a mask. No big deal."

"Stop it and just take the compliment."

"Okay, I will. Thank you. It did, um, feel pretty good. Maybe I can do this."

"This was a big day. Remember it. Remember it so tomorrow or the next day or next week you can remind yourself that you can do this. Because the rest of the days are going to get harder, and probably won't be as much fun."

"Being masked and almost naked isn't exactly my idea of fun." Valentina arched an eyebrow. I blushed and hurriedly added, "I'm sure everyone else feels the same way looking at me."

She ignored the self-deprecation and said that I had tomorrow and possibly the next day off, as they would be shooting scenes with the other teens at their homes. I asked if I could watch and she said, of course, and told me to check in with Karson to get the schedule and location maps. She also said that she wouldn't give me more script pages until either tomorrow night or the night after. She didn't want me dwelling on my next scenes over multiple days. She wanted to keep the rhythm of sides coming the night before.

By this time Cleo had finished reviewing scenes with Dan and stood next to Valentina and said, "Sorry to interrupt, but Dan again pressed us to consider shooting all the schoolroom scenes in a row so we wouldn't have to break down and re–set up."

"And you said no, right?"

"Yes."

Cleo and I shared quick *hey there* head nods and then complimented each other's performances.

I said, "Hey, while I have you both. I am a little confused by today's scene. It wasn't what I imagined when you said I'd be wearing a mask for a horror movie. Aren't I the bad guy in this movie? I thought I would be."

Valentina smirked and said, "Maybe."

Cleo said, "We're all someone's bad guy eventually."

Valentina said, "You're so deep, Cleo," which set off a brief staccato back-and-forth between the two of them.

"Like a river."

"Or a lake."

"No, a river."

"Most rivers are shallow."

"Not all."

"Why not an ocean?"

"Too deep."

"How about a fjord?"

I didn't exactly interrupt, but if I hadn't said something they might've continued that way all night. I said, "Hey, um, this just occurred to me. Do you think I can stay here, in the classroom, over-night? I have no idea what happens next in the script or anything, but I'm guessing they left the Thin Kid here in the school." I paused, waiting for one of them to say something. Neither did. "Anyway, yeah, just to get more 'in character' like you want, maybe I should stay here, even for just a few hours with no one else around, so I can get in that mind space. I can lock up when I leave. No big deal." The school's entrances and classroom doors were chain padlocked.

Valentina and Cleo looked at each other before responding.

Valentina said, "You don't have to do that. We know you're working hard."

Cleo said, "I don't think it's a good idea." She looked around the room, as though afraid we were being overheard.

I rambled about how if I stayed, even just for a few hours, I might dissuade local kids from breaking in, because they'd see my car parked outside and maybe a light on up here.

Valentina said, "There'll be no light. We can't afford to keep the generator running all night."

"Right. I meant a flashlight anyway."

Cleo said, "Won't you be scared staying here by yourself? I'd be terrified. No way."

"Says the one who broke in here and found a mask, right?"

"Exactly!" Cleo shouted and spread her arms.

"Oh, believe me," I said, "I'll leave when I get too freaked out, probably after ten minutes. Look, I think I need to do this, to try this. Really."

Valentina shrugged and said, "Fine by me. Cesare wants to spend some time in his cabinet."

"Who's Cesare?" Cleo asked, which set off another rapid-fire two-woman skit.

"Dude, watch some movies."

"I watch a shit ton of movies."

"Watch some old movies."

"I watch old movies."

"'70s flicks don't count as old movies."

"Yes, they do."

"Watch black-and-white movies."

"I do! *Young Frankenstein*."

"That doesn't count."

"*Psycho*, *Night of the Living Dead*, *Creature from the Black Lagoon* . . ." Cleo continued listing films as they walked away, leaving me standing alone by the blackboard.

INT. CLEO'S HOUSE, BEDROOM - NIGHT

A different dark room.

Cleo flicks the wall switch, a dim CEILING LIGHT fixture flickers to life, perhaps recalling the sparking electric arcs within Frankenstein's lab.

She does a circuit of the room, turning on nightstand LAMPS, one on each side of her bed, and a STANDING LAMP in one corner.

Her room is small and generally neat, or "teen neat." At least her bed is made.

A small wooden DESK nests under a WINDOW. That desk is cluttered with small JARS of paints, brushes, other materials, including what appears to be a human HEAD. We briefly see the desk and the head in our greedy sweep of the room.

Maybe we only subliminally see the head, as we're distracted by the swarm of POSTERS on the walls. They're all blank, rectangles of white empty space.

She removes the lower thumbtacks from the corners of the largest poster, the one on the back of her closet door. She flips up the bottom, revealing the printing on the poster's other side.

Cleo inspects the inverted image of Leatherface on a TEXAS CHAIN SAW MASSACRE movie poster. Her expression is focused, intense, but inscrutable. We cannot know what she is thinking. We can never know what exactly she is thinking. Her mind -- just like anyone else's mind -- is a turned-over poster.

We assume the other posters in her room are also horror-movie posters. She must be hiding them from her overbearing, overprotective parents.

Consider: maybe the reason for the flipped posters is more complex. Maybe she doesn't like many of the movies on the hidden posters. In fact, she thinks most of them are terrible movies. The terrible ones are predictable, follow a pattern, and make her feel safe but in an unsafe way. Horror movies should make us feel the opposite, shouldn't they? Still, she watches all the horror movies she can, repeatedly, and she buys the posters and stares at them until she flips them over to be re-scrutinized later at the time of her choosing. The hope is she'll find a movie that changes her in the way she didn't know she wanted to be changed.

There's a KNOCK on her bedroom door.

Cleo refastens the poster back in place and answers the knock.

> CLEO
> Yeah?

The door remains closed. She flops onto her bed.

> MOM (O.S.)
> Did you eat anything?

> CLEO
> I will in a little bit.

> MOM (O.S.)
> Your friend's mother just
> called. Asking if he was
> here.

CUT TO:

INT. KARSON'S HOUSE, KITCHEN - NIGHT

> KARSON
> (as though answering

Cleo's Mom)
He's not here.

The kitchen is small and earth-toned in color.

Karson is at the KITCHEN TABLE, eating leftover chicken,
rice, and corn, and drinking a tall glass of chocolate
milk. He sits turned away from the DOORWAY, a portal that
leads to the rest of his house.

We see him from behind his DAD, who is an indistinct, blurry
shape. From this vantage, Karson is small, a child, and Dad
is broad-shouldered, with thick arms. He's big and scary
like all dads are. Maybe we are to assume that Karson's dad
is extra scary, that his dad is the minotaur that stalks the
maze of his house.

                    DAD
          No shit, Sherlock. I can
          see that. But weren't you
          with him earlier?

                                        CUT TO:

INT. VALENTINA'S HOUSE, LIVING ROOM - NIGHT

                    VALENTINA
          I haven't seen him since
          school, Mamá.

Valentina scribbles in a NOTEBOOK and doesn't look up when
she answers. She is on the floor, lying on her stomach,
head and torso propped up on her elbows. SCHOOLBOOKS and
HOMEWORK spread out before and around her like a Rorschach
test.

The living room is cavernous, like the rest of the house.
The THROW RUG that Valentina is on might as well be a life-
boat in a sea of hardwood.

MAMÁ (O.S.)
Oh. I hope he's okay.

CUT TO:

****SCREEN SPLITS INTO THE THREE HOME
LOCATIONS OF THE TEENS****

CLEO   KARSON   VALENTINA
I hope so too.   I hope so too.   I hope so too.

The CAMERA holds on the three teens.

MOM (O.S.)   DAD (O.S.)   MAMÁ (O.S.)
I'm sure he's   I'm sure he's   I'm sure he's
fine.   fine.   fine.

We don't know who to look at, who is lying the best, whose look
clearly communicates that nothing will be fine, who might be
itching to crack, to tell the truth. We don't know who will be
believed by which parents. We don't know who is the most dedicated to what they have planned, who is the most resigned,
who is the most afraid, who is the most ashamed.

CUT TO:

INT. CLEO'S HOUSE, BEDROOM - CONTINUOUS

Cleo puts a PILLOW over her face.

MOM (O.S.)
Dad wants to know if you
talked to the tennis coach yet.

CLEO
No, Mom. And I'm not going
to. Please explain to Dad
what "I quit" means.

                        MOM (O.S.)
          You mean, you'll talk to her
          tomorrow after school, right?

Cleo doesn't answer, gives the door the finger.

                        MOM (O.S. CONT.)
          I'm only teasing. Please
          don't forget to eat.

                                        CUT TO:

INT. KARSON'S HOUSE, KITCHEN - CONTINUOUS

                        DAD (O.S.)
          Don't bother your mother
          with any of this yet, if she
          calls. She'll freak out, and
          baby you more than she
          already does.
                    (laughs, even though
                    this is not particularly
                    funny, and his laugh
                    sounds like a bull's
                    snort, a threat)

                        KARSON
                    (a tone of attempted
                    defiance)
          So I can't call her now?

                        DAD (O.S.)
          I wouldn't.

Dad's shape is still blurry, an indistinct person, a manifestation of a father's dangerous disappointment in a son
who isn't like him, isn't going to be like him. It's not that
Dad thinks of himself as a paragon of maleness, quite the

contrary, he's confused by it, even as he dreams of indoctrinating his son with it.

Dad's murky form leaves the doorway. His footsteps are heavy.

Karson gets up from the table stiffly, wearily. Some trap has been set, and he can't see the tripwire. He empties his half-full plate into the trash. Covers the evidence of wasted food with a paper towel.

                                                    CUT TO:

INT. VALENTINA'S HOUSE, LIVING ROOM - CONTINUOUS

                        MAMÁ (O.S.)
                I bought you some new
                clothes I want you to
                try on.

                        VALENTINA
                Mamá . . .

                        MAMÁ (O.S.)
                They're nice. You might
                like them. *And* they're
                actually in colors other
                than black and gray.

This is a conversation Valentina has had a million times. Mamá is spurred on by unfathomable motivation somewhere between cruelty and good intentions, never missing an opportunity to audibly wish Valentina would dress like the rest of her classmates.

                        VALENTINA
                Then I will hate them.

                                                    CUT TO:

INT. CLEO'S HOUSE, BEDROOM - CONTINUOUS

Cleo walks to her desk carrying the paper bag of the Thin Kid's clothes.

We can better see/inspect the arts-and-crafts mess on the tabletop now: a painter's PALETTE with a mix of dried PAINTS of the mask's coloring, tubes of MAKEUP, bits of unformed LATEX (painted and unpainted), stray scales as though the mask had shed them, a leaf pile of POLAROID PHOTOS, and a green Styrofoam HEAD propped on its neck.

She picks up one photo:

Her three friends, outside, beneath a tall tree, the trunk wide, the leg of a giant, the teens frozen in silly poses. The Thin Kid makes pistol hands, pointed at the camera, and he has a sweatshirt on backward. His face is lost inside the hood.

Cleo pins the photo to the head.

She opens her desk drawer and takes out a pack of MATCHES.

She leaves her bedroom again carrying the paper bag.

We stay behind in the lonely bedroom. All teen bedrooms are lonely.

The ceiling light flickers.

                                            CUT TO:

INT. KARSON'S HOUSE, FIRST FLOOR - CONTINUOUS

We follow behind Karson as he wanders through the first floor of his house. No lights are on.

His decisions to turn left or right seem random, but also, there's no hesitation or change within the speed (slow, methodical) of his gait.

We follow and we follow.

His house couldn't possibly be this big.

We begin to recognize some of the rooms we pass through are the same as the ones he passed through earlier, but the order in which these rooms appear and reappear doesn't make spatial sense.

Karson continues walking.

                    DAD (O.S.)
                (sounding distant
                and monstrous)
            Karson?

                    KARSON
                (answering in a
                conversant, mid-volume
                tone)
            I'm going to bed early.

We continue to follow Karson as he wanders, lost in the maze, with the minotaur howling his name.

                                        CUT TO:

INT. VALENTINA'S HOUSE, LIVING ROOM - CONTINUOUS

Valentina remains on the floor, writing in her notebook.

Offscreen, Mamá storms out of the living room, mumbling to herself.

We do not leave with Mamá. We remain in the hovering POV spot she vacated, looking down on Valentina as though we are Mamá's ghost.

We slowly float down closer so we can see Valentina's notebook. She has drawn a rough but clear pencil sketch of the Thin Kid in the mask. He's crouched, sitting tucked in the corner of a room. But not in a threatening, monster-waiting-to-get-you way. His long arms are wrapped around his knees, hugging his legs into himself.

We know/interpret this drawing because of context. We know where the Thin Kid is and what has happened to him.

Because of our POV, however, the image is upside down, and if we didn't know better, it would appear the Thin Kid has floated to the corner of a ceiling, like an untethered lost balloon.

                                        CUT TO:

INT. CLEO'S HOUSE, BEDROOM - CONTINUOUS

Her bedroom is empty, but it's not static. The ceiling fixture's light flickers, flickers, and dies.

With the light in the room dimmed, we must stare at the head on her desk and the window behind it.

Outside, beyond and below the window, there's a muffled WHOOSH. Orange light of small fire flares and settles into a low glow.

                                        FADE TO:

INT. ABANDONED SCHOOL, CLASSROOM - NIGHT

Moonlight filters through the windows to our left, throwing tiger stripes of weak yellow light across the blackboard.

The CAMERA mimics its prior slow approach through the classroom to the supply-room door and focuses its cruel stare on the sliver of opening.

The Thin Kid is inside the supply room. He hasn't dared leave. For the moment, he is our proxy; like him, we are following, obeying the rules of whatever this is.

We do wonder if he left the mask on. Is he sitting with his arms wrapped around his legs as in Valentina's sketch? Is he asleep and dreaming? Is he awake and dreaming? What is he thinking?

We can't know what he is thinking. We can't know what anyone else is thinking, even when they tell us.

FADE TO BLACK:

THEN:
THE SLEEPOVER

Some lighting equipment and cables in milk crates were stacked against the classroom's rear wall by the door. The mask, along with the rolling wardrobe, had been packed up into Dan's van.

I felt silly immediately upon being the last one left inside the classroom, but I worried I'd be sillier if I locked up and vacated right behind everyone else. The classroom windows overlooked the cracked pavement-turned-parking-lot, and I watched the cars, their drivers woozy with fatigue and the work that lay ahead, leave one by one until my shitbox was alone. That hunk of junk wouldn't scare off any would-be nocturnal explorers. They'd assume it had been abandoned.

The classroom was warm, the air sticky. I shuffled around the room, the floor creaking under my weight, and I followed the dusty beam of my flashlight, searching for the reason why I'd stayed. I questioned who I thought I was. Did I think I was a real actor? Was I this precious? My request to stay in the classroom was a momentary lapse of impulse control, something so cliché to my age that I was embarrassed all over again. I promised myself that I would later discuss this evening in such honest terms when asked about how my sleepover went. I could already hear Valentina dismissively describing this, whatever this was, as my sleepover.

I scanned the floor for the marks that Cleo had described when she found the mask. I didn't believe her story, but I wanted to. I eventually made my way to the supply room, which had been left open. The flashlight illuminated a rash of scratches and gouges on the rear wall. Had they been there before? I didn't notice them earlier. Did Valentina have the marks made for the film? Did Cleo? Were the marks supposed to mimic what Cleo had claimed to have found on the floor beneath the mask? (At that point in the shoot, I didn't know there wouldn't be a scene related to the finding or creating of the mask.)

I once had a substitute teacher in third grade who gave us the following art assignment: We were to scribble randomly all over a blank page with a black crayon. When we finished that, we were to color the page in, filling gaps and spaces between the arbitrary lines with whatever color we wanted. We weren't supposed to be actively drawing or creating anything. She wanted an abstract explosion of shapes and color. The teacher claimed that when we finished, she would be able to see a secret picture emerge from the patternless mess we'd made, and she would be able to get us to see it too. I accepted her assignment as an ultimate challenge, and I scribbled and scratched and colored and made something I thought was as indecipherable as static. When I presented my page, she squinted and looked and looked and I thought I had won, but she said, "Ah, there," as though disgusted with herself for not seeing the obvious sooner. "A bird sticking its head through a cocoon-shaped nest." I blinked, unable or unwilling to initially see the image, but then I saw it too. The multicolored bits of shapes, like the digital blobs of an old tube television when your face was inches from the screen, formed a bird with a wide pumpkin-shaped head peeking out from its cavelike nest. It looked too big for its nest and angry at having been discovered or disturbed. I was angry too. I couldn't articulate this at the time, but the teacher demonstrated that I wouldn't always be able to see, to really see, what I was looking at.

The memory of that monstrous bird image struck the first chord of fear. Standing alone in the dark classroom of a dead, condemned school, I didn't want to see the secret within the supply room wall's slashing pattern. I didn't want to see that same bird; maybe this time its head would be larger, beak opened wider, and finally free from its nest. I aimed the flashlight beam back to the floor.

Stripping down to my underwear again was not part of my re-enactment plan, if only because I wanted to remain dressed and ready to sprint from the room. I cleared my throat and said, "Okay," out loud, the verbalization a trespass. I stepped inside the closet, turned my back to the rear wall, but was careful to not brush up against it. Before I could lose my nerve, I swung the door most of the way closed, leaving a gap an inch or two wide, like there had been in the final shot, the final scene of the day. The flashlight was clutched against my chest, beam pointed up and out, and the boxy space glowed a ghostly, jaundiced white. Keeping my mind preoccupied with my assignment, with my next steps, I slowly sank to the floor and sat with my legs crossed. I slid backward until my back was supported by the rear wall. I panned the flashlight right and left. Toward the right, ceiling and wall tapered into a shallow crawlspace meant for forgotten boxes filled with old, graffitied text-books. I briefly imagined the Thin Kid with his mask still on, un-able to sleep sitting up, so he'd lie down, stretching his matchstick legs and flipper feet into the crawlspace void. To my left, the space kept its height for another five feet. Built into the back wall was a warren of empty shelves and, across from them, two crooked coat hooks set at child's height.

I said, "Okay," again, a whisper this time, and I shut off the flashlight. The sudden darkness was total and disorienting. I tried to blink away leftover ghostly images caused by inadvertently looking directly into the flashlight. Unmoored, I reached for and spread my fingers on the gritty floor as I momentarily thought I might've somehow been spun upside down. My breaths were fast, nasal, and obvious. I concentrated on my sputtering machine sounds, attempting to recalibrate, and I stared at where I thought the sliver of open door would be. Eventually my light-starved eyes adjusted and found weak light from within the classroom, or the weak light that filtered into the classroom. With the eyesight toe-hold, that slash of vision into the lighter dark outside the door, my breathing became more under control and shallower, lower in volume. Then there was a scrabbling within the wall behind me.

Waves of chills ran up the length of my body, converging and crashing onto my neck and head, pulling me into an undertow. Dizzy, I was convinced that I was experiencing the aural after-shocks of what had originally made the looping, slashing scratches on the rear wall, or worse, that I was hearing more of them being made. I could feel the claw depressions and grooves on the cold skin of my back, and everything inside me screamed to get up and run. I briefly imagined the frenzied path through the school and the doom-leaden salvation of my first breath of night air outside. But I stayed.

I wasn't a brave person, and I am still not a brave person, and I don't know if sitting in that tiny supply room qualified me as being almost brave, but I willed myself into staying by pretending I wasn't me. I was him.

The Thin Kid listened to the small claws, scratching their way toward the right, to the walls outlining the crawlspace, and beyond, before returning partway and pausing. That the sound was consistent and changed in timbre and volume with distance made him feel, if not in control, then at least tethered to the present. The sound was real and not imagined. He could identify what the animal source might be. He could now focus on other sounds: sharp creaks and groans from the ceiling and somewhere out in the hallway, the low whistle of wind entering the classroom, and most concerningly, a delicate clink of chain against the classroom door. Those noises were harder to explain and too easy to extrapolate into phantasmagoria. The Thin

Kid's circumstances were already fraught and fearful enough without supernatural intrusion. That thought resulted in a cynical brand of comfort. He listened and watched and waited, expecting someone—maybe one of his friends—or something to step into the small, fuzzy field of vision. He regretted unlatching the door, leaving it open, and perhaps the sounds and their accompanying paranoia and fear were his punishment. But what was he being punished for? What had he done to deserve this?

He felt an odd sense of relief when the scratching noises in the wall approached his space again. He rapped his knuckles on the wall, and the scrabbling rodent (a mouse? a small gray squirrel?) stopped as though to acknowledge that they both were frightened, confused, and alone.

The Thin Kid didn't want to hear more secret noises, so he spoke, his voice dusty from disuse. He wondered aloud why his friends were doing what they were doing to him. He wondered when they would come back for him. Would they let him go home after one night? Would they, in the days or even years later, talk about why this happened? He asked himself why he was staying there and what it meant that he would do whatever his friends asked of him.

I didn't remember falling asleep. I awoke early the next morning, lying on my side, my cramped, cold hands my pillow, and my feet stretched into the crawlspace. I'd taken off my clothes at some point in the evening and found them in a discreet pile underneath the blackboard.

INT. HIGH SCHOOL CLASSROOM - NEXT AFTERNOON

Their high school is not abandoned, though they wish it were.

It's a late-in-the-day study hall. Valentina, Cleo, and Karson sit in the back row. The other DESKS -- there seems to be an infinite number of them -- are occupied except for the one in front of Cleo. That desk is empty.

The other STUDENTS are fuzzy and out of focus. They are working or sleeping or passing NOTES or staring off into space, anything and everything but looking at the three teens in the last row.

Valentina still wears her beanie over her thick hair. She has pulled her arms out of her sleeves and hidden them inside her sweatshirt. In the initial moments we look at her, an image of a straitjacket comes to our minds. One empty sleeve is a sash across her chest and stomach, the other sleeve is draped, like a dead snake, over her desktop.

Cleo sits posture-perfect, her hands folded. The muscles in her jaw clench and unclench.

Karson has his BACKPACK on. The pack is overstuffed, almost comically overfilled. He is sunken, curled into his chair so that he looks like a slouched turtle.

The three teens trade looks with one another and occasionally glance at the empty desk that we assume belongs to the Thin Kid. Some movie viewers won't understand that the empty desk is where he usually sits, even though it should be clear from context and visual cues. But we can't spoonfeed, can't be totally obvious about everything; not in this movie, a movie that isn't for everyone.

The BELL rings. School is over for another day.

INT. HIGH SCHOOL, HALLWAY – MOMENTS LATER

The three teens walk down the middle of a hallway, through another tunnel, this one made of lockers and shadowed classmates so blurred-out that individuals meld and morph together to give the appearance of a single amoeba-like organism, ready to spring and lash out flagella.

The teens walk in a careful cluster, not the confident, bold line in which we were introduced to them in the opening scene.

They walk tightly huddled together. We fear for them as they walk as a pack to protect whoever is judged to be the most vulnerable to predation.

DISSOLVE TO:

EXT. SUBURBAN SIDE STREET – AFTERNOON

The teens walk in the middle of the sleepy street, the same one with the entry to the path in the woods at its end.

They are back in their line formation, although today's line is more spaced out. The teens don't talk, don't joke, and they don't playfully bump into one another.

Karson is in the middle, flanked by Valentina and Cleo. He adjusts and readjusts his heavy backpack.

Valentina cradles a paper bag.

Cleo carries a yellow BEACH PAIL/BUCKET.

The teens overtake and walk past the static CAMERA, leaving the briefest view of the empty street behind them.

CUT TO:

INT. ABANDONED SCHOOL, FIRST-FLOOR HALLWAY/STAIRWELL –
MINUTES LATER

The teens flow through the length of the hallway and to the
base of the stairs.

Cleo steps onto the stairs last, after hooking the beach
pail's plastic handle over her wrist and putting BOTH HANDS
into her pockets instead of using the railing to aid the
climb like her friends do.

Valentina is the first one to reach the sun-dappled landing
between floors, and she watches and waits for her friends
to make the pre-summit base camp.

She lets Karson pass her.

She stops Cleo with a hand on her shoulder, then tugs at one
of Cleo's wrists.

> VALENTINA
> (a whisper that isn't
> a whisper)
> I know this is your death-wish
> stairs thing, but you can't do
> that here. If you trip and fall,
> these aren't the fluffy,
> carpeted stairs of your house.
> This is serious. You could
> really get hurt.

Cleo nods and takes her hands out of her pockets.

[It will be difficult to convey the following by the actor's
performance -- unless we include the below in a scene -- but
it is important information about Cleo that all the actors
should know:

Toward the end of winter, a week after having found the mask and not knowing what to do with it, Cleo and Valentina were sitting in Cleo's bedroom, listening to cassettes. Cleo admitted to Valentina that she'd been feeling like she wanted to die for a long time, but -- and this *but* is important -- she would never actively hurt herself because she knew how that would devastate her parents and her friends. However, if Cleo were to be killed in an everyday kind of freak accident, then it wouldn't be her fault and she'd be okay with that. In fact, she thought about small ways in which she might increase her chances of dying in an accident, increase those chances ever so slightly, without being *active* about it. For example, whenever Cleo walked up or down stairs, she hid her hands inside her pockets. That way if she were to trip and fall, it would solely be chance that she smashed her head or broke her neck and died. Who was she to overrule chance by having her hubristic hands ready to play the hero? Valentina tried not to betray her alarm, but Cleo could tell. Whenever her best friend talked with a shrunken, tight mouth, she was upset. Cleo apologized and told Valentina not to worry; like she already said, she would never hurt herself purposefully. Valentina said that thinking and planning as she was, *was* being *active*. Cleo said, "Let me explain it this way: They say lots of people die by slipping in their showers or bathtubs, right? So, before showering, I once considered squirting soap onto the floor of our tank of a clawfoot tub. But I didn't because that would be too active. I would be forcing or aiding an accident into being instead of just letting it happen. Making the tub more slippery is *active*. Putting my hands in my pockets is not. See the difference?"]

Valentina smiles, a weak one, a sad one, and as a show of trust, walks up the second flight of stairs ahead of Cleo.

Cleo puts her hands back in her pockets and ascends.

INT. ABANDONED SCHOOL, SECOND-FLOOR HALLWAY, OUTSIDE OF
CLASSROOM - MOMENTS LATER

The teens gather in front of the closed classroom door.

                    CLEO
          Do you think he's still here?

                    VALENTINA
          Yeah. Definitely.

                    KARSON
          What if he isn't?
               (drops to a
               whisper)
          I kinda hope he's not.
          What if he's already . . .

Cleo reaches out and holds one of his hands.

Karson leans into the hand-holding, then pulls away and
readjusts his backpack. The contents audibly RATTLE.

                    KARSON (CONT'D)
          This is fucking heavy.

Valentina opens the classroom door. The hinges SCREAM.

INT. ABANDONED SCHOOL, CLASSROOM - CONTINUOUS

The room appears the same as it did yesterday. Hazy with
the afternoon sun and the ghosts of students past.

                    CLEO
               (horrified)
          It smells awful.

She spies a wet mark on the wall above a small puddle in the back corner of the room.

The teens walk to the front of the classroom.

Karson unshoulders his pack, and it lands heavily on the floor.

Cleo drops the beach pail next to the pack as Karson unzips it.

Valentina opens the supply-room door.

> VALENTINA
> Come on out. Come on.

The Thin Kid is masked. In the always and forever of this film, he will wear his mask. He emerges slowly from the darkened space. He's crouched and huddled against himself and doesn't stand to his full height.

No one says anything, and he raises a tentative hand, a heartbreaking "hello" hand while the monster mask leers dementedly. In another context, if we were to encounter this same masked person in our dark bedroom, waving at us when we woke, when our eyes opened, we would not feel the pity-tinged dread we are feeling now.

The three teens point at the corner behind him, the corner made by the supply room and blackboard walls.

The Thin Kid obeys, walking as though in slow motion. His long, thin legs remain bent partially even as they stretch over distance, languid and sloth-like. Once in the corner, he stands to his full height. He folds his arms across his chest, then not-so-nonchalantly folds his hands in front of his underwear. His hairless, narrow chest expands and shrinks with each breath. The curled-up bottom of the mask vibrates at the neck.

Karson drags the backpack closer to where the teens stand, between the upturned teacher's desk and the supply-room door. They are ten feet away from the Thin Kid.

The pack is filled with BOTTLE CAPS, small STONES, bits of PAVEMENT, broken or empty LIGHTERS, and even chunks of BOTTLE GLASS. The kind of stuff you might find in an abandoned schoolyard.

It is unclear if the Thin Kid sees the pack's contents. He has gone statue, his rising and falling chest his only movement.

The teens each pull out a single GARDENING GLOVE from their pants pockets. They don the protective glove and scoop debris from the pack. Bits drip and plink to the floor as they open their hands to inspect what they've salvaged.

They each choose a single item with their other, bare hand. They share another look, their wordless recommitment to what they'd already committed to do.

Cleo steps forward and throws a bottlecap at the Thin Kid.

He doesn't shield himself. The cap bounces off his chest.

Karson is next. He throws a stone, hard, and it glances off the Thin Kid's right bicep and smashes loudly into the wall.

The Thin Kid flinches, hisses in pain, and holds the spot where the rock hit him.

Valentina throws a lighter. It thwacks into the Thin Kid's thigh.

After a beat, an acknowledgment, the teens rapid-fire throw their items at the Thin Kid, reloading from the backpack when their scoop hand is empty.

Under the unrelenting hail of objects, the Thin Kid shrinks into the corner, lowering into a tight ball, arms wrapped around his knees. If he cries out in pain, we can't hear him over the teens' exerted breathing and the sounds of the items SMACKING and CRASHING to the floor.

There are hundreds of items within the pack. The teens throw and throw in a frenzy, and the bombardment goes on and on and on until finally the empty pack sags, loses its shape, and collapses to the floor.

The teens are hands-on-knees exhausted and gasping for air.

The Thin Kid shivers and whimpers in the corner. His skin is mottled with red welts and small scrapes. The weaponized debris pond-scums the floor around the Thin Kid.

Valentina retrieves the paper bag she carried and empties the contents onto the overturned teacher's desk: WATER AND SODA BOTTLES, a bag of POTATO CHIPS, POP-TARTS, assorted CANDY BARS, PASTRY SNACKS.

                    VALENTINA
          You can use the bucket and the
          bottles when they're empty
          to go to the bathroom from now on.

Karson gathers the empty pack quickly, on the verge of tears, unable to look at anyone, and runs away.

Valentina follows at a steely-eyed, steady walk.

Cleo initially follows but turns back, crunch-walks over the rocks and bits, and helps the Thin Kid up into a semi-standing crouch. She leans in and pulls him closer.

                    CLEO
          (conspiratorial
          whisper)
          I'm coming back tonight.

> VALENTINA (O.S.)
> What are you doing, Cleo?

Cleo darts away from the Thin Kid and jogs to catch up with her friends, who are already at the rear of the classroom.

The teens leave and close the door behind them.

The Thin Kid sinks back into a squat and scans the scratches and bruises on his body.

> VALENTINA (O.S.)
> We're doing this because we
> have to.

The Thin Kid idly picks up a stone and tosses it to the side. He does the same with a bottle cap, a piece of glass, slowly clearing a path for himself.

> FADE TO:

INT. CLEO'S BEDROOM, KARSON'S KITCHEN, VALENTINA'S LIVING ROOM - EVENING

THE SCREEN SPLITS INTO THE THREE PREVIOUS HOME LOCATIONS OF THE TEENS

The CAMERA focuses on the teens' faces, which are turned away from us. They can't bear to be seen, to be judged.

**When the PARENTS speak, their partial phrases are TIMED to complete a kind of group statement or question.

When the teens speak, they speak in UNISON.**

MOM (O.S.)	DAD (O.S.)	MAMÁ (O.S.)
His mom called	again. He still	hasn't come home.

CLEO	KARSON	VALENTINA
He wasn't in school.	He wasn't in school.	He wasn't in school.

MOM (O.S.)	DAD (O.S.)	MAMÁ (O.S.)
Have you heard where	anything from him? he might	Do you know be?

CLEO	KARSON	VALENTINA
No, I don't.	No, I don't.	No, I don't.

MOM (O.S.)	DAD (O.S.)	MAMÁ (O.S.)
This is so	terrible.	Are you okay?

CLEO	KARSON	VALENTINA
Yes and no.	Yes and no.	Yes and no.

MOM (O.S.)	DAD (O.S.)	MAMÁ (O.S.)
I want you to come No	home right after going	school tomorrow. out.

The teens do not respond to the edict.

FADE TO:

INT. ABANDONED SCHOOL, CLASSROOM - EVENING

The Thin Kid sits in the same corner in which we'd left him. But he has cleared away most of the debris.

On the teacher's desk are a few empty FOOD WRAPPERS, one
EMPTY WATER BOTTLE, and another WATER BOTTLE that is full
of a yellowish liquid we are to assume is urine.

Offscreen, there are approaching footsteps in the hallway.

The Thin Kid stands. Unsure of what to do, unsure if he
should hide, he takes a step toward his food supplies, then
a halting step toward the supply closet, then freezes.

Someone with a flashlight enters the classroom.

                    CLEO
          Hey, it's me. It's okay.

Cleo approaches the Thin Kid and shines her FLASHLIGHT
on him. She sits down, legs crossed, and pats the floor.
She balances the flashlight on its base, light pointed to
the ceiling.

                    CLEO (CONT'D)
          You can sit. Please.

The Thin Kid sits, the flashlight between him and Cleo. He's
close. He could reach across the glowing expanse and grab
a fistful of her red hair.

                    CLEO (CONT'D)
               (matter-of-fact)
          I'm not going to tell you the
          whole story, but I found
          your mask. It is yours now.
          It doesn't matter where I
          found it. Imagine I found
          it in this room, or in the
          basement of another
          abandoned space. It must
          be an abandoned space though.

Cleo unslings a small SHOULDER BAG. While she speaks, she removes a small PAINT JAR, the paint green, the same green as the mask, and a thin PAINTBRUSH.

She draws an intricate set of looping and crossing marks on the floor between the flashlight and her crossed legs.

> CLEO (CONT'D)
> What's more important is that
> I also found some markings,
> symbols drawn under the mask.
> I didn't have a camera with me,
> or even a notebook to copy any
> of it down, so I had to memorize
> it. I made myself memorize it,
> as nervous and awful as it made
> me feel. I'm not sure if I have
> it all down perfectly. I've been
> practicing at home, but I think
> I've got it down. I worried
> being off in the slightest
> would lessen its power, or
> change what it means or does.
> But I drew what I remembered,
> over and over and over, every
> night for weeks and weeks, until
> I got it right. Until I felt
> in my bones that it was the same.
> Then I practiced and practiced
> until I could draw it in my sleep.

Cleo wipes the paintbrush on a RAG and closes the cap to the paint jar. She blows on the paint to dry it. A set of symbols is contained within an ellipse shaped like an eye. She grabs the flashlight and holds it above the symbol.

> CLEO (CONT'D)
> These marks might look
> random at first, but they're

not. Those marks are from a
language not meant to be spoken.
I don't know if the language
is ancient, older than our
tongues, or maybe something new,
new to us anyway. What I do know
is that the marks have meaning
and are powerful and you'll be
able to sense that even if
you can't describe it.

The CAMERA doesn't allow us to get a long, clear view of the
symbol, toggling back and forth between Cleo, the symbol,
and the Thin Kid. In the glimpses we do get, some of us think
we see the mask embedded within the arcing loops and some of
us see nothing, see nonsense and meaninglessness, and some
of us see the terrible, incomprehensible future, and some of
us see all of the above and realize they are the same.

Cleo resets the flashlight on its base. The two teens remain huddled at their makeshift battery-powered campfire.

> CLEO (CONT'D)
> You don't have to go to the
> bathroom in the bottles and
> bucket. You can sneak out to
> the woods if you're sure no one
> is around to see you. But don't
> go deep into the woods, and you
> come right back to this room.
> Promise? You have to promise.

The Thin Kid nods, almost imperceptibly.

> CLEO (CONT'D)
> Once the paint dries --
>   (touches the paint,
>   looks at her finger)
> it's almost dry already --

you are to stand or sit on
top of this symbol. Sit
like we are now: crisscross
applesauce.
> (giggles, then regains
> composure)

For any of this to work, to
be worth it, you must do that.
Okay? Doesn't have to be,
you know, all the time, but
some of the time. I can't
tell you exactly how long.
Go by what feels right, by
what you need.

Again, the Thin Kid nods. He reaches out with a shaky hand
to touch the symbol. He looks at his finger, then wipes it
on his thigh.

> CLEO (CONT'D)
> I'll come back here at night.
> Sometimes.

Cleo grabs the flashlight. Stands. Points the beam directly
into the Thin Kid's masked face. He doesn't flinch, doesn't
cover his eyes.

Cleo walks out of the classroom, taking the light with her.
Her footsteps fade with the light, and we're left with the
Thin Kid's hunched, shadowed form.

He touches the symbol with a finger, then presses his palm
against it. He checks his fingers and palm for wetness. He
scoots and slides forward until he's sitting on the painted
symbol.

Then we leave him too.

FADE TO:

NOW: FERAL FX PART 1

9

Can you believe all these years later I still have the mask?

Blown-up stills from the original movie and detailed sketches of the Thin Kid in various forms and poses fill one wall of Feral FX Studios. A group of makeup artists buzz the hive, and they tinker with various character busts and mask replicas. I stroll in with my mask inside a crinkled-up paper grocery bag. I lift the bag like it's a lantern, letting its light lead the way. Or maybe I hold the bag like there's a gorgon head inside and no one will be the same after they see it. My walk-through earns leery gawks and whispers. I'm long used to being invisible or being an ooh-there-he-is kind of monster or being, simply, *the* monster. There are no cameras around and there won't be any for another two weeks, but my performance for the reboot has already started.

Janelle Ko is the head of the team. They're tall, but not as tall as me, wearing a red *Fire Walk with Me* T-shirt and black joggers. They are in their late thirties or early forties. That decade I have on them is the longest ten years. They clap excitedly at my entrance and say, "I can't wait to see it, but Jesus fuck, please tell me you don't keep it in a paper bag. I'll have you arrested for mask cruelty."

I assure them I don't store the mask this way, that I keep it in an airtight storage box, and I stuff the mask with clean cloth to help it maintain shape. I say, "I only take it out and wear it on the first and third Tuesday of every month."

People can never tell when I'm joking. It's a me problem.

Everyone in the studio crowds to witness the reveal. Janelle dons latex gloves, opens the bag, and removes the mask. I expect expressions of disappointment; a slump of tensed shoulders, a head tilt, a release of breath trying not to be a sigh, a furrowed brow communicating the interior monologue, a debate as to whether they'll ask if this is really it. The mask lacks a presence or essence that is only there when I put it over my head, which is part of its genius. The mask is both vessel and void, and it drudges a vital aspect of the wearer that it lays bare upon its surface.

Janelle and her FX team are not disappointed. There are reverent, call-and-response oohs and aahs as Janelle inspects the mask. Several of the artists reach tentatively toward the holy relic and ask questions about its origin that I cannot answer. I reiterate Cleo's claim about finding the mask in the school, which has become part of *Horror Movie*'s folklore canon thanks to an interview I did with the website *Bloody Disgusting* in 2019. I also tell the FX team that I've moved eight times in the years since filming the movie, and each time I tried to leave the mask behind. I tell them moving on is important, despite what it is we're doing now with the new version of the movie. I also tell them how after every move I'd somehow find the mask inside some random box when I unpacked at my new place. I tell them that most recently, after I'd relocated to L.A., it was in the "kitchen" box, nestled within a covered saucepan, blank eyeholes facing out toward me. I tell them a found object is always cursed. My embellished (embellished doesn't mean "not true," by the way) addendum chips away at the believability of Cleo's found-mask tale, which is why I now tell it. Belief in that kind of thing should be difficult and should require its adherents to actively overcome doubt.

By the way, I'm not saying Cleo made it all up. She never copped to not finding the mask in the manner she'd described.

The youngest of the makeup artists don't know how to take me, and I don't either. Janelle barely listens to me as they delicately fit the mask over a life cast of a young actor's head, his name I've purposefully forgotten. Without the mask, he doesn't look like me, or like I once did. His nose isn't prominent enough and he has way more of a chin than I ever had. Sorry, but he shouldn't be the Thin Kid, even if for only half the film. I'm sure he's a fine actor, or at the very least looks broodily appealing onscreen. The Thin Kid will be a character name he tries on and wears for a few hours a day, and when filming is finished, the Thin Kid will not be an inextricable part of who he is. The Thin Kid will be as easily forgotten as the unremarkable, aging man he will become.

I say, "It looks better when I wear it."

The line gets a few laughs even if it wasn't a joke.

Janelle leads me toward the back of the workshop, and I can't help but look over my shoulder at the mask, maybe twice.

Showing off the mask wasn't the sole purpose of this visit to the FX studio. I'm here to make a life cast of my own head and upper chest. After I'd repeatedly insisted that I'd never gone through this process before, Janelle's coworkers explain that they'll fit a gum-based bald cap on me before they apply the silicone that will cover me from just below the collarbone and up, leaving my nostrils open so I can breathe. Janelle interrupts to say that they'll be the only one working around my nostrils. They say, "I'm a nostril pro. Years of practice. You're not claustrophobic, are you? Pretend I didn't ask that." Once I'm covered in silicone, they'll apply plaster strips to create an outer shell that will come off in two pieces. The whole process should take a little more than an hour. All I need to do is take off my T-shirt, put on the garbage-bag poncho, sit still, and breathe.

I'd hoped for a changing room, but I wasn't offered one. Maybe it's my imagination, or my increased awareness of the moments to come as I peel my shirt over my head, but the studio's buzz goes quiet, and the lighting lamps turn brighter, colder. I'm handed the poncho and it's too late to dive inside, to hide what they've already seen. I act like none of this is a big deal, that I'm not the real cursed object, and I ignore their stares, gird myself for their questions, as the black plastic baggie slowly parachutes down over me.

MONTAGE
QUICK CUTS:

--The teens, new day, same afternoon study hall, staring at the empty seat. A student named SHARON in a row ahead turns, faces the teens with a sad look.

                    SHARON
          Sorry about your friend.

                    VALENTINA
          Thanks, Sharon.

--The teens walking down the high school hallway. Other STUDENTS turn their heads and watch.

--The teens walking down the suburban street.

--The teens in the abandoned school classroom, throwing COINS, as hard as they can, into the back of the Thin Kid.

--The teens at their homes, in the evening, ignoring their parents.

Cleo in her bedroom crying or holding her head or staring blankly. She turns over a horror-movie poster so its print side faces out. The movie is obscure, the art garish.

Valentina on the floor in her living room, drawing the Thin Kid on PAPER (**later, when we return to her living room, the drawing will be different and will hint at a future scene of the movie; the last drawing will feature a rough sketch of the Thin Kid from behind, arms out wide and his legs and feet held up, slightly bent, in a way that makes us think he is *floating***).

Karson walking from the kitchen, wandering the dark maze of his house, and his turns are random and frantic and there are only more blurred-out rooms.

--New day, repeat of study-hall scene (but another STUDENT turns -- with classmates watching, engaged -- says, *Sorry about your friend*), the hallway scene (the STUDENTS who walk by half wave, mouth *Sorry* and *Are you okay?* at them), and the suburban street scene.

--The teens in the abandoned school classroom shouting cruelties into the face of a seated Thin Kid.

--Teens at home, in the evening, as described earlier.

--New day, repeat of the study-hall scene (multiple STU-DENTS are talking to the teens with concerned, pained faces), then the hallway scene (teens walking proud now, accepting condolences with head nods and waves), and the suburban street scene.

--The teens standing with their backs to the Thin Kid, laughing and talking and having a great time.

--Teens at home, in the evening, as described earlier.

--New day, repeat of study hall (teens talk with more classmates, the back of the room crowded now, desks pulled into a tight cluster, and one student drops a NOTE under Sharon's desk and she doesn't notice it, but Valentina does and stretches her foot out toward the note), then the hallway scene (teens stop, accept hugs and pats on the shoulder from other students), then the suburban street scene.

--The teens club the Thin Kid with plastic WIFFLE BALL BATS.

--Teens at home, in the evening, as described earlier.

The pattern of scenes continues and loops, and the cuts are quicker, gaining speed, momentum, and we fear this will never end, and we begin to glimpse a kind of understanding that won't be fully clear until later, but we think, perhaps, everyone in the film is in hell even if the teens don't realize it themselves.

Then the pattern breaks, if only momentarily . . .

INT. ABANDONED SCHOOL, CLASSROOM - AFTERNOON

We are focused on the closed entrance door from inside the classroom. This is not the Thin Kid's POV. It's ours, as though we stayed with him overnight, like we do every night, to make sure he didn't disobey, that he's still there. We're doing to him what the teens are doing. We're complicit.

The door opens. The teens walk in.

The Thin Kid is sitting on his symbol-decorated spot. Maybe he goes back to the supply room to sleep at night. Maybe he stays sitting on the symbol.

His skin is bruised and scratched. He lifts his head wearily.

The mask around his neck no longer fits loosely. The rubber latex folds that once dangled and flapped almost comically at the base of his neck are FUSED, melded into his skin. There are no sharp lines or hard borders that we can see between mask and the Thin Kid's neck.

If the teens see the melding of mask and skin, they don't react to it. They encircle the Thin Kid and sit.

None of the teens carries a backpack this time.

Valentina produces a PACK OF CIGARETTES from a pocket. Karson pulls out a LIGHTER and gives it to Valentina.

The Thin Kid stays seated in his symbolled spot.

Valentina lights a cigarette and puffs it expertly, though she coughs after exhaling, and giggles.

Without warning, she stubs the cigarette out on the Thin Kid's shoulder.

He squeals with pain, a fucking terrible sound. He scrabbles onto his feet and retreats into his usual corner of the classroom.

The teens stand too, and again enclose the Thin Kid within a semicircle.

Karson lights his own cigarette, doesn't cough, and stubs it out on the Thin Kid's stomach.

Cleo follows suit, and while the Thin Kid works to shield his body, she jabs forward, getting him on the chest.

When one teen is stubbing out their cigarette, the others reshape and relight theirs. They stub out cigarettes all over the Thin Kid's body.

The Thin Kid's cries and whimpers fade, diminish, like he's a dying clock. He stops trying to block their glowing-ember snake-strikes.

The classroom is cloudy with smoke. The teens cough and grunt and burn the Thin Kid with their cigarettes until finally (this scene lasts an uncomfortably long time; the first burns shocked and thrilled us, but now we don't know what we want, don't know what we must endure) the pack of cigarettes is empty.

The teens walk out of the hazy classroom.

The Thin Kid stays behind, like he must. He is pocked and polka-dotted with red, angry welts. Dead cigarette butts are a pile of snow at his feet.

He teeters out of his corner, limbs shaking. He inspects his arms and legs and body. He covers his masked eyes with his hands and trembles. Then he arches his back, lifts his head toward the ceiling, as though pantomiming a wolf howling at the moon.

He turns, now facing the blackboard and the chalk writing.

He knows it's all written here; what has happened and everything that's going to happen.

The Thin Kid reads, allows himself to read. We follow his head following the path of the text. He pauses, somewhere in the middle, looks at his left hand, and then smears and erases the board.

When he's finished, his palms are chalked white. He cowers, and shuffles to his supply room and closes the door apologetically.

He knows there will be consequences for what he's done.

Or worse, the forthcoming punishment is arbitrary. There's nothing he could've done or can do to stop or change what is coming.

Most of my cuts and bruises were real. Makeup Melanie told me I must bruise easily, and she jabbed a finger into my shoulder to test her thesis. She said, "No bruise."

I said, "Yeah, but my arm will fall off tomorrow."

Mel and Karson added a few fake cuts and marks to my body. They applied the mask and neck makeup next. Then, when I was ready, it was discovered that no one had brought a carton of cigarettes to set. Oops. Everyone pointed at everyone else, like we were suddenly in a locked-room mystery farce. In a moment of quiet, I attempted to break the tension and said, "Smoke 'em if you've got 'em," the delivery muffled by the mask. I got more laughs than scowls. This is my memory being generous, I think.

Valentina pushed her beanie higher up her forehead and gave me the look of death. My mask returned the look, but I withered on the inside. Bad joke or not, she was upset I was speaking at all, that the Thin Kid was talking. I broke the rule about always being in character when wearing the mask. Valentina was angry at everything, and for the first and maybe only time on-set, visibly flustered. She ripped off her hat and frisbeed it against the windows, then paced in small circles.

Dan, our voice of reason, said there was a 7-Eleven about fifteen minutes away, he'd send one of his grips. We had only one official grip even though he used the plural. Dan tossed the van keys to Mark as he walked toward the classroom exit. If I am to make this more dramatic, imagine a young and bored Jacob Marley shuffling down the lonely school hallway, dressed in a black T-shirt and jeans, the links in his chain wallet jangling for our future sins. Mark was a good guy, a lurching metalhead and engineering graduate school dropout, one of the few on-set who would talk to me when I had the mask on, usually to offer $5 bootlegged live cassettes from any band I could name.

Dan also said, loud enough for everyone in the room to hear, that if this was the worst mishap we'd have on-set, we should consider ourselves divinely lucky.

Cleo mumbled about someone needing to knock on wood. We were wary of real curses. I obliged by miming knocks on my head. So fine, I'm not a comedic talent.

Dan pulled out a crumpled, nearly finished cigarette pack of his own and said, "I guess I get to smoke on-set today. A first."

I wanted to tell Dan and everyone about how my mother used to smoke all day long and that she would send me on the short walk down our road and dashing across the busy and treacherous Elliot Street to the White Hen Pantry to buy her cigarettes. She'd send me with enough money leftover so I could buy myself a pack of baseball cards. I wanted to tell Dan and everyone I wasn't a smoker because Mom let me try one when I was ten, knowing that I'd cough, get sick, almost puke up the radioactive-green Hi-C I'd been drinking, and I'd never want to try it again. But when I was masked, no one wanted or needed to know anything about the real me.

Valentina asked Dan to hold off on lighting up as we'd need that smoke in maybe twenty minutes. Having regained control, she announced we'd flip the day's order and first shoot the Thin Kid alone with his burns and his retreat to the supply closet.

It was back into the makeup chair for me, which was in the rear of the classroom. Karson questioned the new plan, complaining that after this scene they'd have to remove the burns only to have to put most of them back on again later. Valentina asked, "Is that a problem?" dropping the temperature in the room by a gazillion degrees. Karson shook his head and shrugged. Of our group, he was the least enthusiastic about what we were doing, what we were making. I wish I could go back in time and ask him why, ask him what he knew.

Cleo had previously given Melanie and Karson a map of my body, detailing where the burns would be placed. They set to adding small red circles to my skin, and they went about the task somberly, not speaking to me other than to describe what they were doing, what I might feel.

Valentina wandered over to the makeup area and looked me up and down. At the time, I assumed something was wrong. Now I know she was sizing me up, readying to put me to further use.

She called Dan and Cleo over and said she wanted to talk about tomorrow morning's schedule at the high school. Dan had finally convinced Valentina it didn't make practical or financial sense, or even sense sense, to film everything in exact order. They were to crank out all the high school set scenes tomorrow, so they'd need the school and the student extras for just the one day.

Valentina wiped her face, but the pooled undereye shadows betraying lack of sleep remained. She said, "Something occurred to me last night, and I want to run it by you." She briefly described the multiple-day montage as written in the screenplay, which were scenes I had yet to read and would not read until 2008, after she posted the screenplay online. "I guess it makes story sense that our teens have a little emotional arc," she said, "and they enjoy the sympathy and attention they get from their classmates because their friend is missing. But I don't know. Now I'm thinking that feels too *something*. Too armchair psychology, maybe. Too 'movie,' for sure."

Valentina, Dan, and Cleo were framed within the eyeholes of my mask, which made everything seem less real, or more real. I can't decide which. I wasn't a player. I was the watcher, the audience, which had been the entirety of my role thus far. Their movie, the one they imagined in their heads and the one they saw playing out before them, was different from the movie I saw, that I lived in. I don't know if they understood that.

Dan asked what Valentina meant by "too movie."

Valentina said, "The audience expects the classmates to react to the Thin Kid's disappearance, and having the teens feed off it plays into the trope of the loser teens who just want attention. Attention is not what they really want, right? More importantly, do *we* want to communicate that? Attention or social status is not why they're doing what they're doing to the Thin Kid. Maybe the montage as written works as a red herring as far as their motivation goes, or maybe it'll just confuse things later because none of this is about motivation. Not really. I mean, some people are going to think what they do to the Thin Kid is because of their classmates, and that's fine. But I don't really care about motivation. Neither do you, Cleo. We talked about how the teens do it because they can and because they're inexplicably driven to do it and the viewers will be driven to ask *why why why* and not have a clear, easy answer. That's what's scary, that's why I want to make this movie. So, I think we need to go stark. I want to go weirder." Valentina looked at me, and I didn't know if I was being tested because the masked me wasn't supposed to have opinions, was supposed to accept his treatment, at least until further notice, but her stare elicited a shrug from me.

Mel, who worked in and around my chest and reeked of patchouli, poked my arm and said, "Don't move, please. Hey, can we put a burn on his nipple? I want to put one on his nipple."

Valentina and Cleo said "No" at the same time.

Cleo said to Valentina, "Okay, what would be weirder? I'm all for weirder."

Mel whispered, "A burn on his nipple."

Karson, applying burns somewhere down below my knees, laughed. I wanted to laugh too.

"What if, in the montage," Valentina continued, "their school days never change, always stay the same? Their classmates still avoid and ignore them. We see the same exact shots and actor staging. Then it would be like they really are stuck in a loop—stuck in hell, like you wrote, Cleo—and the only thing that is different is what they do to the Thin Kid." Valentina stepped between Dan and Cleo, which is an important staging detail of my recounting. No one said anything, but it wasn't an awkward silence. Valentina continued. "Having no bullshit character mini arcs, having zero change in anyone's reaction and behavior during the montage, them going through the motions, that's more unexpected, more horrifying, more hopeless for everyone."

Cleo flipped through the script. Lost somewhere between the pages, she was her usual inscrutable self. I keep saying that I couldn't read her, which implies that no one could. I know that's wrong. Given what was to happen, saying that she was inscrutable is, perhaps, a mealymouthed defense on my part.

Valentina stared at me.

I swallowed and my mask-and-makeup hybrid throat palpitated with almost-speech. I'm not overstating this. I was afraid, but also, I thought she wanted my opinion, and I had one. I said, "And then everyone would be the monsters."

Valentina pointed at me and said, "Exactly. Fucking right." She left her center-stage spot between Dan and Cleo, and walked toward me, washing up at my side. Dan and Cleo closed together, like a curtain, heads ping-ponging between me and the screenplay.

Valentina was worried that the other two had become a team. While I wasn't privy to earlier discussions about the scenes not involving me, it was clear that Cleo sided with Dan over the scheduling changes. Valentina felt outnumbered and needed to balance the power dynamic on-set, even if it was only symbolic. I had zero issue with Dan or Cleo, but in that moment I wanted nothing more from life than to say something brilliant to bolster Valentina's argument. But Dan jumped in.

Dan said he liked what was in the script because it was a grounding flash of realism and empathy or connection, and it would be fun for the viewer to break the visual pattern. He said the viewers always needed some fun.

"Fuck fun," Valentina said. "Fuck it to hell." She laughed, and we did too.

Dan said, "Well, you say 'fuck fun,' moviegoers say 'fuck your movie.'"

"Eh, fuck them too," Valentina said. "We're not making this for them."

"You better be making this for them," Dan said.

Valentina and Dan continued to joke/not-joke, trading volleys, trading personal mission statements regarding expression and commercial reality hidden inside Trojan horses of humor and sarcasm.

Cleo, the perpetual peacekeeper, crowbarred herself into the exchange and said she saw merit in both approaches to the montage.

Valentina, satisfied, suggested they reconvene after the shoot, or sleep on it and make a final decision in the morning. The morning bit meant that Valentina planned to get Cleo on her own later that night to make and manipulate her case.

Melanie suddenly popped into my mask's eyehole frame. She wore a sunflower-bespeckled purple T-shirt big enough that the short sleeves were half sleeves. She said, "My masterpiece," and made a swashbuckling rapier flourish with an applicator.

Rough burn makeup covered my left nipple.

We shot the cigarette aftermath scene in one take, on Valentina's insistence. Mainly because Dan had only three cigarettes with which to smog our corner of the classroom. After, to appease the makeup-team duo, we did a few close-up shots of my hand covering a spot on my chest and then the hand lifting away to reveal the injury, which would later be intercut within the cigarette attack scene. We were finished not too long after Mark returned with the carton of cigarettes and a couple of fresh bootlegs to show me.

We shot the teens entering the classroom, again one take. Then we spent a considerable amount of time choreographing the attack scene. The plan was for quick shots/cuts of the actors lunging at me with lit cigarettes. They were to get as close to my skin as possible without making contact, close enough that by proximity and camera angle it would appear the cigarettes contacted skin. I was to slap my hand over the spots that they appeared to burn, blocking camera view of my unblemished skin. The rehearsal was shaky at best. Our timing was off. When I slapped my hand over an imaginary wound, I was too quick, or the other actor was too slow retracting their unlit cigarette and I ended up slapping hands and crushing a few cigs. Valentina made us stop, as the rehearsal was seconds away from regressing into a silly slap fight.

Go time. We were just going to shoot it and see what happened. Dan coined the term "fuck-it filmmaking."

Later, much later, on our last day on-set, Dan would present Valentina and Cleo with black T-shirts proudly sporting the phrase FUCK-IT FILMMAKING, and Valentina shouted, "This is the best!," ducked into the makeshift wardrobe area, and changed into the new shirt.

I sat on the symbolled mark on the classroom floor. The teens sat around me. Valentina lit a cigarette, puffed it, the smoke framing her face along with her curls, then she jabbed the glowing end at my shoulder, got close enough that I felt the hungry heat of it. I squealed and scrambled to the corner of the room. Cut.

Dan adjusted the lights for the next shot. While we waited, Valentina casually mentioned that for the past week she had experimented with stubbing out cigarettes on pig skin, hoping they could use that for an on-camera close-up of a burn.

"Do you have that shot in the storyboards?" Dan asked.

Valentina said, "No. I didn't include it because I wasn't sure if it would look right."

"If you'd given me a heads-up I could've tried to pull something together," Karson said, ever the aggrieved makeup and effects artist. "Also, where'd you get fucking pig skin? The deli?"

Valentina waved a hand, as if to say *No big deal.* "I have a tattoo artist friend. Newbies and apprentices practice tattooing on pig skin. She gave me some."

Melanie, sitting in a chair and holding a cardboard platter of cigarette burns, said, "Ooh, bacon."

Cleo asked, "How'd it look?"

"Pretty gnarly. But there's no way we can make the pig skin look as pale as his skin." She flashed an accusatory hand in my direction.

I flinched, and I imagined her inside her hotel room, late at night, the kind of late that became early, unable to sleep, to even think of sleep, as she smoked and stubbed out cigarette after cigarette into the pig skin, into the Thin Kid's skin, my skin, and this wasn't about a special-effects test, not really, it was how she prepared for her dual role as the director and character Valentina, blurring and stubbing out the lines of separation.

Dan said he could try to work magic with lighting, but Valentina was dubious. She continued lamenting not being able to get that kind of simple but effective shot. Recalling what Dan had said earlier, she said that would've been the cool moment of grounded realism Dan wanted, the violence being what grounded this movie. She kept on talking in circles about the shot, and she never asked me to become a half-assed stunt man, didn't ask me to volunteer to let a cigarette actually burn my skin, but I knew that was what she wanted.

I can't explain why I would let a cigarette burn me other than to say if you were there in a mask, that mask, and if you felt the way I felt about myself both in and out of that mask, you would've said what I said and the way I said it.

"Hey, we can do it once. Stub one cigarette out on me," I said.

The funny part is everyone knew I wasn't joking, despite my previous jokes. Everyone said no, told me to stop it, to shut up. But I didn't. I said it wouldn't be a big deal if they stubbed it out quick, if they didn't leave the burning part against my skin too long. There were more *noes* and *no ways*, but fewer people were saying them. I asked, "Who hasn't stubbed out a cigarette on themselves before?" and no one answered. The implication was I had done so before. Therefore, the question was a kind of lie, as I hadn't burned myself like that. But it wasn't a full lie, either, because the Thin Kid in my head had had it happen to him, many times. Because he and I had already read the scene we were about to shoot, it meant the scene had happened to him, to us. I kept saying, just do it quick, and like I was a burn expert, I said it would only be a first- or second-degree burn if you were quick, and those burns healed, didn't leave scars. The *noes* and *no ways* stopped.

With everyone gone quiet, watching their movies inside their heads, Valentina said, "You don't have to do this."

Now, here's what I think. Everything that had happened that morning was purposeful: forgetting the cigarette carton, the discussion about the montage scenes, Valentina pulling out my opinion in support of her rewrite position, and her pig-skin story all were to get me to a place where I would volunteer to have a cigarette stubbed out against my skin on film. I wasn't mad then and I'm not mad now. This wasn't manipulation, it was direction. The Thin Kid needed direction.

Mel said, "I'll do it!"

I said, "Hell no. It's gotta be Cleo. Her character would be the quickest, I think, wouldn't press as hard, would leave the cigarette on me the least amount of time."

Valentina rolled her eyes and slumped her shoulders like she was jealous of a sibling getting to do something she wasn't allowed to do.

Cleo blinked at me, processing. I thought she would protest, and I'd have to keep asking until I wore her down, but all she said was, "You sure?" Maybe she was pissed that I'd sided with Valentina on the suggested script change. Maybe motivations were simple sometimes.

I said, "I'm sure."

Dan and his camera cornered me. Valentina perched over his shoulder. Mark hovered the boom mic over my head. Cleo pinched the cigarette, her eyes wide, fixed on the spot we agreed to use, left chest, over my heart.

After this shot, the unspoken rules for my speaking with the mask on would go back into place for the rest of the day, and really the rest of the shoot but for the times I was hurt or could answer a question with one word or a grunt. One of the last full sentences I ever said with the mask on was "Don't worry, I won't feel it."

Cleo puffed the cigarette until the embers glowed redder than her hair. Valentina told Cleo to be slow on the approach, to pretend she was trying to pin a tail on a butterfly. She came in slower, slowest, and hesitated, and I don't know if anyone else saw the hesitation but I lived there and I've lived there ever since, and I looked down into her face, not for the first time and not yet for the last, and she wasn't looking at the spot on my chest, but at my eyes, the mask's eyes, and yes, I know how boring and impossible it is to describe a look on someone's face so I won't, but I'm being a coward because I'm choosing not to describe that look, not yet, not now. Maybe the hesitation meant she didn't want to do it, or it meant she really wanted to do it and was dragging it out. Either way, I stepped in, or I leaned into the cigarette. And I felt it. I still feel it. The bright, searing pain electrified my nerves into a ball that expanded from my chest, filled my body, and I gasped to let it free and into the world. I flinched and fell back into the corner.

Cleo dropped the cigarette, covered her mouth with her hands, and stumbled backward, bumping Dan. Valentina helped steady him and the camera.

Dan said, "Don't worry, I got the shot," even though no one asked.

A few minutes later, or maybe it was more like a half hour later, I don't remember, it was the full cigarette-frenzy-scene time. Cast and crew gathered in the front of the classroom and lit up to fill the room with smoke.

The burn on my chest throbbed with my heartbeat. I suppressed the urge to touch the blistering, dead skin with a finger, to press that button. This burn marked where the rest of the movie began, where it spooled out on its own and into forever. The cigarette attack is one of three scenes that Valentina eventually uploaded to You-Tube. One minute and twenty-five seconds in duration, it appears well choreographed, like we'd spent hours carefully mapping out each movement, and almost in one take, due to the clever, cold, calculating, unobtrusive editing, which includes a stinger of a shot on Cleo's cigarette burning my skin. When I watch and rewatch it, I don't see me leaning my chest into the cigarette, and it's almost enough to change my memory of what happened. Almost. But I know what I did. There's no changing or editing that. *When* Valentina had edited this scene along with the other two is subject to much online debate and speculation, as though pinpointing the time and level of technology at her disposal would bring meaning, order to the world. The scene is difficult to watch, I'm told, although it has over 20 million views online.

Cast and crew's smoke clouded the front of the classroom, and I remained in the corner. I shallowed my breath because I could.

Melanie extended her cigarette toward me, filter first, and said, "You can put it in your mask hole if you want to help out with a puff."

I stood tall, taller, and tilted my head, just slightly. The tilt was subtle, so subtle that if we'd been filming, the camera might not have registered the movement.

Melanie retracted her offer, her arm, and the smile on her face withered, died, and was then reborn inside my mask.

THEN: THE CONVENTION PART 1

11

Of course you already know about Cleo.

In December of 1998, Karson died in a car accident. Based on the braking-tire marks on the street and curb, authorities concluded he'd fallen asleep at the wheel and woke as he was about to career off the road, through a guardrail, and death-roll down a steep embankment. There were no drugs or alcohol in his system. I didn't know he'd died until after Valentina's death from pancreatic cancer in 2008 and after the horror community discovered the assorted materials from our movie she had released online. Melanie had become a long-distance marathon swimmer in her thirties. She competed and placed in the top ten in four national events in the early 2000s. In 2006, she was training alone in the waters off Newport, Rhode Island, and presumably drowned. Her body was never found. Dan sold his production company in the summer of 1999 and dove into local politics. He was a second-term Rhode Island state senator and a weekly guest on a popular local talk-radio station when he died of a massive coronary in his sleep, February 2007. He was fifty years old, married, had three children. With Valentina's passing, I was the sole remaining major participant from *Horror Movie* who was still alive.

The deaths fed the lore and interest in *Horror Movie*. Scores of websites, blogs, YouTube channels, and Reddit threads were dedicated to the movie, conspiracy theories regarding what had happened on-set, the screenplay, and all things related to the actors and characters, especially the Thin Kid. Artists posted and shared their fan art: the Thin Kid as the goth, emo little brother of Jason, Michael, Freddy, and Leatherface; the Thin Kid walking hand-in-hand with Cleo, or Valentina, or Karson. I avoided reading the fan and slash fiction, and later, a randomly trending Twitter discussion about the Thin Kid's big dick energy. What's wrong with you people? In 2017 a popular true crime podcast produced by NPR featured Cleo, our film, and the aftermath. I'd declined to be interviewed, which made me look guilty in some people's view. I'd also declined to be interviewed for a proposed documentary called *Cursed Films*. Post-podcast, the size of our fandom grew exponentially. *Horror Movie* became as famous for not being made as Jodorowsky's *Dune*. The Thin Kid even started showing up in memes.

Cleo's family signed with one of Hollywood's largest agencies to field offers on her screenplay and to legally force YouTube to take down the scores of amateur filmmakers' attempts and interpretations of scenes, including three poorly made full versions of the film. My email inbox swelled with interview requests, and messages from agents and writers and directors and producers wanting to talk to me about the movie, wanting me to help with their reboot pitches. I hired a manager named Kirsten Billings. She was in her early forties, five-foot-zero, bragged about owning five weekday pairs of the same jeans, and swore like a character in a Tarantino movie. Her first act was to arrange my paid appearance at a regional horror-fan convention in Virginia. Her second act was to convince me it would be worth the investment of time and funds that attendance required.

August of 2019. I drove eight hours to the sweaty chain hotel at which Summer Scares was being held. I was paid a nominal

appearance fee, a fee that Kirsten promised would go up after my
maiden con voyage. The pandemic had put the kibosh on live appearances for a few years, but now that we pretend Covid isn't a
thing anymore, she's been proven correct about the fee escalation.
She also assured me I would make a lot of money by signing the
stills of the Thin Kid that Valentina had released into the world.
I was to charge forty bucks a pop for a signed official set photo.
Kirsten suggested fifty. Part of the reason I drove and turned down
the offer of a free flight was I didn't trust hotel mail with the boxes
of photos I'd outlaid good money for, and I certainly didn't trust
the mail with my mask. I planned to charge twenty bucks if an
attendee wanted me to sign something of theirs and twenty if they
wanted to take a picture with me. Again, Kirsten wanted me to
charge more, but I was dubious. I was convinced I'd take a loss on
the stills and the slick professional banner we'd made to display
behind my autographing table.

I arrived at the hotel around 1 P.M., checked in, and received my
neon-pink wristband, guest badge, and lanyard. I dollied my boxes
of stuff to the celebrity room, which was to open to the public in
an hour. The movie celeb tables lined the walls of the generic hotel
ballroom. Black curtains hung in front of off-white/beige parti-
tion walls, and the carpeting was a similarly inoffensive bland color.
In the middle of the room was a small rectangle of horror-author
tables. Celebs and writers milled around and caught up with one
another as presumably they'd all done this kind of thing before.
My table was stationed between one of the *Friday the 13th*'s Jasons
and a woman who as a teen starred alongside a kid Stephen Dorff
in *The Gate*.

I unpacked at an empty rectangular table covered in black felt.
I arranged a selection of black, white, and silver Sharpies and then
displayed my selection of three glossy photos I would sell and sign.
One was a pic of the Thin Kid standing in the classroom's corner,
covered in cigarette burns. You couldn't tell from the picture which

burn was real. The night before the con, Kirsten had suggested *step right up, step right up, and guess which burn is real for five dollars off* could be my carnie-like pitch if things were slow. I'd pointed out to her that she'd promised things wouldn't be slow. She'd said "fuck" a few times, pretended to have a bad connection, and then hung up. The second glossy was of the Thin Kid standing silhouetted in the doorway at the other end of a long, darkened room. It's the scariest image and scene of the movie, if you ask me. You couldn't see any mask details, but it was a creepy-ass picture. I didn't like looking at it. My third glossy was not the most famous on-set photo of the three that Valentina had uploaded online, which some have dubbed the "impossible shot," but was instead my brand-new headshot in which I held a foam mannequin head wearing my mask. That was me: B-Movie Hamlet with Yorick. Kirsten had insisted on having the picture taken, and it was what she was sending around Hollywood.

After setting up my photos and the price list, I unpacked my mask, which was housed in a clear acrylic display case. I wouldn't let anyone touch the case or hold it for a photo, but if they wanted to take a picture of me holding it, that would be okay, I guess, and maybe I should've included that option on the price list. I had a cash box and a Square for my phone so I could accept credit card payments. I hadn't tested that out yet. Fucking hell, I didn't know what I was doing or why I was doing it, beyond money. Fifty years old with no career to speak of, I was adrift, and had been so since the last day on-set, if not before then. I briefly thought about packing up and hiding in my hotel room all weekend. Instead, I wrestled with my banner and its antagonistic folding stand. I was losing the wrestling match badly.

The writer at the table across from me asked if I needed help. I said, "All I can get."

His banner proclaimed he was "The Nightmare Scribe" in a slashing, spooky font. He had book blurbs not from Stephen King but from people and zines I'd never heard of declaring him to be the next Stephen King. He wore all black in the author photo and there were photoshopped wisps of ghosts flowing out from behind his head. Yeah, cheesy as fuck. But what did I know? I didn't even know how to put up my own banner.

He made quick work of hoisting my banner sail. It looked okay. Black matte background, the title *HORROR MOVIE* in white block capital letters, Arial font, my name underneath followed by "the Thin Kid" in quotations. The banner featured the three surviving photographic images from the original set. It was hard not to feel a bit like a fraud, given no one ever saw the movie, but at the same time, the movie existed. We had spent five weeks making it. Just because our movie was the tree falling in the forest for no one to hear or see didn't mean we didn't fall.

I thanked the horror writer for his help, introduced myself, and shook his hand. He was a head shorter than I was, his black hair was clearly a dye job, his Vincent Price goatee trimmed short like he'd been eating chocolate cake messily, and he dressed the same as he did in his banner. He asked if this was my first time doing a convention like this.

I asked the rhetorical, "Is it that obvious?"

He inspected my wares and said that I would run out of photos. The first-timers always did well at shows like these.

He wanted to talk more, and he was nice enough, but I felt trapped behind my table already and I had hours and days of being trapped behind the table to go. I wasn't good in forced social situations pre-movie, and that certainly hadn't improved post-movie. I could handle crowds but only when I could hide in them. I excused myself, went to the bathroom, splashed water on my face, bought a tea from a vendor cart, and took a quick stroll around the celebrity room. I got head nods and half waves when there was eye contact, which I assume were acknowledgment of my guest badge, no real recognition, or begrudging recognition if some of them knew who

I was and didn't think I deserved to be there for myriad reasons, which would've been fair. But at the same time, fuck them, man. I put in hard work on that movie, left pieces of myself at that abandoned school, and like everyone else involved in the film my life was if not ruined, then changed irreparably. So what if no one saw the final cut, or any cut? That didn't mean I'd cheated or short-cutted and was less deserving of the inexplicably strange fandom that had cropped up without any prompting from me. Not until Summer Scares, anyway. It would've been a hell of a movie. Five hundred thousand (more or less) Thin Kid fans can't be wrong.

Anyway, let's finish the celeb-room tour. Svengoolie was there, Joe Bob Briggs, too, plus a slew of famous slasher victims, the great actor Tom Atkins, who had a T-shirt with his cartoon visage and his last name under it (a brilliant T-shirt, and if I wore anything other than white T-shirts I would've bought one), two characters from the early seasons of *The Walking Dead*, and the guy who played Fuchs from John Carpenter's *The Thing*. Fuchs I wanted to talk to, but time was running short. I scurried back to my table.

In the final minutes before the doors opened, I played three-card monte with my photo arrangements, and there was a loud bang to my right. I jumped out of my fucking skin. The Jason actor hammered his sheathed machete into his table like a judge's gavel and announced there was one minute before the room opened. People laughed and applauded.

The Nightmare Scribe stage-whispered from across his table, "Get used to it. He'll do that at least once an hour."

Once the doors opened the flow of people at my table was near continuous. The first fans were a young man and woman, presumably a couple, both of whom had to have been born after the filming of *Horror Movie*. Fans. Do I call them fans? Fans of what, precisely? Fans of a movie that existed purely within their imagination? How different was that from the movies you've seen, really? After you've viewed them, they only existed in your head too. Bullshit dime-store philosophy or criticism or whatever you want to call it, but I thought I might try that line or something similar if confronted by a cynical non-fan. The couple wore matching round, black-framed glasses and garish *Horror Movie* poster-style black T-shirts, and they stood there blinking at me. Kirsten had instructed me to be kind, patient, and approachable and she didn't want to see any shit online about how I was an asshole, but she'd also said, in an eerie replay of a conversation I'd had ten years prior, I had to be mysterious, to "have an aura of mystery," and I wasn't to give everything away (what did I have to give away?), and to treat each interaction as a mini first date and that I desperately wanted the second date. Fucking hell, okay. In my most kind, approachable voice, I asked the young couple where they got the shirts, which I thought was a good opening line, one to get them talking about themselves. They said, "Online," sheepishly, as though they expected me to scold them. I then brought the mask case to the front of my table for them. They didn't say anything. I wasn't sure if it was awe or disappointment. I said in my older man's mysterious voice, "The mask looked better when I wore it," which is a villain's line if there ever was one. The fan couple giggled nervously and said the mask was amazing. They asked a question that I would field all afternoon: Was there a reboot of the movie in the works? I told them the original screenplay had been optioned and was in the early stages of development. One bounced on her toes, the other mini-clapped his hands, and they said they couldn't wait. Each one bought a photo, and because they'd done so, I didn't charge them for a selfie with me, and let them take a photo of the mask too.

The Jason guy had a fan in a headlock and his machete tip pointed at the fan's neck. Sure, he was having fun and his fans were eating it up, but I didn't like him. He was a bit obnoxious and full of himself for playing a character that had already been established. Look at me with my semiprofessional jealousy already.

The afternoon blurred by. I signed photos and fan art and had some fan art given to me.

A shy teenage boy who looked and dressed like Karson gave me a detailed pencil drawing of Cleo staring off blankly, eyes angled away from whoever might be looking back at her, and she carried the Thin Kid in a reversal of the famous picture of the *Creature from the Black Lagoon* carrying the white-bathing-suit-clad Julie Adams in his arms. Cleo's look somehow was her look. I thanked the artist, my voice quavering, and I couldn't look at the picture for long. I had to hide it in a cardboard box underneath my table before I started full-on ugly crying, and I quickly moved the Karson look-alike along. Jason slammed the table with his machete again. I gave him a look I couldn't back up. Sales were brisk, and the Square thingy on my phone worked. I shook hands and forced smiles for selfies. The Nightmare Scribe cut the line to give me three of his signed books. I thanked him and pretended like getting books from him was a big deal. A woman in the darkening forest of her forties asked if I'd kept in touch with Valentina after the trial. I told her the truth: mostly no, but I visited her a few weeks before she died. Nightmare Scribe popped back over, briefly described the plot of each book he'd given me and how they'd come so close to being optioned for film. I wished him luck. A twitchy guy showed me a tattoo on his arm of the Thin Kid sitting in the corner of a room. It was like looking at a memory. He asked if I had been in any other movies and that IMDb had me listed on a few things as being in preproduction. I told him they were mistaken. Nightmare Scribe returned with a bottle of water for me, and he asked if I had an agent or manager. I thought he was working up to ask me to give Kirsten one of his books. A young woman and her toddler in a stroller were next. The kid absently chewed on the head of a plush Cthulhu. She said that I should be blurring my face out, not revealing my identity, like in the movie. She kept saying "like in the movie," and it was all I could do to not say, "There was no movie," to be rid of her. She lingered. I offered clunky answers to questions that weren't questions, and the thudding silent aftermath should've been a cue for her to move on. She didn't leave my table until she bought one of everything and took a staged photo of me with her drool-slimed kid, and I had to open my mouth wide and pretend I was going to eat the squirming little grub. Her I charged full freight for everything. After a few more people, Nightmare Scribe returned to tell me his manager was pitching him as a *creator*, not a *writer* because no one in Hollywood respected writers. The Jason actor overheard, slammed the table with his machete, and bellowed, "The only good writers are dead ones." Someone in my line whispered, "Too soon." Nightmare Scribe laughed too loudly. I ignored Obnoxious Jason and made commiserative noises and said things to the writer like "That must be tough" and "They always fuck you at the drive-thru." This time he didn't go back to his table but edged over slightly so the next person in my line could step up. The writer kept his half of the conversation going, saying actors like me had it easy, all things considered. That, I didn't like. So, I asked him if he in fact had considered all things. I signed photos and Nightmare Scribe told a story about a friend who'd had their contractually due credit scrubbed from the film's posters, and another friend who had a movie come out on a streamer and the streamer was trying to cut her out of sequel rights to both films and books, and another friend who had a movie tie-in edition of one of her books squashed by the studio and egomaniacal director. The guy for whom I was signing photos was himself a young writer. He was riveted by the tales of writerly woe and likely secretly thrilled as being the righteously aggrieved makes good daydream fodder. The fan ended up following the horror writer to his table. Well played, Nightmare Scribe.

I got plenty of disgusted and appalled looks and heard disapproving whispers from folks who scurried by my table. The one openly antagonistic fan (well, I probably shouldn't call him a fan, right?) wasn't my last visitor of the afternoon, but I might as well pretend he was for the purposes of this audiobook retelling.

This guy was a part of a group of three. The other two, a man and a woman in their twenties, both sporting multiple piercings and many tattoos, were excited to talk to me. They were friendly, and conversation with them was not awkward or uncomfortable in the least. They were fun and disarming, and honestly I began to relax for the first time that afternoon, thinking, Okay, this isn't so bad, I can do this. Then their friend stepped between them. He wore a gray *The Shining* T-shirt emblazoned with a maze and a red baseball hat backward. On one hand, he was one of the only people in the room not wearing a black T-shirt. On the other hand, man, the douche-bro hat was a warning sign, a red flag worn backward. He had that sneering, dismissive expression unique to dudes who know more than everyone else in the room and they can't wait to tell you about it.

He said more than asked, "Mind if I look at your hand? Up close."

INT. CLEO'S HOUSE, STAIRWAY - MORNING

Cleo, wearing an empty BACKPACK, walks slowly and quietly up and then down her carpeted stairs, her hands in her pockets.

This is Cleo wishing, begging for fate to intervene, to stop her from what she and they are doing, what she and they will do.

She stumbles once, but athletically quickens her pace to keep from pitching forward, from tumbling headfirst down the stairs.

She sighs at her feet, which were autonomically fast enough to prevent a fall, and to add insult to noninjury, her feet were heavy, loud enough to tattle on her.

> MOM (O.S.)
> (sound of bedroom
> door opening, then
> slippered feet,
> hesitant steps)
> Cleo? What are you doing?
> It's Saturday. Why are you up
> so early?

> CLEO
> (frozen in place,
> halfway down)
> I'm going over to Valentina's. We
> have a big project to work on.

> MOM (O.S.)
> Well. Okay. But what are
> you doing on the stairs?

                  CLEO
I -- I forgot something in my
room, and, um, had to go
back up.

                  MOM (O.S.)
How many times did you
forget?

EXT. KARSON'S HOUSE, BACKYARD - MORNING

Karson closes his BACK DOOR and SCREEN DOOR, careful to not wake the dad-minotaur. He pauses on the stoop, adjacent to overflowing GARBAGE CANS, and he listens for stirring noises inside.

Karson walks across the small patch of cracked BLACKTOP to the dilapidated, sagging GARAGE. There's a weathered, disused BASKETBALL BACKBOARD AND RIM hanging above the twin boarded-up DOORS.

He slowly lifts one door, the rusted hinges complain and echo, but not as loudly as they would if he had roughly tossed the door above his head.

Now we are inside the dark, dusty, and cobwebbed garage, watching Karson's silhouetted form lift the door over his head. Behind him the narrow driveway rivers away from the garage and is flanked by his house and a row of patchy, craggily-branched six-foot-tall BUSHES.

We're in another tunnel, and at its end is the street. Stepping into that end is a blurry Cleo.

Karson looks over his shoulder, sees her, then steps inside the welcoming darkness of the garage with us.

EXT. LARGE SUBURBAN HOUSE, FRONT YARD - MORNING

Valentina stands on the sidewalk in the shadow of a large, verging on ostentatious, impeccably kept, colonial HOUSE with gables on its main and garage roofs.

She silently considers the home and isn't worried if anyone were to spy her spying.

Her fingers are hidden inside the folds of a fortune teller-style NOTE, a note that she intercepted during study hall a few days prior. The paper petals sport numbers or the names of colors. The petal labeled ONE also reads "For Sharon's eyes only!!!"

Valentina silently picks a number and moves the folds back and forth accordingly. She mouths, *Blue*, and switches the folds again. Then she opens a petal and finds a circled heart with a line through it. She dispenses with the rules of the game and opens another petal, finds a name, "Gabe," and a smiley face with heart eyes. Opens another petal, finds a foaming beer. Opens another petal, finds "Party!!!" and another petal, "Next weekend!!!"

She crumples the note, stuffs it into a back pocket. She crosses the front lawn, walking toward the adjacent SIDE YARD concealed by a healthy, impenetrable wall of SHRUB-BERY. On the other side is a large PATIO or garden or per-haps a pool area, as a PERGOLA is visible above the living green wall.

Valentina goes to the green wall, sinks her arms to her elbows in the shrubs, trying to pry open the branches, to make a secret passageway, but is unable to.

She drifts along the shrubbed perimeter, heading toward the back, and is suddenly aware that she's being watched. She turns.

Karson and Cleo are on the street behind her. Cleo offers a half wave.

INT. ABANDONED SCHOOL, CLASSROOM - LATER THAT MORNING

We are again focused on the closed CLASSROOM DOOR from inside the classroom.

The door opens. The teens walk in.

No one is in the front of the room. The teens stare at the smeared, cloudy blackboard.

> CLEO
> (mournful, but not
> surprised, and we
> won't know, won't
> ever know for sure
> if his act of erasure
> had been written on
> the board too)
> He erased it all.

Valentina angrily stomps to the front of the classroom.

> VALENTINA
> Hey! Hey, come out here!
> Now!

The supply-room door CREAKS open in a way any child who has been yelled at knows, recognizes.

The Thin Kid leaks out, hunched over. If he had a tail, it would be between his legs.

He looks at the teens and then looks away, at them, and away.

He's pitiful. We're afraid for him, for what might happen to him. But we want to see what the teens will do to him.

We need to see it. Maybe we've been influenced by the established rules within the movie. Regardless, we agree his transgression should be addressed.

The mask remains fused to the skin of the Thin Kid's neck. The green, scaled flesh reaches lower than it did before, past his Adam's apple, almost to the base, where neck becomes chest. The rest of his white skin is dotted with burns. Two of the burns look like GREEN splotches.

> VALENTINA
> (points at the
> blackboard)
> Why did you do that? Who
> said you could do that?
> Who said you could do
> *anything*?

The Thin Kid cowers, sits in the corner, shaking his head *no no no*, and then covers his head with his arms.

> KARSON
> Do you need to --

> CLEO
> (interrupting)
> No. We already know what's
> going to happen.

The teens, not without struggle, flip the teacher's desk back over onto its legs. It's a little wobbly, unsteady.

Karson goes to the corner, grabs one of the Thin Kid's arms, and drags him next to the teacher's desk. His raw strength is frightening, unexpected.

> KARSON
> (his voice sounds
> adult, and we can

                    too easily imagine
                    his dad saying this)
          This is your fault. You're
          making us do this.

What he says is a lie -- the logic of punishment is always
a lie. Why did the teens bring what they brought if they
didn't know the Thin Kid had erased the board?

The Thin Kid is dragged until he knocks against the desk. He
looks around the room wildly and he doesn't make any sounds.

Karson pulls the Thin Kid's right arm across the desktop,
while at the same time, he adjusts the Thin Kid's squirming
position on the floor, until he's on his knees, sitting on
the backs of his feet.

Cleo unshoulders her PACK and pulls out two dingy BATH TOWELS
and a pair of giant GARDEN SHEARS, its hungry mouth closed.

Valentina takes the shears, pulls them open, then closes
them. The SNICK of the blades and the levering handles is
audible. Satisfied, she passes the shears to Karson.

The Thin Kid quivers but otherwise doesn't move, doesn't
retract his arm from the desktop.

The rest of this happens quickly. There will be no time for
the hope of disbelief.

Karson opens the shears, places the bottom of one blade and
one handle horizontally against the desktop.

Valentina grabs the Thin Kid's right hand, manipulates it
into a fist with the pinky finger sticking out. She positions the pinky with the first knuckle flush against the
horizontal blade.

Karson grips each handle, flexes and adjust his fingers
once. Twice.

Then he pushes the upper handle down with all his might.

SNICK

HALF OF THE PINKY shoots out from between the closed blades, along with a gout of BLOOD.

The Thin Kid falls away, curls into a ball, leaking red as he rolls and writhes, and he screams and screams and screams, and it's the worst sound most of us have ever heard.

The screams go high-pitched then low and guttural, the screams impossibly jumping octaves without hitting the octaves between.

The Thin Kid sounds human, though. Never once does he sound like an animal bleating. He sounds human, terribly human.

And worse, buried in the din of his agony, we might hear him say "Oh God!" and "Why?" and "I'm sorry!"

Cleo rushes to the Thin Kid with one of the TOWELS and wraps his wounded hand tightly until it is cocooned. She squeezes, applying pressure, and blood darkens the towel.

He is still screaming. Won't somebody make him stop?

Valentina plucks the half pinky from the table and carries it the short distance to the ceremonial symbolled spot on the floor. She holds the pinky so that it drips blood onto the symbol. The drops fall at random.

Karson and Cleo half lift, half slide the Thin Kid onto the marked and blood-dappled spot.

This, whatever this is, isn't over yet.

The Thin Kid is still screaming.

He tries to roll onto his back, but Karson props him up in a sitting position. Cleo holds his head.

The Thin Kid is still screaming.

Valentina jams the severed pinky, slowly, into the mask's open slit, the mask's mouth.

The Thin Kid stops screaming. He shakes his head. The teens struggle to hold him in place, to keep him in his place.

Valentina pushes and mashes and jams the pinky into the mask mouth with the palm of her hand until there is no more pinky.

The Thin Kid coughs, chokes, grunts, coughs more, and then he goes silent and still.

His body and mask mouth are splashed and smeared with blood. He stares straight ahead at no one.

Cleo unwraps the Thin Kid's right hand and tosses the blood-soaked towel away, and then quickly rewraps his hand with the other towel.

After she finishes, the teens leave the classroom.

We stay behind with the Thin Kid, but we cower in the back of the classroom.

He remains rooted, unmoving.

From our distance across the room, his masked face is out of focus, and the red smear around his mouth looks like a smile. His white skin is marbled red.

We stare and we stare, but make no mistake, he is looking at us too. He knows who and what we are, and we are afraid.

DISSOLVE TO:

12

The following—or versions of it—is what I've told interviewers about my missing finger. For the purposes of this audiobook, I went back and reread some of those interviews to see what I'd said and how I'd said it.

I don't remember much from that morning on-set and the chaos during and after the accident. I don't remember who drove me to the hospital. I don't remember who had the severed half of my pinky. I do remember Cleo sat in the backseat with me, holding my other arm while I had my wounded hand wrapped and raised. She asked me random questions about the street I grew up on, my favorite ice cream flavor, and got me talking about bands I liked. When I ran out of things to say, she told me about how in fifth grade she found an abandoned, sickly baby squirrel in her backyard. It was so thin its head appeared too big, as though the body were failing under the strain of sustaining such a head. She tried to nurse the squirrel back to health. Her trying equated to placing it in a big cardboard box, padded with dish towels and newspaper. In one corner of the homemade terrarium was a plastic bowl of water, grass, and some granola. Her parents wouldn't let her keep the squirrel and the box in the house, so she left the box in their beat-up garage. I assumed hers was the garage referenced in the screenplay. Cleo slept terribly that night and was up before the sun the next morning, which was cold enough for frost, and when she went out to the garage, the squirrel was dead. Cleo had teary eyes and ended the story by saying she didn't know why she was telling me any of that. I asked if I was the baby squirrel now, and she said no, of course not, and, "You're all grown up." We laughed. I think we laughed, or I choose to remember we laughed. I think we're in more control of what we remember and what we don't remember than we assume.

After being seen and treated in the ER I was given a private room in the adjoining hospital. Visiting hours were supposed to end at 7 P.M., but Valentina and Cleo showed up after 8 P.M. I was exhausted and groggy on pain medication. My memory of the conversation within that room has a dreamlike quality, insofar as the logic of what was said and who said it and in what order is all off. Consequently, what follows is a forensic-like reconstruction of what might've been said, what should've been said.

Valentina spent a solid five unbroken minutes apologizing, promising to pay current and future hospital bills that insurance wouldn't cover, and took full responsibility for the accident, that the safety and care of everyone on-set was her priority. Yes, we had staged a shot of my wriggling real finger between the blades, but the blades were locked in place then. To Valentina's credit, she did not ask how my real finger ended up between the blades after the fake finger rigged with a blood-spurting tube under it had been attached to my entirely closed fist. She did not ask how my real pinky somehow ended up between the blades when they closed. If she had asked (maybe she did and it was what precipitated an argument between her and Cleo), I wouldn't have been able to give an answer. Cleo and Valentina argued about the movie itself. Cleo said they should shut it down, and Valentina asked for how long and said they could shoot other scenes while I recovered, and Cleo said, shut it down for good, and speaking for me, she said that there was no way I could go on filming after this, and she mentioned how

upset Karson was and didn't think he wanted to continue either.
I interrupted, at some point, to say that the doctors would be by
anytime now to tell me if they could reattach the half pinky, which
meant longer recovery time, but they also thought the chances were
slim that they could, that the reattachment wouldn't take, my body
might reject the old piece. I didn't tell them that I'd already decided
I didn't want the half pinky reattached because I knew we couldn't
afford to postpone shooting for what would be weeks of recovery.
Without the pinky, I'd be ready to go tomorrow, metaphorically
speaking. Maybe I did say all that out loud, because I remember
Valentina's cagey and wary facial expressions along with Cleo's horrified and confused ones. Valentina said they'd wait for me, and I
said that I would wait for them, which didn't make sense, wasn't
what I meant to say, but they must've taken it as my saying I would
continue to be in the movie and there was no way I was quitting
now, that I'd sacrificed too much to not continue. They said *okay,
okay* and soothed and shushed me as though I'd been yelling. Hourglass sands of silence dripped until they started talking again, this
time about stuff not related to the movie, so I left them and went
back to the movie set in my head, to piece it all together. Not sorry
for the pun. Did Valentina insist on a second shot with my real finger between the blades while they weren't locked in place? Maybe?
I think so? While my finger was inside the metal beak—that's what
the opened shears looked like to me, a giant bird's opened maw,
the same bird that hid within the drawing I'd made in third grade,
inexplicably that magical thinking/random connection made sense
and soothed me—did Valentina lie about the shears being safety-
locked? Did run-of-the-mill garden shears have a safety feature like
that? What was so safe about locking blades open? Those doubts
were preferable to my inexplicably sticking my finger out, hiding it
under the fake pinky, planning to retract it the nanoseconds before
the blades closed, before the beak closed, just so I could be the real
Thin Kid for those extra moments, those real moments. Maybe

that's why I left the pinky there, hidden under the fake finger. Maybe it had nothing to do with the Thin Kid and I wanted to see and feel what would happen. I told Valentina I didn't blame her or anyone else, that it was an accident. My mouth was dry, full of that hourglass sand, and my hand throbbed with my heartbeat, and I tried a joke, I said maybe I blamed Dan and the crew for cursing us, and when Valentina asked, "What curse?" I reminded her that on cigarette day they said if forgetting the cigarettes carton was the worst mishap we'd have on-set, we'd be lucky. Cleo agreed. We were totally cursed.

INT. ABANDONED SCHOOL, CLASSROOM - LATE NIGHT

We're alone in the back of the dark classroom. The supply-room door is slightly ajar, but we do not see the Thin Kid.

As if awakening from a nightmare, we blink to adjust to the dark and we wait and we hold our breath. Our waiting and staring and listening to the NIGHT SOUNDS and wanting and fearing is practice for later.

Approaching STEPS ECHO in the hallway. The footfalls are gentle but determined. We remain focused on the room. The classroom door opens and Cleo walks inside.

She has a FLASHLIGHT, a JUG OF WATER, and her BACKPACK. She walks to the front.

She shines the light between her feet, onto the ceremonial marked spot on the floor. The green symbol is almost entirely covered with blood. It's difficult to make out the original marks she'd drawn.

Cleo sits on the spot, legs crossed. Instead of facing the blackboard, she faces the supply-room door.

The door CREAKS open a few inches, then a few more, then stops. The opening is large enough for someone to slip through while turned sideways.

It's too dark to see the interior of the supply room.

Cleo sits and watches. She blinks and squints her light-starved eyes. She is patient, though, knowing that she will see him eventually.

>   CLEO
>   You can stay in there if
>   you want. It's totally
>   up to you. Really.

No movement or response from the Thin Kid in the supply room.

                    CLEO (CONT'D)
          I have this theory.

She pauses.

She doesn't think her theory is original or revolutionary or anything like that. Worse, she fears it's a rationalization for what she is doing, for what she has set in motion, and if she were being honest with herself, she never dreamed it would've gotten this far. She thought someone would've stopped it all by now. Why couldn't she stop it? Thoughts and events have a way of gathering momentum, and the brain's natural state is one of perseveration, not preservation.

Cleo wants to say, *My theory is that we're in hell. Some of us are demons and some of us make demons because we don't know what else to do*, which she knows is such a teen-angsty thing to say, but that doesn't mean there isn't a kernel of truth to it.

                    CLEO (CONT'D)
          Never mind. It's a dumb theory.
          Even if it was true, it wouldn't
          help anyone.

Cleo stares into the supply room. She still can't see the Thin Kid and she doesn't hear him either.

Our pity and empathy for the Thin Kid is turning into fear for what might or could happen to Cleo now. We've seen all the horror movies, and we know what is supposed to happen.

Cleo unzips her pack, removes some FOOD, including a grease-stained FAST-FOOD BAG; a cloudy but clear PLASTIC BAG that appears to contain MAKEUP and BRUSHES and bits of LATEX; and, last, a FIRST-AID KIT.

                    CLEO (CONT'D)
          Let me bandage up your hand, add a
          few bits, then I'll go. Me and the
          others won't be back for a few days.

The Thin Kid sticks his right arm through the door opening.
His hand is balled in a bloody TOWEL. His arm is long and
telescopes into the room.

Cleo stands, leaves the marked spot, goes to the disem-
bodied arm. She balances the flashlight on the floor so it
spotlights the arm. She unwraps his hand to the point where
the towel meets wound. The cloth is stuck in the clotted
blood. Like removing a Band-Aid, she yanks the last of the
towel free.

The Thin Kid's bloodied hand tremors.

Cleo cleans the wound with HYDROGEN PEROXIDE, then wraps
his hand in GAUZE, but in a way that covers and swaddles
his mangled pinky but leaves his other fingers open,
free.

She gently guides the Thin Kid out of the closet a step
or two, so he stands with his toes almost touching the
flashlight. In the odd lighting, his body appears gaunt,
ghostly; the mask remains mostly in shadow.

Cleo applies small, squared bits of GREEN LATEX to his
arms and chest, covering old burn marks and scratches.
Using larger strips and pads of latex and a brush and palette, she fills in then blends areas with makeup at the
base of his neck, working down toward his collarbones and
shoulders.

*We don't get a clear view of her makeup. Despite the
poor lighting, Cleo does not appear to struggle with the
work.*

                          CLEO (CONT'D)
        All done.

The Thin Kid recedes into the supply room, and the door
closes, latching shut.

Cleo steps to the door, reaches for the knob, but decides
not to open it. She leans forward, presses her forehead
against the door.

She wants to say something again. She wants to tell the
Thin Kid about a line in Peter Straub's novel *KOKO*, in
which the killer thinks that demons are made to love and
be loved.

Instead, she leaves him food, then packs up her stuff, purposefully steps once on the bloodied symbol on the floor,
and leaves.

                                              FADE TO:

EXT. SUBURBAN SIDE STREET - DAYS LATER - AFTERNOON

The three teens walk in their horizontal line down the
middle of the road again, toward the path in the woods, the
same path, the one they've always been on.

                          VALENTINA
                    (impatient, playful)
        Where is it?

                          KARSON
        You'll see.

                          VALENTINA
        You did get one, right?

                    KARSON
          Yup.

                    VALENTINA
          Took you long enough.

Karson sticks his tongue out at her and blows a raspberry.

The three teens giggle.

                    VALENTINA (CONT'D)
          Tell me how. You got it
          from your dad's store, yeah?

                    KARSON
          Don't worry about it.

                    VALENTINA
               (rolls her eyes)
          You're killing me.

                    KARSON
          My dad's gonna kill me.

                    VALENTINA
          Obviously.
               (then looks to
               Cleo)
          Did he tell you how?

                    CLEO
               (laughs)
          Nope!

                    VALENTINA
          Ugh.

More laughter from Cleo and Karson.

EXT. FOREST PATH - MOMENTS LATER

Karson walks in the lead. Valentina and Cleo follow closely
behind.

> VALENTINA
> You better not be lying.
> We're running out of time.

Karson dashes into a sprint, initially remaining on the
path, then suddenly plunging into thick brush off-path.

Valentina and Cleo call out to him, and they jog to catch
up, stopping where he disappeared.

> VALENTINA
> (looking into the
> brush, but not
> stepping into it)
> Karson! Come on, this isn't
> funny.

She listens and only hears Cleo breathing and BIRDS CHIRPING.

Cleo taps Valentina on the shoulder.

> CLEO
> (whispering)
> I told him he could leave the
> room and go into the woods
> if he promised to go right
> back to his room. Maybe --

A white FIGURE (not Karson) bursts out of the brush inches
from Valentina.

> KARSON (O.S.)
>> RAAAAAWRRRRR!

The figure is a full-size MALE MANNEQUIN that Karson holds
in front of himself like a shield.

A finely timed jump scare. The only cheap one in the movie.

Cleo jumps, even though she knew it was coming.

Valentina is unfazed, however. She barely blinks.

> KARSON
>> (peeking out from
>> behind the mannequin)
> I totally got you.

He shakes the mannequin hesitantly.

> KARSON (CONT'D)
>> (a small voice)
> Rawr?

Valentina smacks the mannequin, knocking it out of Karson's
hands.

> KARSON (CONT'D)
> Easy! He's delicate.

Karson gathers the unwieldy mannequin. The teens laugh and
trudge forward on the path, toward the school.

>> CUT TO:

EXT. ABANDONED SCHOOL - MOMENTS LATER

The teens emerge from the wooded path onto the cracked blacktop of the schoolyard. The Thin Kid spies the teens walking
and joking to each other from his voyeuristic distance, from
the second-floor classroom.

He focuses on the mannequin, and we wonder along with the Thin Kid: What is the mannequin for? Is it going to replace the Thin Kid?

He and we can't help but jump to the conclusion that we're all replaceable, expendable.

INT. ABANDONED SCHOOL, CLASSROOM - CONTINUOUS

The Thin Kid leaves his perch by the window, creeps and crouches across the room, and sits on the bloodied marked spot.

While he waits, the Thin Kid slouches and stirs a finger on the floor, like a bored child, tired of sitting, tired of waiting.

Offscreen, the teens clomp up the stairs and down the hallway.

Finally, the teens enter the room.

The Thin Kid straightens his posture and goes still.

Karson carries the mannequin awkwardly, as it is taller than he is. He knocks it into the doorframe (swearing as he does so) and once inside the classroom, the mannequin's feet drag on the tile.

He carries it to the front of the room and lays the body atop the teacher's desk. The desk is an altar and the mannequin is an offering.

The mannequin is also a compass: its head points toward the Thin Kid, legs point toward the classroom windows.

The Thin Kid shakes his head No. But he does it slowly.

The borders of the mask have leaked/spread deeper onto his body, taking over more of his skin. His shoulders are now green and scaled. The rest of his skin is pocked not with cigarette burns but with more SCALES. These scales look more realistic than what Cleo had been applying to his body, but we still see, or believe we see, an amateur makeup job.

VALENTINA
Stand up. Please.

The Thin Kid obeys. He stands, but not to his full height; he's curled, a posture of fear and shame stirred together, and his legs are spread, knees bent.

Valentina inspects his makeup scales and his other wounds. She nods approvingly.

Karson pulls a flathead SCREWDRIVER out from the back pocket of his jeans. The shank is the length of his hand. The handle is wrapped in MASKING TAPE gone grimy with all the hands that have twisted it.

Karson extends his arm, offering the screwdriver to the Thin Kid.

The Thin Kid flinches and pulls away, cowering.

Karson moves quicker, though, and grabs the Thin Kid's right arm and places the screwdriver's handle in the palm of his bandaged hand.

The Thin Kid doesn't close his fingers around the handle, and the screwdriver clatters to the floor.

Karson picks it up, puts it into the Thin Kid's hand again. This time his four unbandaged fingers shakily grip the tool.

KARSON
Come on. Come over here.

Karson leads the Thin Kid to the teacher's desk and the mannequin, continuing to prod him forward.

The Thin Kid stands next to the desk and appears to be confused, looking back and forth between the mannequin and the screwdriver, and he holds up his hands, miming that he doesn't understand what he's supposed to do.

Despite ourselves, even if we don't know what it is he's supposed to do, cruel anger flashes in us. How can the Thin Kid not know what's going on, not know what he's supposed to do? Our worst selves, the ones some of us hide better than others, think, *He deserves this.*

Karson points at the mannequin and sighs like an adult, like his dad does when his expectations aren't so clear, but his impatience and disappointment are clear.

The Thin Kid shrinks and shrivels as if weighed down by his inability to understand, to please.

> CLEO
> Maybe you should demonstrate
> for him.

> VALENTINA
> Yeah, *demon*-strate for him.
> > (pronounces as "demon,"
> > as in a demon from hell)

> KARSON
> Really?

He sighs again. It is unclear if he's bothered by the pun or by the fact that he must show the Thin Kid what to do, or both.

> KARSON (CONT'D)
> > (sounding like himself,
> > sounding scared)
> If I have to show him, doesn't
> it mean that none of this
> is working?

> CLEO

It's working.

Karson shrugs an I-surrender shrug. He delicately takes the screwdriver out of the Thin Kid's hand. His calm and care are notable.

> CLEO (CONT'D)

Oh, don't forget the tape
recorder.

Cleo approaches the desk and the mannequin with a hand-held TAPE RECORDER. She presses Play and then leaves it by the mannequin's head.

The recorder HISSES for four or five seconds, then there is a WOMAN SCREAMING long, one-note screams, with a breath between each scream.

> VALENTINA
> (to Cleo)

That's you?

> CLEO

Maaaaaybe.

Valentina nods, lips pursed, impressed at the volume and realism.

With the screwdriver in hand, Karson approaches the manne-quin. He manipulates the screwdriver so it's held like one would hold a knife, a stabbing knife. He gives everyone in the room a look, then he plunges the tip and shank of the screwdriver into the plastic chest of the mannequin.

Karson steps back, the screwdriver buried up to its handle.

He stares at the Thin Kid, and the Thin Kid stares blankly back.

Karson returns to the mannequin, pulls out the screwdriver, then, striking like a cobra, he stabs the mannequin repeatedly and in the same area of the chest. During the furious attack, Karson grunts and his sounds/words are loud, difficult to understand, though we think we hear some fuck-yous in there. His fury is not difficult to understand.

The attack ends, and Karson is breathing heavily. The screams stop and the tape hisses. Karson stares at the Thin Kid until he stares back.

Karson points at the mannequin with the screwdriver.

                    KARSON
          Do that.
                    (he's loud, Dad
                    loud initially,
                    but then gets
                    self-conscious,
                    goes quiet)
          But, um, be more
          composed. Less, um,
          emotional. And make less
          noise.

Karson returns the screwdriver to the Thin Kid. Both boys have shaky, tremulous hands.

Cleo darts back to the desk, rewinds the tape recorder, presses Play.

The Thin Kid holds the screwdriver with his bandaged hand and slowly approaches the desk. He walks in *front* of the desk, blocking our full view of the mannequin. *The staging is important here and will be replicated later.*

The screams start again.

The three teens stand shoulder to shoulder and they move back a step or two.

The holes in the mannequin's chest are grouped closely together; combined, they form a larger hole covered with a
few connective webs and wisps of plastic.

The Thin Kid stares as though he can see inside the mannequin, see its unbeating plastic heart.

The Thin Kid slowly lifts his right hand and brings it down.
The screwdriver doesn't penetrate, is knocked loose from
his bandaged hand. The Thin Kid jumps up in pain and shock,
and he hides his bandaged hand beneath his left arm.

Cleo quickly bends to the floor and retrieves the screwdriver, brings it back to the Thin Kid.

> CLEO
> It's okay. Try again with
> your other hand.

Before accepting the screwdriver again, the Thin Kid slowly
knocks his forehead with the palm of his bandaged hand; an
aren't-I-a-dummy gesture.

The tape finishes screaming a second time.

The teens laugh, even though they don't want to, and they
attempt to cover it up, like they're trying not to laugh at
a toddler who swears.

The Thin Kid repeats the gesture, eager and desperate for
their approval. The teens aren't laughing anymore.

Cleo puts the screwdriver in his left hand and she rewinds
the tape again. Presses Play.

The Thin Kid walks in front of the desk, faces the mannequin, faces away from us. There's no hesitation this time.

The tape screams. He raises the screwdriver and brings it
down hard and fast.

WHOOMP, then a muffled CLATTER.

The puncture sound is louder than Karson's had been. The power of the strike is unexpected and frightening.

The Thin Kid stands to his full height. He's as tall as the screen. Taller. He stares at the hole he made in the mannequin's left chest. The hole is as wide as the screwdriver's handle. He'd struck so powerfully, the screwdriver went all the way through, is now trapped within the mannequin.

The Thin Kid tilts his head as he continues to stare, and the tape continues to scream.

This is not a confused head tilt. This one is different.

The Thin Kid grabs the mannequin by the neck and lifts it off the desk, the screwdriver rattling inside the plastic torso. The tape recorder falls to the floor, cuts out. He holds the mannequin so that the head is a few inches above his.

The Thin Kid's skinny arm doesn't tremble or betray any hint of strain. He isn't breathing heavily, if he is in fact breathing at all.

The teens silently watch as he inspects the mannequin. Then, with an eerie economy of motion and exertion, he throws the mannequin against the blackboard.

SLAM!

One of the mannequin's legs is ripped from its torso with the force of impact, then the body crumples to the floor.

The Thin Kid turns and faces the teens. His head is tilted down, toward them. Then he lifts his bandaged hand, stares at it as he flexes it slowly.

Cleo breaks from the group, gently loops one of her arms around the Thin Kid's left arm, and we see, really see, how much shorter she is than him. Cleo leads him to the supply room.

The Thin Kid doesn't resist and almost meekly shuffles inside.

Cleo shuts the door.

Karson has already picked up the mannequin, awkwardly hugging the one-legged body with one arm and holding the severed leg with his other hand.

The two girls look at him.

> KARSON
> What? You guys need to
> help me fix him.

The teens briefly try to put the mannequin back together again. They give up.

The tape recorder is broken too.

Valentina carries the leg. Karson lugs the rest of the body, and the screwdriver RATTLES as he walks.

The teens trudge silently out of the classroom.

                                        CUT TO:

13

"Reprising my role?" I ask. If I sound incredulous it's because I am. I can't go back, even if I wanted to. "I understand stunt casting and all that, but I'm a little old to play a teenager even if I still imagine myself as one."

Marlee crosses her arms and says, "Oh, no offense, you're a lot old to be playing a teenager."

"Obviously, but now I'm confused. Well, I'm always confused, but I'm extra-super confused."

Marlee finishes her water. Her cup clinks against the glass tabletop, and the well-tuned engine of a luxury car buzzes by the house, up the mountain, toward even more expensive homes. All the details are important, especially the ones we miss. She says, "We have a young actor cast as the Thin Kid for, roughly, the first half of the film. You would take over as the masked Thin Kid at a certain point in the movie, after his transformation has begun."

"What certain point?"

She says, "I haven't fully decided. I wouldn't ask you to go through either the cigarette or finger-cutting scenes again." Marlee pauses and openly watches for my reaction.

I nod. I don't know what I'm nodding at, and I cover my right hand, the one with the missing half pinky.

"Likely with the mannequin-training scene," she continues. "By that time, your hand will be wrapped in gauze and your body will be partially covered in burns and scales. Your more mature physique would add a nice practical effect we couldn't otherwise replicate."

"'More mature physique.' That's a nice way of saying my older man's body brings extra body horror."

She asks, "Is that a problem? You don't have to do anything you don't want to."

The latter statement is not true. She knows it too. We're already reading lines, playing out a scene. My audition. The idea of wearing the mask for real again is terrifying and intoxicating. I try not to let on that I want this, need this, have dreamed of this, because she's testing me. If I'm too eager, too desperate, she'll change her mind. I say, "Showing off the dad bod is not a problem as long as I'm wearing the mask."

It's Marlee's turn to nod. I can't tell if my answer was expected or disappointing or both. She says, "There's a version of this movie where I use young, age-appropriate actors and I also use actors who were semi-famous teen actors in the '90s for all the roles. I shoot two versions of the film with both sets of actors. Then in editing, I intercut them, switch them around, scene by scene, maybe shot by shot. To show us who we were and who we are at the same time. Maybe by the end of the film, we'll have killed nostalgia dead."

"I like it," I say. "But you didn't pitch that version, did you?"

"Oh, hell no." She laughs. "But the studio went nuts over my other idea."

"The idea of using me."

"Yeah. That's exactly the correct way of putting it."

This blast of honesty is both refreshing and off-putting. "I'm eager and willing to be used." I say it with a smile, like a joke. Like I'm the joke.

"Good. I think?" Her smile flashes, then fades. "You will not play the Thin Kid through to the very end of the film. The teen actor playing the Thin Kid, Jacob—he's quite talented, and I'm looking forward to you two meeting—he'll return to the role for the final kill scene. Having you participate in that scene wouldn't be . . . appropriate."

"I agree," I say. It doesn't sound like the sincerest "I agree" that has ever been uttered. I'm a better silent actor.

She narrows her eyes and can tell I'm not committed to my verbal agreement. She says, "I'm all for exploitation, but only up to a point. And I don't mean to joke, because I'm taking this movie and everything around it seriously."

"I appreciate that. And I'll do or not do whatever you need me to, um, do. Sorry, that's a lot of *do*."

"It is a lot. And thank you." She exhales and rests her hands on her lap, smiles again, which normally is Hollywood for *We're done talking now*, but she asks, "Do you have any questions for me? I have tons more for you, but they can wait."

My typical, defensive response to the I-have-more-questions-but-they-can-wait tactic is to answer preemptively and obliquely the anticipated questions about what happened on the set and later at the trial. An I-know-that-you-know bit that is more than a little paranoid on my part, but hey, I gotta be me. But here on my new director's back patio, I resist my typecasting. I say, "As an associate producer, may I ask what the budget will be?"

"You didn't hear it from me, but between twenty and twenty-five million."

"Holy shit." If I'd had a mouthful of water, I would've done a spit take.

"Holy shit is right."

"Fucking Hollywood. Don't get me wrong, spend the money, and pay me, please." I pause to laugh, the kind that doesn't go beyond my seat. "That seems excessive, considering how little we needed to make the movie, or almost make the movie, the first time. Unless the plan is for a shit ton of digital effects. Which would make me sad."

"I plan to spend it on sets, locations, actors—present company included, of course—and practical effects. We'll shoot on film. And I want to keep the digital effects to the absolute minimum."

I don't know what to say. Being paid and paid well wasn't necessarily part of my plan.

Marlee continues when I don't say anything. "This kind of budget will allow us to do everything the way Valentina and Cleo intended. Including filming the big scene in Karson's house as written in the screenplay and not what you ended up shooting."

I say, "Valentina never said so, but I could tell she wasn't happy with the throat-slash compromise. She'd hoped to use lighting and prosthetics, and even showed me the storyboards, which she normally didn't do. Once I saw the boards, I knew there was no way they'd be able to replicate what Cleo had written, at least not without it looking utterly silly."

"Can I admit that I'm afraid what the effects team and I came up with still might look silly? But I want to try. That scene is one of the many reasons I want to make the movie. If you don't mind me saying so, how the filmed scene currently ends is anticlimactic. The buildup is so unbearably intense and scary and unhinged. If you watch it under the right conditions, it breaks time. But after all that, the onscreen kill is a letdown." For a moment, she's a wide-eyed, enthusiastic, filterless, unselfconscious fan of horror films, and then her formidable intellect catches up with her "onscreen kill is a letdown" phrase and she is horrified at the words and at herself, and her hands move to cover her mouth but they're too late.

I jump in before she can apologize or dilute what she'd said. "Spoken like a true gore hound. You sound like one of the super-fans that accost me at conventions." I smile to let her know I'm making fun of somebody, or something, but not her.

She waves a dismissive and relieved hand in my direction and says, "I'm not, generally. And when I first saw that scene on You-Tube it was brilliant, and I loved it. I was obsessed with it and watched it repeatedly, but later when I read the screenplay and saw what the scene could be, I wanted *that* end to the scene. I still re-watch it, but only up until the throat slash. Even the timing of the slash feels off."

"It does. It's subtle. The editing isn't obviously off continuity-wise, but it's like there are one or two missing frames, somehow."

"Yes, exactly."

"I think Valentina put it together that way purposefully."

"Did she tell you that?"

I say no, which isn't exactly a lie because I can't remember if she did or not. So, it's the truth with a few missing frames. I continue, "But everything she did was purposeful. Including her choosing to upload that scene to YouTube. If she was truly disappointed in that scene, she wouldn't have released it."

"Maybe. I didn't know her like you did, obviously, but filmmaking is sometimes about proudly showing off your almosts and your failures. I'm guessing she knew that after people viewed that scene and the others, they'd debate the merits and meaning."

I say, adding to her riff, "Putting the idea of the movie, her movie, out into the world, planting it in people's heads, letting it grow into a life of its own, calling it back fully into being."

She says, "Looks like it worked."

"We're not there yet. But it feels like we're getting close."

Marlee shakes her head and says, "All right, I need to ask about the party scene, how you all filmed that. It seems impossible without a crane."

MONTAGE

It's Friday. Do you know where your teenagers are?

--A brief tour of the suburban town's quiet streets and side-walks. MISSING POSTERS dot telephone POLES and TREES and the automatic glass doors of a GROCERY STORE. People pass between the doors without a second glance at the posters.

The name and photo of the Thin Kid is never shown, or if shown, is blurry, out of focus so we can't see his face. Without his face, it has been easier to do terrible things to him, and it will be easier to be afraid of him.

--At the high school, a POLICE OFFICER stands at the front of a classroom. The scribbled words filling the chalkboard are out of focus. The officer asks if anyone has informa-tion on the missing boy.

--High school hallway, Cleo at her locker, invisible to a small pod of CLASSMATES excitedly discussing the big party happening later that night.

--More Missing posters about town.

--The police officer at the front of another classroom, advising the teens to not go out alone at night, to be on the safe side.

--Karson, blank-faced, in the NURSE'S OFFICE, having his temperature taken.

The NURSE tells him he is fine. Normal.

--More Missing posters, these ones taped and tacked to the hallway walls and bulletin boards around the high school.

--Study hall. Valentina hides her head behind an open TEXT-BOOK placed vertically on her desk. She fiddles with the crinkled-up fortune-teller note, that party invitation she intercepted the previous week. She opens the petal that reads "Party!!!"

--The tired, bored police officer is in the study hall after school with only the teacher, Karson, Cleo, and Valentina in the room, sitting in their usual seats in the back. The officer asks questions, holds a NOTEBOOK.

The teens shrug and shake their heads no.

FADE TO:

INT. CLEO'S HOUSE, BEDROOM - EARLY EVENING

Cleo flips over the reversed movie posters hanging on her walls so that the images face out, are no longer hidden. Good movies and classic movies are mixed in with and out-numbered by terrible ones.

When she's finished, the walls are splashed with the garish fonts and rictus grins and knives and monsters and chain-saws and bloody mouths and screaming, hapless victims.

Cleo slings her pack over her shoulder, leaves the bedroom, shuts the door behind her, momentarily trapping us with the familiar monsters.

INT. VALENTINA'S HOUSE, KITCHEN - EARLY EVENING

Valentina's kitchen is large, brightly lit, sparkling clean.

Her back is to us as she opens a DRAWER as stealthily as she can. She plucks then deposits a mysterious item into her canvas bag.

She grabs a COOKIE from a nearby JAR and takes an unenthu-siastic bite. Then she navigates around the counter to a SLIDING DOOR. She pulls it open.

VALENTINA
(shouts)
I'm going to Cleo's!

From somewhere within the home, Mamá responds, but Valentina shuts the slider behind her before we can register what she says, is trying to say.

Valentina walks through her YARD, eating the cookie.

INT. KARSON'S HOUSE, FIRST FLOOR – EARLY EVENING – CONTINUOUS

Karson wanders through the dimly lit first floor of his house. The lights are on in most rooms, but the wattage is as weak as Karson's resolve.

KARSON
Dad? Hey, Dad?

We've taken this trip through the maze of his house before. It's just as disorienting as it was previously. The colors of the wallpaper and rugs or exposed floors don't match or fit any decorative pattern, as though each room is in a different house.

Karson doesn't follow a discernible circuit, a clear path, and seems to be taking random turns, sometimes doubling back into a different room somehow, even as we reenter the same room we'd been in moments ago. The layout is illogical, impossible to follow.

But we follow Karson, and he continues to call out to his dad.

Karson stops within the entryway of what appears to be a long DINING ROOM. The lights are out. A small -- too small for the room -- stained wooden TABLE huddles in the middle, the CHAIRS pushed in so their backs press against the tabletop.

There's a corresponding doorway ARCH across the dark valley of the room. Behind that arch, a few feet away, is a plain WALL. Dim light shines from the left of the doorway.

> KARSON (CONT'D)
> You there, Dad?

Dad's shadowed form steps into the archway. He's not tall, but he fills the space with his width. Thick arms, legs, torso; he's built like a bull.

> DAD
> What? What do you want now?

His voice is deep, vibrating through the expanse, directly into our chests.

> KARSON
> (statement spoken
> like a question)
> I was going to meet Valentina
> at Cleo's?

> DAD
> Are you telling me or are
> you asking? Your mom says
> you shouldn't be out alone
> at night.
> (he doesn't sound
> overly concerned,
> more annoyed that
> he's forced to
> interact with his son)

> KARSON
> Asking. And please. Also.
> Cleo's dad wants to borrow
> your chainsaw to cut down

some rotting branches. Is
that okay?

Dad releases a heavy sigh. This bull might charge at any
moment.

> KARSON (CONT'D)
> At least I'll be safe out there
> by myself. I mean, I'll be
> walking down the street with a
> chainsaw, right?

We laugh. We have to.

> QUICK CUT TO:

EXT. SUBURBAN SIDE STREET - EVENING

The three teens walk in slow motion down the middle of the
familiar road. Streetlights spotlight their parade.

As they strut like rock stars, one of the following songs
plays: Buzzcocks, "What Do I Get?"; Dead Kennedys, "Forward
to Death"; PJ Harvey, "50ft Queenie"; Elastica, "Connection."

Karson is in the middle, carrying his CHAINSAW proudly. Big
smile, puffed chest.

Cleo has an amused expression.

Valentina's face is blank. Or pissed off. She adjusts her
hat and hair.

The slo-mo and music cut out abruptly.

> VALENTINA
> We're not using a fucking
> chainsaw. Are you high? What
> are you thinking?

Karson deflates, crestfallen.

We have one last laugh, maybe our final one, as the music kicks back in and they continue striding down the familiar street to their collective destiny.

There's no stopping this now.

                                                    CUT TO:

INT. ABANDONED SCHOOL, CLASSROOM - CONTINUOUS

We're at the front of the room, hovering over the sacred marked spot on the floor, facing the rear wall of the classroom. It's as though the teens left us here to change us too.

The classroom door opens, and we only see the bright cyclopean eyes of two FLASHLIGHTS. The light blobs are oversized fireflies, and they dance until they focus on our spot, on us.

                    KARSON
            It's fucking creepy here at
            night.
                    (he says it with
                    self-awareness,
                    hopelessness,
                    regret)

We flip to the teens' POV.

Their flashlight beams are pinned to the classroom's front, and we itemize: the bloodied symbol on the floor; the teacher's desk; the clouded chalkboard, a precursor to the violent storm to come; the *open* supply-room door.

                    VALENTINA
            Shit. Is he in there? Where
            is he?

                    CLEO
        Maybe he's in the woods.

                   KARSON
        What do we do now?

Cleo shuffles forward and her two friends follow, flashlights focused on the open door and the sliver of empty
space it exposes. Why must we always peer into those spaces?
Why do we *need* to know?

The Thin Kid's bandaged hand materializes out of the darkness, grabbing hold of the doorframe.

There's an unbearable body-being-dragged SLIDING SOUND
that lasts too long and pools at the bases of our skulls.

The Thin Kid's head finally appears *below* where his hand
is secured.

We realize he stuffed himself within the cramped space to
the far left of the supply room. We don't know how little
space is there, but we can imagine it, even if we don't
want to. We think about other dark corners and unexplored
spaces in our lives, and we wonder what might live there,
what might *choose* to live there.

And worse, he left the door open, meaning he wants the
teens to see and know where he was.

The Thin Kid finally pulls himself onto his feet and emerges
from the room.

He is no longer crouched, cowering, curled into himself.
He stands to his full height. His limbs are as long as a
spider's.

The flashlights crawl over him. Cleo's makeup and latex
scales have spread, covering roughly half his body. In the

weak, almost strobing light, the exposed patches of his actual, pale skin look fake. His mask looks more real, like a living skin.

Cleo approaches, aiming her flashlight beam toward the floor, slowly takes his right arm with her free hand, and leads him to the symbolled floor spot, though it's no longer necessary to do so. She knows this, but there's a comfort in surrendering responsibility to continuing ritual.

The Thin Kid obliges. His chest expands and contracts, but his breathing isn't audible.

Cleo leaves him standing on the spot. She steps toward Karson and turns, so her back and backpack face him.

>   CLEO
>   (to Karson)
>   Can you put that down and
>   get the tape out of my pack?

Karson looks at the chainsaw in his hands like he forgot it was there, then walks to the teacher's desk and puts it down with a CLUNK. He idly wipes his hands on his pants, as though the chainsaw had left some sort of residue behind.

The Thin Kid turns his head, watches Karson intently.

Karson walks behind Cleo and roots through her pack.

>   CLEO
>   (almost a whisper)
>   Should be on top.

>   KARSON
>   I can't see anything.

The Thin Kid is as still and as patient as a statue.

Karson fishes out a roll of DUCT TAPE. He tosses it up in the air and catches it, to show that it was no big deal, that he was in control all along.

Valentina pulls a BUTCHER'S KNIFE out of her bag. The blade in silhouette appears to be an extension of her arm.

> VALENTINA
> (to Karson)
> You helping?

> KARSON
> Um, yeah. Yes.

Karson flanks the Thin Kid but is careful to not get too close.

Cleo holds the flashlight on the Thin Kid's bandaged hand. The bandages are dirty, crusty. The exposed fingers are still and not scaled like much of the rest of his body.

Valentina places the knife's handle into his bandaged palm. The blade, caught directly in Cleo's flashlight beam, flares sun-bright, flash blinding us as we hear Karson rip and tear lengths of duct tape.

Valentina manipulates and moves the Thin Kid's compliant fingers, closing them around the handle. Then she holds his forearm steady.

Karson applies and rolls the tape over hand and knife handle, taking time, taking care, smoothing down corners and seams.

Once they finish taping the knife to the Thin Kid's hand, the teens fall back into their group.

The Thin Kid, his arms initially slack, lifts his right arm, and the knife blade again catches the flashlight beam and throws it back in our faces.

Valentina fills her hands with the fortune-teller note, her
fingers hidden in the paper folds.

> VALENTINA
> (talking to the
> Thin Kid)
> What's your favorite color?

Silence.

> CLEO
> His favorite color is blue.

> VALENTINA
> (moves her fingers
> and the note as she
> spells)
> B-L-U-E.

Valentina holds the note in place for a beat.

> VALENTINA (CONT'D)
> Who is your secret crush?

The Thin Kid doesn't answer, remains motionless.

The three teens share a look, passing secret knowledge
among themselves.

Valentina opens and closes the note as she silently spells
out a name. We could count her movements and attempt to
figure out what name she is spelling, but she stops before
we can try.

> VALENTINA (CONT'D)
> Pick a number between 1
> and 4.

The Thin Kid surprises us with movement, and he holds up three fingers with his left hand.

Valentina moves the note, then unfolds a petal, and shows it to the Thin Kid.

                    KARSON
               (whispers)
          Isn't he supposed to pick --

Cleo elbows him.

We don't see the petal, but we can make a good guess at what is on it.

Valentina crumples the note and tosses it away.

                    VALENTINA
          Come on. You're coming with
          us.

The teens all move at once, knocking into one another. Their clumsiness is not comedic; it reflects their fear and panic and excitement. They whisper apologies to each other, and Karson awkwardly deposits the duct tape back into Cleo's pack as they meander slowly to the back of the classroom.

The Thin Kid does not follow. He stays rooted to his spot.

The teens don't notice he isn't with them until they make it to the classroom door. They point both flashlights at him; at this distance the beams diffuse, giving the room a ghostly glow.

We wait and watch, and we stare at his mask, suddenly convinced its features might twitch, might move.

                    KARSON
              (whispers what some
              of us think is
              a non sequitur)
         This is definitely Mr. Whalen's
         room. I want to forget the
         crocodile poem.

                    VALENTINA
              (annoyance and
              concern in her
              voice)
         Dude? Are you gonna be all
         right?

                    CLEO
              (calling to the Thin
              Kid)
         Hey, it's okay. It's time.

The Thin Kid walks forward, knife in hand, neither halting
nor in a rush. We linger with his walk to the front of the
classroom just as we linger with the possibilities of what
might happen next.

                                        CUT TO:

14

In mid-April of 2008, fifteen years after her out-of-the-blue call and answering machine message that had led to Valentina and Cleo pitching me my role in *Horror Movie*, Valentina called and left me another message. This one a voicemail on my cell phone. We hadn't spoken since the brief trial. I don't know how she got my number this time, and she never told me.

I didn't recognize the phone number associated with her voicemail, of course, but I recognized her voice, despite it being reedy, weak, and distant, as though she were speaking to a phone that was on the opposite end of a large room, maybe the dining room in Karson's house. It's difficult for me, especially now, not to relate everything that happened and happens in terms of our movie.

On the voicemail, Valentina said she had a proposition, and she laughed. Her laugh turned into a cough. She didn't apologize for laughing or coughing. She said the proposition was serious. This was a knowing, canny replay of the message she'd left on my answering machine in 1993. The *uncanny* part was that I hadn't remembered what it was she'd said originally until I heard her repeat it. We were trapped in another script, one that was self-aware and echoed what had taken place earlier.

In retrospect, maybe Valentina, nearing her end, couldn't resist thinking in the language of film.

———

I didn't know anything about what Valentina had done with her life post–*Horror Movie*. I was surprised she still lived in her hometown. Given everything that had happened on-set and afterward, and her complicated relationship with her parents, I thought she would flee this town as fast as a final girl fleeing the killer. Maybe on some level she enjoyed being the local pariah, the cautionary tale. She wasn't exactly conflict-averse. I always admired and loved that about her.

On the way to her place, I swung by the old elementary school we'd used in the movie. I expected to find a skeletonized husk, or a pile of rubble, or an empty lot for sale. But the brick school building survived and had been converted into condos with an adjoining apartment building and parking lot on the footprint of the old schoolyard. Ah, you can't stop progress, you can't stop change. I wondered who lived in the classroom we'd used, what the supply room had been converted into, and what might lurk in its corners.

Cut to my arriving at Valentina's house, which was a modest Cape, maybe a half mile away from where her parents lived. It was three blocks from the road we had used for the various shots of the teens walking.

I parked on the street. There was no curb to delineate the road from a cracked, narrow sidewalk. Her house's exterior was freshly painted yellow, the trim a bright white. Larger neighboring houses leaned in, keeping it in line. New, early-spring grass patched the muddy front yard. The front stoop was red brick. I wiped my feet on a straw welcome mat and rang the bell.

Valentina opened the door, and the sight was so shocking, I took a step back. She was always short, and I had not expected her to grow taller in the intervening years, but now she was *small*. Her shrunken body was adrift in plaid flannel pajama pants and a billowy hooded gray sweatshirt. Her long, dark curls were gone. She wore an orange winter beanie over her obviously bald head. Her cheeks had deflated and sunk below her cheekbones. Her skin was sallow and jaundiced. Her moon-sized eyes settled on mine and her expression was blank, a deathly vacancy that was more than unrecognition; it was a despairing incomprehension at the unfairness of her physical degradation. I thought about asking if she was home alone, how someone could leave her alone like this. Then, with great effort, as though drudging up a lost memory, she smirked, and her face became one I recognized, if only as a sickly echo.

"I know. I look that good, right?" she said. There was anger and sorrow and grit and a gallows charisma if not humor in those few words. Valentina held out her arms, pivoted on her heels, posing like a supermodel.

I wanted to cry but I was also a little bit mad at her for making me confront her illness after years of not seeing her, of bursting my delusionary fantasies that, of all of us, she was and would be okay. She was supposed to be the one who survived.

I said, "Hey, um, it's great to see you, but fucking hell."

"Exactly. Sorry, I should've warned you." She paused and had that look, that almost-smile she used so often on-set. Maybe she was still directing me. "I thought about putting jeans on at least, but then, well, I spent most of the morning puking. Come on in." She stepped aside and held the door open. She didn't make any sort of move that communicated she wanted a hug or a handshake.

I followed her slow shuffle through the sparsely decorated house, which was clean and well-kept but for a small, cluttered office space into which I had the opportunity to briefly glance. I thought I saw a reel-to-reel projector among boxes and paper piles, and I wanted to linger there, but she led me to a living room that had a television, a half bathroom, a wooden dining-room chair, plus a puffy love seat and pull-out sofa bed both covered in sheets and blankets. A bottle of Pedialyte, assorted prescription bottles, and a half-eaten plastic sleeve of saltine crackers cluttered an end table. The room's smell was something I'd like to forget.

Valentina cratered onto the love seat, and I settled into the wooden chair.

She told me she had stage-four pancreatic cancer that had spread pretty much everywhere. She had maybe two months left, but they'd said that to her one month ago. She had opted for home hospice care, something her parents were able to help pay for. Normally her mother and the day nurse were there, but Valentina had managed to convince both to leave so she could have some time alone with me.

I told her I was sorry. And I didn't know what else to say. I knew nothing of her too-brief adult life, and it felt wrong to barrage her with questions about who she was and what she had done now that both her past and future were dead. But I still asked her, because I wanted to put off whatever her new proposal was.

Valentina said that "after everything"—here she paused to honor our experiences—she had moved to Denver and worked admin for Learningsmith, a short-lived educational toy and game store, then moved to San Diego to work for Petco, and in between she married and divorced a guy named Jeremy who didn't do her the favor of disclosing he was a high-then-low-functioning alcoholic. He wasn't a monster, but it became impossible to live within his constantly draining whirlpool. They remained in touch, and he was doing better as far as she could tell. After the divorce, she moved back to the East Coast, settling in Providence. She worked for her father, helping to manage the car washes, and the experience wasn't as terrible as she had thought it would be. Of all the things she told me, her voice sounded the saddest at that. Her cancer was diagnosed last summer, already in stage three, and none of the treatment prevented the aggressive disease from worsening, spreading. Her eyes were too big now, could see too much, and they blinked and rolled out of focus. Her parents wanted Valentina to move back home so they could help care for her. She would've rather stepped in front of a bus, but she didn't tell her parents that. Renting this house was the compromise. She started most days with a hard cry in the bathroom. The duration of those bouts diminished with each passing day, just like her.

Her candor was a shock and not a shock. I couldn't help but feel there was a purpose to it. She thanked me for letting her say what she couldn't to her mother. Her thank-you was cold though, an employer thanking an applicant for the effort.

With her flash autobiography completed, she asked, "So quid pro quo, yeah? What have you done with your life?"

I said, "Keeping a low profile. Walking the earth."

She smiled again. It was both wonderful and horrible. "Right. Walking the earth. Are you Cain or *Caine* with an *e*?"

"Maybe both. I have a few marks," I said.

"Don't we all." She wrapped her thin arms around her chest and shook her head. "I never blamed you. Ultimately, I was responsible. I failed to make a safer set."

"I still blame me." I wished I had my mask, so I could hide. But that's a lie because the mask was never about hiding.

She said, "I know you tried reaching out a few times, but the years of no contact wasn't about you either. I just wanted to, needed to—"

"Forget. You needed to forget. Which was and is impossible. But I totally understand—"

Valentina interrupted. "May you be blessed and cursed with a long life, my friend, one over which to continually pick at the corpse of regret. Anyway, no, I didn't want to forget. Certainly not in the way you mean it."

"I'm not sure I understand."

Valentina waved a never-mind-what-I-said hand at me. "Being so close to oblivion makes me think and say portentous things." She pointed a finger at me. "Not pretentious though."

"Of course. Never."

"Now that we have that out of the way. I do have something to ask. A new proposition. But I also wanted to see you, see how much you've changed."

"Well? What's the verdict?"

"It's too early for a verdict. Clearly you've filled out, and good for you that you still have your hair."

I said, "Thank Christ," a little too enthusiastically, and then immediately felt guilty given Valentina's bald head. "I mean, I'm not that old yet."

"Overall, I'd say you're more the same than not."

"Is that a good thing? It sounds kind of pathetic." I was never very good at self-deprecation because I was too honest.

"To be determined."

"Nice."

Valentina struggled to stand up. "Okay, sorry, but I need to use the bathroom—"

I stood too. "Don't be sorry. Do you need any—"

"No. I don't need any anything." Once she was upright, she closed her eyes and breathed deeply, then shuffled away from her seat. "If you want anything, please, head into the kitchen and get it yourself. Take your time. I'll just be on the toilet, trying to decide if I should bother reupping this place's rental agreement."

I stood with my arms out like I was ready for her fall, like I could catch her.

She waved me away and said, "Go, please."

Her more than strongly worded hint taken, I wandered into the kitchen and got myself a glass of tap water. Instead of expending mental energy on what her proposal was going to be, I tiptoed through the house to her office. At the doorway, I listened for sounds of Valentina emerging from the bathroom, but all was quiet. I walked inside. There were two tabletop Macs on an elongated and overloaded wooden desk; one of the computer screens was double the size of the other. On and around the desk and shelving were a chaotic array of wires and other equipment, including a reel-to-reel projector and stacks of boxes piling toward the ceiling in a losing game of Tetris. I focused on the reel-to-reel projector, the gargoyle on the top shelf. Its exterior shell was metal, painted a light brown color, and in decent condition other than a few rusted patches at the base stand. The empty reels perched vertically above and below the projection lens. I didn't know anything about it, but judging by the appearance, I assumed it wasn't functional, was a collector's item, though haphazardly stored. I decided the carefree placement of it looked *too* carefree. The projector was cherished, but she didn't want anyone else to know how much she cherished it. Maybe it was a carefully placed prop to seed movie thoughts in my head prior to her new proposal. Later, when I finally returned to my apartment, I searched for projectors on eBay and found an 8mm film model from the 1940s that looked similar, but not quite the same. I moved on to the sieged desktop and a rubber-banded stack of papers print-side down. Not daring to set my glass of water on the desk, I flipped the stack over with one hand, accidentally nudging an unseen computer mouse. Both Mac screens woke from their slumber with a loud, crescendoing note from a bombastic classical piece. Frightened by the audio jump scare, I stumbled away from the desk, splashing water onto the throw rug. I wiped the wet spot with my foot and listened for Valentina. The toilet flushed on cue. Fuck. I still had the paper stack in my hand. I took a quick peek at the print and saw the telltale screenplay typeface and the capitalized character names from *Horror Movie*. There were red-ink underlines, circles, and notes in the margins. I returned the screenplay to the desk. The glowing computer screens displayed the same home page, cluttered with folders that had roman-numeral names, the letters lowercased.

I walked back quickly to the living room, and Valentina was already settled in her love seat.

She said, "Welcome back. I'd offer to give you a full tour of the place, but, you know."

I sat down on the wooden chair again, feeling caught. By "caught" I mean "ensnared." "Sorry. I'm a snoop," I said, and added, "That's a cool projector, in the office," as though she didn't know what she had and where she had it. "Does it still work?"

"It does. I don't have a lot of 8mm film stuff to show on it, but yeah, it works."

I wondered about the projector's origin. Had she bought it for herself recently, a lonely online, secretive purchase? Had one of her parents given it to her as a housewarming present, which seemed both thoughtful and terrible at the same time? We're always compelled to invent stories that make sense of the unknown and meaningless. If we were in a movie, Valentina would tell me that Cleo had given the projector to her as a congratulatory present in the days before filming started. If we were in a horror movie, the formulaic, comforting, cheap-thrill kind, one that followed the dumbass rules of having a *scare* every ten or so screenplay pages, Valentina would *flash back* to how she used the projector to obsessively watch and rewatch the flickering final death scene of *Horror Movie* on the dingy wall of her office.

She asked, "Do you still have the mask?"

"Yes, I do."

"I hoped you would say yes. I also hoped you would've said no."

If there was, unsaid, a moral judgment, that was probably fair, but it was one I had no interest in exploring. "I just couldn't bring myself to throw it away," I said.

"You don't have to explain why you kept it."

"Good. Because I can't."

"You mean you don't want to explain or—"

I interrupted and finished the sentence for her. "Or I won't explain. Maybe that's right. Honestly my opinion on the matter changes daily."

"Fair enough," she said. "Is it in good condition?"

"Pristine." I luxuriated on the two syllables.

"You didn't bring it with you by any chance?"

"If you had asked, I would've brought it with me."

"Is that an answer to my question?"

I held up my glass of water and an empty hand. "I don't have it with me."

If I were to describe her face as having an I-don't-trust-you expression, you should rightly ask, *How would he know that?* The answer: I was projecting. Her expression registered as distrust because I didn't trust myself.

She said, "I almost did ask you to bring it. I wish I had." Her wish was a casually dropped penny into a well, and she followed it down into the water, zoning out. She wasn't there in the room with me anymore and her body slumped into the love-seat cushions and I worried the slump might take her down to the floor. I called her name and started up out of my chair.

She came to and readjusted in her seat. "I'm fine. Just got a little light-headed." She sipped from the bottle of Pedialyte.

"Are you sure? Should we call your nurse? Can I get you anything?"

She shook her head and drank the fluorescent-colored electrolytes. She said, "If you haven't figured it out by now—but it sounds like you understand, too, since you kept the mask—I didn't and don't want to forget the movie. I want to finish the movie. I've always wanted to finish it."

I put my glass down on her end table, and I asked, "How much of what we filmed do you still have?"

"I have every single frame we shot."

"I thought you had to, you know, turn everything over to the police. Did they give it back? Did you, what, make copies?"

Valentina dismissively waved a hand at me and said, "It took me years to work up to it, to be honest with myself about what I wanted. I finally started working on the movie again, digitizing all the film I had, at the start of last summer, months before my cancer diagnosis. The cancer, of course, was already there inside me without my knowing." She leaned forward and smiled; it was a skull's smile. "Who knows, maybe the cancer appeared the moment I rewatched those first frames, yeah? Maybe it's a cursed film." She sounded way too hopeful in anticipation of my response.

"You don't believe that, do you?" I asked.

"A cursed film? No. But there will be lots of people who will believe and want to believe it's a cursed film, especially when I put it out there."

"Out where?"

She didn't answer me. "I could've rushed together a sloppy, almost-full cut of the movie, but I wouldn't include your and Cleo's final scene. That's the one bit of film I haven't and won't watch again. I can't. I tried, though, because I'm a terrible person. When I first unpacked everything and watched the shots and clips from the start, I planned to watch that last scene and include it for the sake of the movie, for the sake of the thing that we all worked so hard on, you know? It has our literal blood, sweat, and tears. I went through and digitized the last scene, but when I pressed Play to watch and I heard me yell, 'Action!' I stopped it immediately. I couldn't watch." Valentina paused and was breathing heavily, and I knew there was more there that she wasn't telling me, so I filled in for her, imagining her pacing circles in the office, returning to the chair, pressing Play again, then stopping, then diving under the desk and unplugging the power strip and sitting in the suddenly stilled room.

She continued. "Without that scene there wouldn't be a full film, not even close. Why bother putting the rest of it together, right? I mean, what would be the point? But I still want and need people to see this movie someday, somehow. So, I came up with a new plan. The long play, even though I don't have any time left. Does anyone ever *have* time? Don't answer that.

"I've cut, edited, and completed three scenes: the cigarette burns, the party, and Karson's dining-room scene. I even made a rudimentary synth soundtrack. That took a lot of time and energy I didn't have. I'm no Trent Reznor, but it came out pretty good, I think. The first two scenes look how I'd hoped they would look. A little shaggy in terms of production value, obviously, but they work. And that arriving-at-the-party scene is magic. Dan was a camera wizard, but I don't know how we pulled it off, how we got it to look so good, how you made that jump. Do you remember?"

I took a moment to gather what I thought she expected or wanted to hear and mixed it with the truth. I said, "Honestly, after the finger scene, I don't remember much about the making of the movie. I only remember the *movie*, as though I was in it. Living it."

"You became the Thin Kid. I love it. So method."

"I had a great director."

She bowed her head, then said, "The third scene, Karson's scene, is almost perfect. That's the filmmaker's lot in life, I think, which is kind of wonderful. Which is why I wanted to make movies. To be almost perfect. We couldn't shoot exactly what was in the screenplay, remember? The technology is here *now* though. Someone else will be able to shoot that scene the right way if they commit to it."

"Someone else?"

"I'm going to upload those three scenes to YouTube, and post stills along with the full screenplay on various horror message boards and my blog. I know horror fans, and this will cause an online stir. A slow-burn kind of stir. And that's probably better for the second life of the film, more organic. I'm guessing it'll take years—years I don't have, but years *you* have—years for the legend of our cursed movie to grow, take a life of its own. I mean, take *on* a life of its own. No Freudian slip there, right?

"People will discuss and dissect the scenes and Cleo's fucking brilliant screenplay, and everyone will know how talented she was and they'll know a little bit about who she was and maybe remember that instead of how she died, and if we're lucky—and if you help— the legend will grow and grow until someone, someday will have no choice but to make this movie. My proposal: I need your help to get *Horror Movie* made."

I didn't say yes. I didn't say no. I asked, "How?"

She described a convention she'd attended in the fall called Rock and Shock, held at the DCU Center in Worcester. The place was packed with horror fans in black T-shirts. Aside from the merchandise vendors there was a large section of booths with B-grade horror-movie actors signing autographs, selling shirts and pictures. Every actor's booth had a line, no matter how obscure, no matter how scraggly they looked, no matter how dimmed the shine of their onetime starring role. She said it suddenly all came to her. She could see me there and at other, bigger conventions. With an oracle-like forecasting of the future, she talked about a cult-like fan interest in the cursed movie and the controversial Thin Kid reaching a point where Hollywood could not ignore the built-in, waiting fan base. They couldn't say no to the easy, cynical buck. Producers would contact me and would want my involvement and Cleo's family would sell the rights to the screenplay because they would be convinced making the movie would honor her memory, that it would be what she wanted, and the money would be too much to say no. She said it all hinged on my participation. I would need to stop *walking the earth*, to come out of hiding, and to be approachable but not too approachable. I'd never be the carnival barker. I'd be the mysterious tease. Make people think I was coy and damaged and dangerous. She said of course people would be drawn to the released scenes, to the what-could've-been, and they'd discuss and dissect her possible motivations for releasing materials, but the Thin Kid would eventually and necessarily become the focal point, the face. The mask. She said she knew what she was asking of me. She knew it would be difficult and horrible. She knew what I would have to live with. She said that people would think I was a ghoul, making money off Cleo's death, and some would argue that her death was my fault no matter what I did or said. But, she said, everything, all of it, would boil over into irresistible momentum toward remaking the movie.

Perhaps my memory of Valentina's last proposal has been embellished by the intervening years. If I step back and am honest with myself there's no *perhaps* about it. If she didn't say everything exactly as described above, well, it was all still there. That was what I heard. That is what I remember.

Valentina lifted her bottle with a shaking hand after she finished.

I was no near-oracle, but prior to the visit, I'd hoped Valentina's newest (and last) proposal had something to do with our movie. I didn't ask follow-up questions. I didn't offer a lengthy retort. My answer was not no. I didn't say the word "yes." I didn't have to.

I stood and said, "I, um, I'll be right back."

She said, "I'm not going anywhere."

I walked through the house, darting through the front door, breaking into a run, fleeing what was behind, desperately running toward something else. I stopped at my car, or my car stopped me. My hands smacked, palms open, against the rear-window glass. I unlocked and threw open the hatch trunk.

I took a moment to breathe, to slow everything down, to make sure that this was what I was going to do, that this was what I was running toward.

I carefully freed my mask from its case.

EXT. SUBURBAN SIDE STREET – EVENING

Our three teens walk down the middle of the familiar street. We've walked it with them countless times now. We know this street by heart, even in the dark.

Our vantage is the same as it was during the prior shots on this street. But this time the teens walk *away* from the school, the path, and *away* from us.

The teens have a conversation that is just out of earshot.

The Thin Kid lurches into the frame, waking ten or so paces behind the teens.

From our perspective, the Thin Kid looks twice the size of the teens.

From our perspective, the Thin Kid represents the teens' uncertain future.

The hastily affixed latex scales are peeling and slough off the Thin Kid's back and legs. As good as some of the makeup looked earlier, it now looks rough and shoddy. He's wearing a costume that a child might make, and it doesn't fit right, and it makes us briefly pity him all over again.

But there's the knife taped to his hand. And its elongated point is glinting.

If we didn't know better, if we were to join this movie *now* and without prior context, we would think the Thin Kid was stalking the teens, and we would anticipate seeing their blood.

Cleo looks over her shoulder to make sure the Thin Kid is following.

FADE TO:

EXT. LARGE SUBURBAN HOUSE, FRONT YARD - MINUTES LATER

We arrive at the PARTY HOUSE, the one with gables on its gables, the one with the long, tall wall of shrubs fortress-
ing a large patio or garden or perhaps a pool area.

Lit up by strings of LIGHTS, white and orange, the pergola
glows above the shrubbery wall.

The driveway and street are crowded with CARS that belong
to the partying teenagers. We don't linger on car makes
and types, but the most observant of us will notice the
cars are nice, the cars are *better* than what their teach-
ers drive, and surely *better* than what Cleo's and Karson's
parents drive.

We subconsciously do a quick party math on the number of
attendees based on the number of cars. We hear MUSIC and
LAUGHTER and high school PARTY SOUNDS. But we're not at
the party, and we're not on the patio with cheap beer, wine
coolers, drinks called Fuzzy Navels in plastic cups, and
for the non-novices in attendance, whiskey and weed and
whippits.

We're the outsiders, on the sidewalk, at the lip of the
front yard's sea of grass, standing with the teens and the
Thin Kid.

> KARSON
> (he doesn't say the
> following like a
> smartass and it's
> not a joke; this is
> not *we're gonna
> need a bigger boat*,
> no one will laugh,
> because he sounds
> honest and terrified)
> So. We're here.

                    VALENTINA
          That we are.

                    KARSON
               (whispering, as though
               the Thin Kid can't
               hear him)
          Do we need to tell him what
          to do here? I mean, we don't
          have to, like, show him,
          do we?

                    CLEO
               (speaking to
               Valentina)
          How is he going to get back
          there? If he goes through
          the bushes he'll tear off
          his scales or maybe even
          his mask.

Cleo turns to the Thin Kid, who looms close behind the
teens, and she inspects the makeup and scale appliance
work she'd done.

The Thin Kid stares, presumably, at the wall of bushes,
and he doesn't acknowledge Cleo's inspection. He's a totem,
shouldering our projections and emotions and meanings. And
fears.

                    VALENTINA
          Don't know.
               (pause)
          Maybe we did need Karson's
          chainsaw.

                    KARSON
          Fuck me --

                    CLEO
                (interrupts)
        -- *with* a chainsaw?

                    KARSON
        I left it back at the school.
        Shit, I can't . . . can't leave it
        there.
                    (relieved, as now he
                    has an excuse to ditch,
                    and he imagines going
                    to the school, though
                    he isn't wild about
                    the idea of being
                    there by himself
                    in the dark, but he
                    imagines getting the
                    chainsaw back and
                    going home and not
                    leaving his house,
                    ever again)
        I can go get it. It won't
        take me that long. I'll run.
        The party will still be
        going when I get back.

                    VALENTINA
        It's too late now.

One more group-stare at the bushes. One more loud burst of
laughter from the partygoers.

The Thin Kid is off like a shot, sprinting across the front
lawn.

We didn't know he could move like that. Still gangly, all
legs and arms, he's not athletic, but he is *feral* with his
commitment to forward motion, to *going* as fast as he possibly can.

The teens are shocked and don't comment. They don't have time to speculate how he might pass through the barrier and if his mad dash will produce enough momentum to break through to the other side.

The teens creep a step or two onto the grass.

We're with them, watching the Thin Kid sprint up the slight pitch of the yard. Because of where we are, the Thin Kid starts off looking taller than the bushes and he shrinks as he increases the distance from us and as he gets closer and closer to the bushes, and as he's about to crash into the bushes, he jumps.

He *jumps*.

He *rises*.

He rises impossibly. His arms are stretched out, away from his body, like wings.

His legs bend, fold up, retract, and tuck under his body, and he still *rises*, and he passes above and over the bushes, and finally, as he falls back down, his legs unfold, stretch back toward the ground, and then his legs and the rest of his body sink from our view somewhere on the other side.

There's no going back now. There was never any going back.

The teens creep a step or two farther onto the lawn, toward the party-house bushes, and we stay with them. We will not *see* what happens now that the Thin Kid is on the other side.

At the party, the music still plays, but the laughing and yell-talking pauses, briefly pauses, heavily pauses.

A teen guy yells something in a high-pitched, mocking voice and there's laughter, nervous laughter. We can tell it's nervous even from the front lawn.

Then there are SCREAMS.

All manner of high-pitched terrible screams that cut out or fade into moans. And there's glass SHATTERING, water SPLASHING, more screams, things BREAKING, the music cuts out, and more screaming and screaming and screaming.

Hearing is somehow worse than seeing.

The pergola shakes, the lights rattle, a bulb or two winks out, then the whole string goes dark.

A trickle of partygoers escapes by clawing through the bushes, that thorny barrier, and they flee, paying no mind to Cleo, Karson, and Valentina.

We stand behind the teens now because we're frauds, acting like we don't stand with them anymore. The three teens exchange looks, presumably of shock and horror, but we don't see their faces full-on. As with the party massacre, we haven't yet earned the right.

Yelling and screaming emanates from the sidewalk and street, from the partygoers running to their cars and then screeching their tires as they flee. We're distracted by the cars. They fishtail and swerve and narrowly avoid smashing into trees and fences and one another.

When we turn back, the Thin Kid stalks down the front lawn.

We don't know *how* he left the backyard, but we know he can be wherever he wants however he wants now.

Even though the Thin Kid is in silhouette, it is clear he has changed, has undergone an apotheosis.

Our front-yard perspective flips what we witnessed earlier with the Thin Kid as he sprinted away from us toward the bushes. The Thin Kid now *grows* in height as he walks toward us.

Some of us will notice his hands right away. The knife is gone. The knife has become his impossibly long fingers, tipped with claws. He spreads his hands flaunting them, brandishing them.

Finally, only mere steps away, the Thin Kid comes fully into focus.

He stands at his full height, towering over us all. There are no more tricks of perspective. No more CAMERA lies. This is how tall he is. How did we not realize he was this tall before?

His body is covered in reptilian scales and mottled bumps, and not a patch of his original skin, of his original self, remains.

He's not wearing Cleo's cheap makeup.

He is what the mask promised he would become now that he has been baptized in blood.

The teens are horrified and terrified even though this is what they wanted, or this is what they had thought they wanted.

Valentina and Karson slowly back away, but Cleo steps forward.

> CLEO
> Wait. Hey, A--

> VALENTINA
> (interrupting,
> shouting)
> No! Do not say his name.

Cleo backs up again, until she is shoulder to shoulder with her friends.

They stand and stare.

There are no more screams. Those have stopped, for now.

> CLEO
> Let's go back to the classroom.
> Okay? Let's all just go back.

No one tells her the answer is no. They don't have to.

Karson breaks from the line, sprinting away, down to the street.

With their group's gravity broken, Cleo and Valentina can't help but fall into Karson's empty space.

The Thin Kid grabs Valentina and he throws her across the front lawn toward the bushes. She lands with a heavy THUD.

Cleo doesn't move.

The Thin Kid plods forward, past Cleo, and onto the street. A fleeing Karson is still within his sights.

The Thin Kid moves in long, smooth, assured strides as he stalks after Karson.

                                              CUT TO:

NOW:
THE DIRECTOR
PART 3

15

I say, "No one ever believes me when I tell them that all we used for the party scene was a well-placed mini trampoline, distance and perspective, and camera angle."

Marlee says, "You're right. I don't believe you."

"You don't think I had the mad ups to get up and over?"

"Ha! No, sorry. I'm convinced she manipulated it in post somehow."

"Well, the party house was her parents' house. Not the *character* Valentina's parents' house but the *real* Valentina's parents' house, just to be clear—"

"Crystal clear."

"Valentina managed to talk her mom and dad into cutting a chunk off the top of the shrub wall prior to the shot so I could make the jump."

"Really?"

"Yeah. The jump was still dicey. How much they trimmed was purely a guess on Valentina's part. It's not like we tested it. Cast and crew took bets on whether I'd clear the bushes or not. Dan Carroll, our DP, didn't think it would work or look good even if I made it over. But I made it. Hardly anyone saw, but I stuck the landing on the other side too, at the cost of shooting pain in my lower back. My proudest moment not caught on film. Not sure how I did it. Adrenaline? Demon power?"

"That's amazing. Well, we're going to use a crane and not rely on demon power."

"Never underestimate demon power," I say.

I don't tell Marlee that after the losing-the-pinky scene, the unwritten rules of no talking or interacting while the mask was on went back into place. Karson could barely even look at me, as though the Thin Kid losing the pinky half was my fault. Even Mark had stopped chatting me up to sell his bootlegs. I stayed in character from the time I was on-set to when I left. When I went back to the hotel I would hole up in my room, read the next day's sides, eat, and sleep, and that's it. The only way I could deal with what was happening to me was to equate it with what was happening to my character. But that bushes jump, I was proud of that, and as surprised as anyone else that I made it. I probably shouldn't have made it. Up to the moment we started filming, Cleo was dubious and kept asking me if I could clear the bushes. I couldn't speak with the mask on, so I nodded and gave her a thumbs-up. Even though they had cut at least a foot from the top, the bushes were still a few inches taller than I was. When Valentina yelled, "Action!" I hesitated, long enough for her to say "action" a second time. The mask and the darkness made it nearly impossible to see where I was going, which loosened any doubts and physical inhibitions I had during my mad, headlong dash. I couldn't see how impossible this was supposed to be. I sprinted faster than I ever had, and I could do so because I wasn't me. I was him. And because I was him, I was partially transformed. There was no question I would make it over the bushes. Maybe it was simply pure belief and commitment that powered me. I hit the trampoline in stride, pushing off and up with both legs, and I rose, and continued to rise, and the upward trajectory was outside of my control. I soared over those bushes and rose so high I thought I might continue up and into the cold forever night, and maybe that would've been the proper ending, an ending in a fair universe. Now, in my memory, the memory is the movie. I saw the teenage partygoers and they saw me ascending, and their beautiful faces were made even more beautiful by their shiny-eyed expressions of awe and adoration, and they would've bowed before me were it necessary but they were already below me, then finally, past the bushes on the way back to the wretched, cursed Earth, the rubber knife taped to my hand got heavier and became real, just as I was real, and those partygoers, they knew what would happen to them—all of them—was real, and their faces filled with the flies of terror and despair, and they knew that their eyes were to be extinguished, that their eyes were to be mine. The landing, which happened before I could prepare with bent knees, jarred me out of the movie, a cruel shock of reality manifesting as my lower back fucking screamed with pain like it had after those miserable summer workdays when I had unloaded the frozen-meat trucks. There were no partygoers with shining eyes in the backyard. Only Mark was there as a spotter, to keep me from falling, though I probably should've fallen and rolled to disperse the energy of my landing. Live and learn. Despite the back pain, I laughed and took off my mask and shouted and celebrated the leap. Mark and I walked around the bushes back to the front yard, and he kept telling me that my leap was amazing. Everyone else on-set applauded when I reappeared, and I took a bow, partly giddy that I could take a break from being the Thin Kid. Mark, without warning, ran at the bushes, and you could tell he wasn't going to make it because he ran like he was drunk and he slowed down before hitting the trampoline, and yeah, he crashed, and we had to pull him out of the bushes. I headed over to the van parked across the street, because as soon as Melanie was finished staining some of the teen extras with blood, she would help fully suit me up. Everyone else prepped to shoot the party and fleeing partygoers. Dan jogged over to me, shook my hand, looked at me side-eyed, shook his head, and said, "Incredible. There's no way you made that jump." I gave him a *Who, me?* smile and shrug. He said, "But you should stop putting yourself on the line for this. It's not worth it." Still full of adrenaline, full of greed for the quickly fading glow of my transcendent moment, I said, "Totally worth it."

I do tell Marlee an abbreviated version of Mark's failed jump, and I add, "I bet if we could watch the scene after my jump, we'd see the mangled shrubs in the shot. Valentina was not pleased, but it was kind of hilarious."

Marlee says, "I wish we could see what Valentina shot for the party scene."

"That was one of the few scenes when I wasn't onscreen that I watched. She shot what was in the screenplay verbatim. You mentioned adding—I think you said *scaffolding*—to the screenplay. Are you planning to show what happens when the Thin Kid crashes the party? A lot of horror fans complain there isn't enough gore, not enough onscreen kills."

"No, I'm sticking with the teens' POV. It's important the viewers know only as much as our three teen characters know. Besides, if we shot that scene, it might look too much like the scene in *Nightmare on Elm Street Part 2* where Freddy crashes the pool party. And—"

"And?"

Marlee pauses to gather her thoughts, then she speaks in careful, measured sentences. "The story will remain set in the early '90s. Like I said earlier, I plan on shooting on film, and even using some cameras from that era if I can get hold of them. But the movie will be coming out, movie gods willing, in the mid-2020s. In the post-school-shooting world this reboot will inhabit, my filming the mass deaths of teens by a teen-monster-slasher created by other disaffected teens strikes me as too close to the blurry line between transgression and exploitation. Not that mass teen deaths aren't part of the formula for so many slasher flicks.

I think the original screenplay being written and filmed six years before Columbine is . . . if not quite prescient, it taps into something terrible burgeoning within the zeitgeist, which makes the not-seeing-the-violence more powerful in a way. I don't know if I'm saying this well. It's difficult to put into words. The difference between screen deaths as entertainment and art, perhaps. And sorry, that's bullshit, too, as come on, *Evil Dead 2* is one of my favorite movies. And people die violently in real life, so they must die violently in our art too.

"So, no, I'm not filming that party scene and I'm not adding any other major scenes, because I want to make *this* movie. What I love about it, as written and as it will be filmed, is that I honestly don't know what it means, that it makes me so uncomfortable but almost joyously so, and it communicates emotions I can't simply describe with words alone."

"Well said," I say. "As Dan our DP was fond of saying, 'It's a fucked-up movie.'"

Marlee laughs, and so do I.

She says, "I'm almost done badgering you. Can you tell me about the last time you saw Valentina?"

I tell her in the briefest, broadest terms about my visit with Valentina.

Marlee asks, "She told you then that she would be releasing scenes and the screenplay?"

"She did," I say. "And she did so hoping that one day someone would remake it. She'd be quite pleased by your planned faithful reboot."

Marlee doesn't acknowledge the compliment as, lost in thought, she stares at some spot above and behind me. After a beat she asks, "Have you reread the screenplay, the one that Valentina released?"

"Yeah, I did, shortly after she first uploaded it, and I've reread it a few times recently to prepare for the pitches."

"The screenplay Valentina released online is what I'm working from. Cleo's family negotiated the option to the rights, as you know, but they did not give us a copy of the script. I'm of the understanding that they have some notebooks she used to sketch out ideas, but they didn't save or have a full screenplay. She wrote it on an old word processor, and there are no digital copies."

I interrupt. "The digital stone age of the early '90s."

"I know, right? I can't even imagine it now. Now, I know you know what Cleo's family had and didn't have in terms of the screenplay, and sorry it took so long to get here, but what I've been working up to asking you is— Did Valentina release the original screenplay that you used?" Before I can answer with a simple "yes," she continues, "Have you noticed any differences—major or minor—between the uploaded screenplay and what you used for the movie?"

"Oh. No, I don't think so. Nothing sticks out in my memory as being changed. But remember, I didn't read the entire screenplay in '93. I was only given the pertinent pages the night before we were to shoot my scenes. According to Valentina, since I wasn't an experienced actor, it was her way of helping me to be in character. I would never know more than what my character did while he was on his journey. Sorry, she never used the word 'journey.' Can you tell I've talked with way too many producers lately? Anyway, I was never given a full copy of the original screenplay, and I only read a handful of the scenes that didn't involve me."

"Did you save any of your sides?"

"No, I didn't. All I have is the mask."

"I wonder how much Valentina changed or added in the years between filming and her passing. Did she mention anything to you about editing the screenplay? I ask because in the comedic scene with the teens walking down the middle of the street and Karson with the chainsaw, the screenplay mentions possible songs to play while they strutted along. One of the songs, 'Connection' by Elastica, didn't come out until 1995. That song couldn't have been included by Cleo." Marlee's eyes are wide and expectant, and she is as infected with the virus of *Horror Movie* as the YouTubers and Redditors who spend their free hours speculating, spelunking, and postulating about the movie and the answers they'll never find. People can't help but want their fiction and its players to be real, and they want their reality to follow the comforting rules and beats of fiction.

I say, "Yeah, I'd been made aware of recent online rumblings about that song and when it was released." I play it cool because I am cool on the subject. Honestly, the truth, as far as I know it, is that Valentina didn't edit much of the screenplay. Not everything is conspiracy. I don't tell Marlee about finding the marked-up screenplay on Valentina's desk. Maybe I should. If I give her that little nugget, it will engender more trust between us. However, the danger of my further validating Marlee's discovery of Valentina's edits might lead her down a rabbit hole into a fruitless and time-consuming search for the original screenplay, the *original* original screenplay, which would delay her movie. I don't want this movie to be delayed. No more delays. It's time to make the thing. It's my job to ensure the film gets made. I am doing my job. I am ready to be him again.

Marlee says, "Occasionally a printed-out script will pop up on eBay purporting to be the original, and I even bought one—okay, two—on a whim. Both were different, had silly add-on scenes that clearly weren't written by Cleo, but the hard proof of their not being the original screenplay was both had the Elastica reference." She pauses, waiting for my response. I don't have one, so she continues, "A minor thing, I know, but with all the camera references and usage of 'we' to stand in for the camera, I spend a lot of time, too much time, wondering how much of what was written was Cleo or Valentina."

To allay her fears, I say, "Beyond cosmetic changes, which I'll allow could certainly be there, I'm confident there's zero difference, storywise, between the released screenplay and what we filmed."

"So, Cleo wrote that aside paragraph in the first act about why she put her hands into her pockets while walking down stairs?"

"Yes. That I remember reading in '93."

"And that unhinged scene in Karson's house? Cleo wrote that?" she asks with a little self-effacing chuckle.

"Oh, hell yeah, she wrote that. The morning of the shoot, I held up the sides, fanned out the pages, and said, 'Seriously?' She laughed a mock-villain laugh and rubbed her hands together fiendishly. It was no doubt the longest sides I'd received. We shot a crazy amount of takes to get that scene, especially given its length and that it was one long mostly static shot. More than ten takes. Maybe twenty. Fuck, maybe more."

"Why so many for that one scene?"

"Maybe she wanted Karson and me to have experienced the . . . the heaviness and gruelingness—is that a word? I'm going with it—of the big wait that the viewers would experience. I can't remember if anyone pushed back on the number of takes. We just kept doing it over and over, and it was like, Okay, this is what we do now, and we'll be doing it forever. It's funny, in general, what I remember from the set I remember in great and terrible detail, but also, there's a lot I forget. After a certain point in the filming, I only remember the filming. I only remember the movie and seeing the movie through the mask's eyes. I don't know. It's all weird. But I do remember they had to peel me out of my costume after we were done with that scene."

There's a pause and we both look at our watches. I can't tell if Marlee is disappointed or excited, or exhausted, by our conversation. Regardless, it's time for me to go. Marlee mentions a call that she has to jump on soon. After an exchange of pleasantries, of *looking foward to working with you's*, she leads me out front, where the eager sun and heat are waiting for us. She thanks me for coming all the way up to her place, and I thank her for hosting our meeting.

At the edge of her driveway, I ask, "Will there be enough money for hedge trimming this time around? I still can't get over that budget number, and that this grim, fucked-up movie is going to get remade using the original screenplay."

She says, "You mean rebooted."

"I'm not complaining, mind you, but it doesn't make sense."

"You're right. It doesn't. It seemed like the longest of long shots when I pitched it. But I don't know what to tell you. I told them I wanted to make this movie and there was no other way to really make it, and they went for it." She shrugs and shakes her head. "They went for it enthusiastically."

I say, "It's almost like this is preordained." Above us, the Southern California sky, blue and impossible. I spread my arms. "The stars have finally aligned."

THEN: THE CONVENTION PART 2

16

After Hat Guy asked to look at my hand, his two friends whispered *Stop it* and *Don't be a dick for once*. Their pleas brightened the wattage of his self-satisfied smile.

I said, "That's not on the pricing menu," and hid my hands behind my back. This was me being mysterious. Given the chatter online, I was surprised it had taken this long for someone with an utter lack of tact to show up and want to inspect my pinky.

"I'll pay. Secret off-menu item, yeah?" Hat Guy said, and crossed his arms over his chest. This guy. He was meant to be a slasher victim, the kind we root for to die and die horribly.

His friends stood behind him, but that wasn't a metaphorical gesture. They were trying to hide their embarrassed faces. One of them said, "Sorry. He's always the asshole."

I said, "You'll pay, huh?" I briefly considered saying something ominous about people being too quick to say *I'll pay* before the full price is known. Instead, I added, "Forty bucks."

"Worth it. Um, do you take Venmo?"

"No. Secret off-menu item is cash only."

Hat Guy sighed. It was so hard being him. He had to borrow a twenty from one of his friends, but, eventually, he dropped two twenties on the table.

Keeping my right hand behind my back, I flourished my left hand and waggled my fingers. I said, "Nothing up my sleeve," and snatched up the two twenties.

Any semblance of cool tough guy gone, Hat Guy lunged for the twenties but he was too slow. He yelled, "You know I was paying for the right pinky! I knew you're a fraud! A scam artist!" He swiped a tantrum hand across my photo stacks, messing them up, like a game of fifty-two pickup with a deck of cards.

His outburst brought over one of the convention's burly security guards. I told the guard that it was okay, that I could handle it, but he stuck around. Hat Guy's friends set to fixing my photo piles. The celebrity room quieted to a hush. Jason and the other celebs froze in mid-autograph or mid–photo pose to gawk at my table. Nightmare Scribe had a little notebook out, and I would have to talk to him later about this scene not making it into one of his shitty books. This scene would be going into my own shitty audiobook. And thanks again for listening. Tell your friends.

Hat Guy and I weren't done playing, though. Especially since he started it.

I said, "All right. What's got you so hot and bothered to see my pinky?"

Hat Guy deflated a bit, likely sensing that I had the, well, upper hand, as he summarized the online conspiracy about my pinky *not* being missing. He used broken, incomplete sentences, and more "likes" and "ums" than a preschooler, so allow me to clean it up for him. He said that I did not lose half my pinky on-set while filming a scene. None of the actors or crew ever publicly verified that the accident had happened, and that included court testimony. He asked why wouldn't the lawyers bring up my losing a pinky to aid the case of negligence, of the set not being safe? He said no one could find the medical records of my injury, which was, of course, ludicrous as medical records are confidential. The most damning evidence were photos of me leaving the courthouse after the wrongful-death suit was settled, and in those out-of-focus, somewhat-distant pictures (that's me editorializing, sorry) you can see a blurry but presumably full pinky on my right hand. Hat Guy at this point held up his phone to show me and everyone else the photo. He didn't hold it up very long. He flicked to another photo that was supposedly of me in the early 2000s.

I laughed and said, "That guy isn't me. I was way more handsome." If the room wasn't on my side before the joke, they were now. In the photo, the guy who wasn't me was standing behind a bar, holding a comically small beer glass with his pinky out, presumably a parody of proper teatime. The camera's flash was a blue orb in the mirror just over the bartender's right shoulder. He wore a white T-shirt and had that terrible early 2000s George Clooney hairstyle, short hair combed flat and forward. Okay, so the bartender did look a lot like me, or the old me. By the *old me* I mean the *younger me*. I even had that same haircut once upon a time. What were we all thinking back then?

Hat Guy was losing his steam, but he kept going. He claimed the story of my losing half a pinky on-set was just that: a story. A story I promoted in interviews and now I wore an obviously stupid wrap over my healthy finger. His big finish: "That wrap is nothing but a cover for the fabricated story of losing your pinky while filming. And you made up the story so you could make *more* money off your fake celebrity. So, let's see it. Prove me wrong."

By this point my right arm was so far behind my back, I was practically chicken-winging myself. Next door, Jason had backed up against the curtained wall and shamelessly stared at my hidden hand. That fucking guy.

I didn't shout. I projected. "Did everyone get all that?" There was good cheer in my voice, and the gathered audience responded with appreciative laughter. Now I raised both arms over my head, showing off my right hand and the strip of flesh-colored bandage over the top half of my pinky. I made quick work of unwrapping and exposing a green foam piece that made up half of the digit. It was and is the same green of my mask, by the way. When one was going to be caught within the tractor-beam stare of the public eye, one must accessorize.

"Let's give him a *hand*," I said, and politely golf-clapped. Then I made a show of looking at my right hand and flexing the fingers in and out of a fist. I said, "Have you ever just sat with your hand, flexed the fingers, wiggled them around, and marveled at how they work? All those tendons, muscles, joints, bones, neurons, working in concert. If you stare at your flexing hand long enough, you can believe it's moving on its own, that it's not your hand. Try it sometime and imagine you're watching a movie about your hand." I stopped moving my fingers and held my right hand up and open. I added, "Okay, so I only do that when I'm, like, super high."

The crowd was—fine, another pun—in the palm of my hand. Scores of phones were held up and recording, which was against the celebrity-room rules, but no one moved to stop them. I was fine with it. I would shortly be going viral on Twitter, which would lead to invites from the biggest conventions before the weekend was over.

Hat Guy was thoroughly defeated, and security was about to escort him from the premises. But I wasn't done yet.

I leaned across the table and I said, "Before this one, I used life-like prosthetics that were, I don't know, so un-lifelike. I hated them. Then a friend of a friend of a friend 3-D printed this bit for me. I thought I would hate it, too, and that it would be uncomfortable. I was wrong. I love it and it fits so well it's like it's not there. But a weird thing happened after I started wearing it."

I made a fist but left the pinky out, and I tapped the center of his chest with it.

He said, "Are you going to take it off? Show us?"

First, I held my right hand flat, like I was going to cover my heart, and then I did that lame missing-thumb trick with my left hand obscuring the right's bent thumb knuckle and I moved my left thumb back and forth across my right hand. That earned well-deserved groans from the crowd.

I said, "Sorry, couldn't resist," and then I took off the green foam piece—there was a rush of exhales in the crowd—and revealed that, yeah, the upper half of my pinky was gone. I balanced the foam piece on the table, so that it pointed up. "Don't worry, friend, you can still have your conspiracy." I grabbed a Sharpie and personalized a headshot for him as I continued. "Maybe I was born this way. Maybe I lost the bit as a child. But right, your photos, sorry, okay. Well, maybe I lost the pinky half in an accident after the movie filmed. That would be a poetic-justice kind of thing. You can make up whatever accident you'd like. Car door. Lawnmower, though I've never owned one. Maybe I worked odd jobs as a landscaper and had to work with all manner of bitey equipment. Or, wait, wait a minute. I mean, we're just riffing and workshopping here, but how about this? What if I purposefully cut the pinky half off? Amazing, right? Imagine it: I'm home, in a dingy one-bedroom, no, a studio apartment, standing in my kitchen. The overhead light flickers because I'm so broken that I can't be bothered to change the bulbs. Doesn't that set the scene and character? On the counter by the sink full of dishes is a half-empty whiskey bottle. Or half-full if you're an optimist. I have a butcher's knife in my hand because that's all it would take, right? Don't they say our fingers are about as difficult to cut through as a carrot? And I'm standing there, swaying in my drunkenness, gearing up for a little chop-chop. I put my finger on a dirty cutting board—no, straight on the counter, my character probably wouldn't own a cutting board—then there's a lens flare in the blade, and it happens quick, the knife cuts through my finger just above the middle knuckle. There, I sacrificed a chunk of flesh to make more money off my fake celebrity, like you said. Wouldn't that be perfect? And what would that say about me, right? Who would do such a thing?"

I gave him the signed photo. "For your forty bucks. Don't want you leaving empty-handed." Along with my signature, I wrote, *Dear Hat Guy, Be careful. Or I will slice off and eat more than your finger. All the best, the Thin Kid.*

Hat Guy took the photo but only glanced at it. He didn't read my message, at least not while he stood at my table.

I said, "Oh yeah, I mentioned a weird thing that happened." I flexed my hand one more time into a fist. "I've since had doctors look at the new end of my pinky and they said it's fine, but they can't explain why it looks the way it looks." I held out the stub of my pinky toward him and everyone else who had gathered at my table. "Okay, I haven't had a real doctor look at it."

Hat Guy said, "Jesus, is that—what, a tattoo?" I let him fill his own pause. "Another cover, like, what, some kind of plate?"

The scarred, rounded end of my half pinky was bumpy, hard, sharkskin rough, and it was green. The same green as my mask.

I snarled. A snarl is a different kind of smile.

I said, "It grew in like that. Weird, right? Do you want to feel it? Go ahead. I won't bite."

EXT. ANOTHER SUBURBAN STREET - EVENING

Karson runs down the middle of a street we haven't seen before. His footfalls are heavy and fatalistic.

He looks over his shoulder and doesn't see anyone or anything behind him. Each look back throws off his already-sloppy running mechanics, and it slows him down.

He runs in the quicksand of a nightmare.

                                        CUT TO:

EXT. FRONT LAWN, PARTY HOUSE - EVENING

With the Thin Kid in pursuit of Karson, Cleo returns to the lawn and rushes over to Valentina, who is facedown on the grass, arms wrapped around her middle.

                    CLEO
          Valentina! Are you okay?!

Cleo flips her friend over, and Valentina groans and gasps. When she's finally able to speak, her voice is strained.

                    VALENTINA
          I'm . . . okay. Wind knocked . . .
          out of me.

                                        CUT TO:

EXT. ANOTHER SUBURBAN STREET - EVENING

We're a few paces behind Karson now. He's not in shape for this marathon sprint. He is panting and slowing down.

He stops running and walks backward to get a long look at the street behind him. He pushes his dark bangs over his forehead, and his wild, desperate eyes fill the revealed space. His cheeks are tearstained.

He spins back and pushes into an exhausted, resigned jog. He mutters to himself in a childlike, high-pitched voice.

He turns left.

EXT. KARSON'S HOUSE - CONTINUOUS

His house was always the last place he ever wanted to be, but there is no place else for him to go, which is one of the many horrors of this film.

Karson leaps the stairs of his front stoop two at a time, opens the creaky storm door, and tries the knob of the front door. Locked. We knew it would be locked.

He strikes the door with an open hand and yells for his dad. He doesn't wait for him to answer.

Karson curls across the postage-stamp-small front yard to his DRIVEWAY.

He briefly pauses at the mouth of this last tunnel. Tall bushes to the left, his house on the right, and at the end, the hulking, dilapidated GARAGE.

                                                        CUT TO:

EXT. FRONT LAWN, PARTY HOUSE - EVENING

                          CLEO
              He's going after Karson!

Valentina is sitting up now, taking deep, greedy breaths.

                        VALENTINA
              Go. I'll be fine.

                        CLEO
          But --

                      VALENTINA
          Just go! Now. I'll catch up.

Cleo runs across the lawn, to the street, into the night.

                                              CUT TO:

EXT. KARSON'S DRIVEWAY, EVENING — CONTINUOUS

Karson half jogs, half walks the length of claustrophobically narrow driveway.

To his right: the dark portals of his house's WINDOWS. A
light breeze stirs the bushes on his left. The driveway
can't possibly be this long and narrow, can it?

He's as skittish as a hunted, haunted rabbit, looking
wildly around for the dangers that surround him. He's
being funneled into a trap, and there's nothing he can
do about it.

With Karson nearly at the drive's end, the garage door
slowly opens.

The rusted springs calamitously CREAK and CLANG, and he
can't help but stare at the growing dark void between the
rising door and the cracked blacktop.

Karson turns and scurries up the house's rickety BACK
STEPS. He flings open the thin-as-a-fly's-wing SCREEN DOOR.

Behind Karson, the opening garage rumbles like the end of
the world.

He finally opens the wooden back door and slips inside as
we suddenly rush toward him, at him.

INT. KARSON'S HOUSE, FIRST FLOOR - CONTINUOUS

Karson pivots in the cramped MUDROOM, slams the back door
shut. There is no deadbolt, only the small, feckless knob
lock he pinches between his shaking fingers and turns.

He stumbles into the KITCHEN. The lights are out. None of
the lights are on in the house.

                    KARSON
          Dad! DAD! Where are you?!
          I need help! Please!

We follow behind Karson as he breathlessly plods through
the dark first floor.

He turns the lights on in each room after he passes through,
and he throws a glance over his shoulder to see where he
has been. The light doesn't help illuminate what is ahead
of him, though.

Karson continues calling out to his father.

(We've seen the exterior of Karson's house, so we know
there's a second floor, but Karson never gets to or finds
stairs.)

There are pounding FOOTSTEPS on the floor above him, and
his father bellows.

                    DAD (O.S.)
          Karson! Jesus Christ, what?
          What have you done this time?

On this trip through the maze, Karson stumbles into darkened room after darkened room, turning on each one's light
as he passes through.

KARSON
Dad! We need to hide! We
need help! We need to go!

Dad yells incoherently somewhere on the second floor above.

Karson jogs into the next darkened room and when he turns
the light on and looks behind him, we recognize the room as
one he'd been in seconds ago. How can he always be so lost
within his own house?

He pauses in the doorway, the portal to the next room, and
he waits and listens.

FLICK.

The sound of a wall light switch, somewhere behind him. The
room goes dark.

FLICK.

The light turns back on.

Karson doesn't dare look behind him, and he sprints through
room after room, and we follow on his heels. Each room is
dark when he enters, and after another FLICK from behind,
the light turns on.

He blurs through the rooms, lights strobing on and off, and
he cries and calls out to his dad.

The manic circuit ends in the long DINING ROOM.

The overhead fixture, a faux chandelier with candleflame
lightbulbs -- two of the six don't work -- is illuminated.

*This is the first room he has entered in which the light
was already on.*

Karson stops after taking one full step into the dining room. We've been in this room before, earlier that evening, when Karson was joking about being okay walking the streets alone with a chainsaw.

A small -- too small for the room -- stained wooden table huddles in the middle, the chairs pushed in so their backs press against the tabletop.

The only sound is Karson's ragged breaths.

He reaches for the wall switch to his right.

FLICK.

The lights go out.

And at the same time, a rush of footsteps echoes from the floor above, loud enough that the RUNNING and STOMPING emanates from directly above Karson's head.

He stares at the ceiling as the steps and thumps continue and build and impossibly multiply, as though there is a group of people stampeding madly around the second floor.

Dad's angry yells turn into guttural, watery SCREAMS.

There's an unmistakably final THUD of a body crashing to the floor.

The ceiling CREAKS under the weight of a single person's footsteps. Karson's eyes follow the progress across the ceiling. Then somewhere in the house, those creaks and footfalls find the staircase.

Then silence but for Karson's panicked breathing.

There's a doorway arch across the valley of the dining room. Behind the arch, a few feet away, is a plain wall. Dim light shines from the left of the doorway.

Karson stares across the room, at the archway and beyond, waiting for it to be filled.

He waits and we wait.

He doesn't run away. It's not that he's making the typical poor decision that horror-movie victims always make. He's not lost within the maze, either. He knows the way out, but he won't take it because *there is no way out*. We, too, will realize this by the end of the scene.

Like us, Karson needs to see what is going to fill the doorway. He needs to see the inevitability.

The wait is unbearable. Each second is a dare. Will the Thin Kid step into the doorway across the room *now*?

Or *now*?

Or NOW?

We anticipate. The anticipation is the first horror of this *waiting* scene.

We brace and we need the release. This is a horror movie, and horror movies have rules, don't they? We need the fulfilled promise, the validation, even if we think we know what we will see, we still need to see it.

Some of us cover our eyes and peek between fingers. Some of us wince and curl into ourselves. Some of us actively disengage and think about other things because we won't be able to handle what we're going to see. Some of us scoff and act like we've already seen it all.

We've been waiting for the Thin Kid to appear for twenty seconds now.

The same image is on the screen: across the dark dining room, a doorway arch, a molding-adorned/outlined empty space, and beyond that a plain wall and dim light from an offscreen source.

Karson's breathing slows and settles into a normal pattern.

We start to wonder if we're missing something, and instead of the archway, we stare hard into the room's dark corners and along the walls and behind the dining-room table, and even at the ceiling. Something must be there hiding, grinning in the dark, watching us without our knowing, and we're scared again, really scared. But we don't see anything other than the expanse of the room and the empty archway.

For those of us watching this movie in a theater, taking part in a communal, shared viewing, we glance at our friends and then, a bit more carefully, at the strangers near us. Is this movie for real?

We wonder which will happen first: the Thin Kid finally stepping into the archway or a member of the audience shouting something. Who will break or blink first? There is little doubt we're engaged in some sort of battle of wills with the movie. But there isn't a single shout from the audience, not yet. Then some of us half giggle to release the tension and incredulity. A low, collective murmur builds. Finally, one guy yells, "BOO!" from the back of the theater, prompting a few startled screams, and most everyone laughs. Not all of us laugh though. Some of us are still staring at the image, realizing something is happening, not onscreen but to us.

Still, we stare at the same image of the room and the archway across from us. One image of thousands within the movie.

We've been watching and waiting for a full minute, which is an eternity in film time.

Some of us get angry. What kind of art-house pretentious bullshit is this? We heard this was a fucked-up movie, and we want fucked-upness. We want blood, guts, and tits, and there's been barely any so far. Yeah, it was cool when they tortured the Thin Kid and all, but now he's the monster/ slasher/whatever and it's time for some killing. Fucking *kill* the Karson kid already. Kill him!

Some of us wonder pragmatically if perhaps the movie got stuck on this frame. We look closer at the image on the screen attempting to determine if it is frozen. We ask a friend if we need to check with an usher or theater man- ager or the projectionist. Has any of us ever spoken to a projectionist?

Some of us need to pee and have had to for a while. Some of us get up to run to the bathroom despite our friends tell- ing us we're going to miss it. *Miss what?* We can't tell if they're being serious or not, if maybe they're making fun of us again. But fuck it, we can't hold it any longer and we say *excuse me* and sidle down our row, bumping legs, then sprint down the aisle as though the image is chasing us.

Who are we kidding? If anyone watches *this* movie, it'll likely not be in the theater but on a VHS tape. Some of us sitting at home try hitting Pause and Play again to un- freeze the image. Not satisfied, we rewind a few frames to verify the tape is still playing. We might even hit Stop and then Eject, then pop the tape back in and hit Play. Some of us flip open the horizontal flap to look at the tape for a mark or a wrinkle or snag or something. Some of us will turn on the light -- because you can't watch a movie at home with the light on -- leave our couch, look at the VCR like we know how it works and how to fix it. We are confused be- cause the VCR counter's numbers tick and accumulate. This close to the TV screen, we can tell the image isn't static even though nothing is moving. We can just tell, and we back away slowly, eyes on the television, newly afraid. Some of us announce we're going to the bathroom and jokily ask a friend to hit Pause so we don't miss anything, but we say the joke because we're more than a little freaked out and we'll take the image with us into the brightly lit bath-room. Some of us have a totally stoned friend who tries to convince us they see weird shit happening in the shadows.

We have now been waiting for two long minutes.

Some of us in the theater throw popcorn and shout dumb jokes and "This is bullshit," and we're shushed by friends or the strangers around us. Some of us leave. For some of us, leaving is a defense, the righteous anger as an excuse to abandon a movie that has been fucking with our heads. Some of us follow the ones who leave because we always follow even if we want to stay.

Some of us at home talk and joke with our friends and sig-nificant others, and we try to scare them with a sudden out-burst and/or shaking them by the shoulders, and the scared friend tells us to fuck off and punches one of our shoul-ders, and we all laugh, then settle, and the image is still there, as though it's waiting for us. We wordlessly recog-nize the power the image has and our fear of images. Some of us ask, "Are they serious with this?" repeatedly, but some of us say it in a way that means something else. Some of us are legitimately confused and are angry that we are confused because life is already enough of a mind fuck, and why can't our movies be straightforward and simple and delude us with their order? Some of us are terrified and are so glad we're not watching this, whatever it is, by ourselves. Some of us say it's the dumbest movie we've ever seen and some of us say this is the best movie we've ever seen.

Some of us are at home by ourselves. Some of us get bored and read the cover and back flap of the VHS tape box, checking the run time against the glowing green letter clock on the VCR face, and estimate we've been watching the movie for over an hour, maybe an hour and fifteen minutes, and we laugh and wonder if this is the last scene, we won-der if the hacky filmmakers are stretching this out to the end. We wonder why the video-store clerk had *this* as a staff recommendation and decide they're just fucking with people. Why do people always need to fuck with other people?

Some of us are at home by ourselves and we turn on the light and think to ourselves that watching this before we go to bed was a terrible, horrible, no good, bad idea and it would be okay to stop now because we're too tired for this bullshit and we have to get up early for work and maybe we'll finish the movie tomorrow and we call our pet to come sit with us, and some of us might have to get up and go across the room to help our older cat or dog onto the couch, and the pet gives us a confused look -- they never understand the whimsy of the universe -- and we don't hit Stop on the remote.

We have been waiting for three minutes.

This movie is not for everyone. This movie is for some of us.

The movie theater settles into easy conversation, as though we are all gathered for a party. Some of us don't talk or have stopped talking. We again look around at the strangers near us, we observe them as one might observe characters in a movie, and we decide that some of them are more likable than others and we are struck by how odd it is that we're there, gathered in rows in the dark. We wonder who the strangers are, who they really are. We wonder what their lives are like and if they're good people. We wonder what their secrets are. We wonder how many people in the theater have done terrible, unspeakable things. We wonder how many human monsters -- because there are so many, varied kinds -- are in the theater with us. We wonder how many of *them* would happily treat *us* like the Thin Kid. Some of us imagine looking at ourselves through a stranger's eyes. Is this imagined stranger afraid of us? Should they be afraid of us? Who or what is a good person, anyway? What does that mean? Then we look at our friends or our significant others, who talk and have stopped paying cursory attention to the screen. We wonder how well we know them, and without articulating the following in a direct thought, it's as though our loved ones sitting in a large, dark room is a metaphor for how unknowable they really are. We wonder about their secrets. We wonder if they have done terrible things like the teens in the movie have. We wonder how well our friends and loved ones know us. We wonder if they really knew us would they still want to be near us. The movie has now achieved the second horror of this scene. The above thoughts are not pleasant nor productive, and to pull ourselves out of the spiral, we have no choice but to engage with the screen again, despite our exhaustion with it. There's the image, the same image, and we look long and hard at it, and at first, it becomes part of the theater scenery, like looking out a window and recognizing that what we see is somewhere else.

Some of us at home, either alone or ignoring the conversation around us, stare hard at the screen and we concentrate, and we think we can see subtle changes, shadows growing or shrinking, changing contour, and some of us are about to shout out, "I see it!" but we blink and the image resets and nothing has changed. Nothing has changed.

We have been waiting for four minutes.

Some of us are lucky -- which is not a purposefully ironic choice of word, here, though it could easily be argued that knowing the truth or a truth does not equate to good fortune -- to be in a theater or our house or our friend's apartment where everyone quiets down. The scene has gone on long enough to let the children play, to burn off the nervous energy, the briefly shared mirth and flippancy as necessary aspects of the continuing experience, and we're again ready to engage and participate.

Some of us are in rowdy, obstinate spaces, and we block out the noise of what is happening around us, not because we want to but because we must.

We stare at the image and the screen. At this point, some of us have forgotten about Karson and only think of ourselves. Everything is about us, and we realize we are alone even when we're not.

Some of us attempt to analyze the image: the empty archway, the expanse of room between the archway and the viewer, the dim light on the other end, the pool of darkness from which we stare. Some of us attach meaning and metaphor, but there is only one meaning.

Some of us dwell on the instinctual fear that we're going to see this image later that night when we shut the lights off as we make our way to our bedroom. Some of us fear a room in our home will be transformed into this dining room. Some of us fear that when we close our eyes, we'll see this image and we'll see it when we have nightmares, and worst of all we'll see it when we open our eyes in the haunted middle of the night.

We've been staring at the image too long; how can it not continue to be there when the movie ends? Love the movie or hate it, we will never forget it.

Some of us remember that Karson stares at the same image, that it looks back at him as it looks back at us. What does *it* see? We don't want to know what it sees, do we?

Finally, now approaching the five-minute mark of wait time, is the third horror.

We know that Karson is going to die at the end of this scene, whenever it ends. We know that *he* knows he is going to die. Whether some of us think Karson deserves what is going to happen to him, it's going to happen to him anyway. We know that what we're watching, what we're experiencing, is Karson waiting for his death. We know death will eventually -- in one more second, one more minute, one more year -- fill the doorway and stare back at him, as it'll one day stare back at us too.

We know Karson's maze of a house is our house. We know and *feel* the truth -- perhaps more viscerally than we ever have before -- that *we* are going to die. The image we have been staring at is a representation of the temporally fickle death trap that awaits us all. We can stare or look away and pretend it's not there, and it doesn't matter, because death will fill *our* next doorway eventually. For some of us, death's arrival will be totally unexpected, until it's not. Some of us will get tired of waiting for death and some of us will want it to hurry up and finally get here for fuck's sake, all the while still being bone-deep, pants-shitting scared of dying.

Then.

Finally.

The Thin Kid creeps into the archway with his long silhouette. Our eyes are fooled initially into thinking that it's not him but merely a shadow resulting from some change in lighting.

But it is him.

His appearance is almost a relief, a balm, as much as his arrival is frightening, because we'd begun to believe and fear our vigil might never end. We're eager to be rid of this horrible glimpse at the madness of eternity.

For some of us, his appearance is more horrifying than we imagined it could be. No, we don't want to see this. We're sorry we waited patiently for the reward.

The Thin Kid ink-blots out the archway space with his height and length. There's no mistaking the nightmare shape of him.

There's no more waiting.

He walks into the dining room, toward Karson.

> KARSON
> (quavering, broken
> voice)
> *How doth the little crocodile*
> *improve his shining tail.*

Karson recites the poem he never wanted to recite when he was a fourth grader.

Karson does not run. He is done running. Yes, he has given up. There are so many ways to give up.

The Thin Kid moves slowly but fluidly. He doesn't make grand gestures or hunch-walk. We project our fears and night-mares onto him. For each viewer, our memories of his walk across the dining room will be slightly different, per-sonalized. Some of us will remember his walk with a giddy thrill and we'll continue to seek out movies and books that make us feel the same way. Some of us will remember that he is inexorable. He will get us no matter what.

> KARSON (CONT'D)
> *How cheerfully he seems to*
> *grin. How . . .*
> (pauses, swallows hard)
> *. . . spreads his claws.*

The Thin Kid's arms are long enough to reach across the room. Blood, the grease in the universe's gears, drips from the tips of his clawed fingers. His height increases with each step.

As the Thin Kid gets closer, we see more details of his transformation. Shadows fill in the gaps and creases be-tween his scales and plates and the wells of his eyes.

The mask/face is the same, but the mouth is different.

The mouth opens, and it's filled with teeth.

>   KARSON (CONT'D)
>   *Welcomes . . . little fishes in*
>   *with smiling . . . smiling jaws.*

Our view changes, and we are *behind* Karson now. The Thin Kid, partially obscured, towers over him.

The Thin Kid's mouth opens, yawns, stretches, expands, un-hinges.

The Thin Kid doesn't strike like a snake. Instead, he takes his time, wraps his fingers around Karson's arms, then fits his mouth around Karson from the neck down past his left shoulder blade and toward the mid-back.

Then, in mid-bite, Karson in mid-thrash . . .

Note on the above: The "how" of Karson's death will be beyond our special-effects budget, or any budget. I'm leaving in the big chomp description, though, for the *feel* of the scene. Replace with a torn-out throat or a throat slash or whatever you think we can achieve effects-wise.*

>   CUT TO:

17

Yeah, they all see me.

I sit on a low-backed stool and Janelle instructs me to raise my arms up and through the top of the garbage-bag poncho. They pull and adjust the covering so my chest, a few inches above the nipple line, is exposed. They glance at my chest, my face, and away. Sometimes I can't bear to look at myself either.

Janelle steps back to take in the totality of me. Yes, I know, I'm a lot.

I say, "I've probably cut too much weight for the role. It's hell being an over-fifty-year-old teenager."

Janelle says, "Losing weight under the care and supervision of a doctor, I hope."

"Nah. Doctors are judgy and are always so disappointed when I can't produce a health insurance card."

Janelle says, "In case you're *not* joking, before you leave, I'll give you the name and number of a friend who helps new, struggling actors with health insurance stuff."

"Am I new or struggling?"

"Clearly both."

"Fair."

They point at my chest, swirl a pointer finger around, and ask, "Probably a dumb question, but are those scales, like, tattoos?"

I answer in the affirmative without saying yes. "It covered up the cigarette-burn mark first and I liked how it looked, so they multiplied over old acne scars." Scales polka-dot my chest, and really the whole torso and parts of my thighs, too, so I'm maybe 75 percent man, 25 percent monster. Don't double-check my math on that. I add, "Though I kind of regret it now."

I don't know if anyone in the room registers how honest I'm being with my not-fully-honest answer about the "tattoos." But hey, I can't give away the whole story. Sometimes you must work for it, earn it.

The legend of what happened to me and my pinky on-set and my role in Cleo's death combined with my body visuals now laid bare makes for a complicated if not disturbing vista, one they were not expecting. One might think that given my experiences, I would not choose to have done to my body what has been done. One might jump to conclusions about why I made those decisions. *Hey, you do you* doesn't quite cut it as a response in this case. My case.

Janelle says, "They look, wow. I mean, they look like real scales. Like little, hard, ridged scales. The color and shading really makes them pop. 3-D almost. Amazing. Who is your artist?"

I give them a fake name from a place I never lived in. Remember, I'm supposed to be mysterious.

Janelle wants to ask if they can touch one of the scales (why not the cigarette-burn one, right?) thinking they might be able to feel the bumps and ridges. Given they have tattoos as well, they know the etiquette of never asking to touch someone else's ink.

My bald cap goes on first, which is glued at my hairline. I joke that if I lose any of my luscious locks, there will be hell to pay. Janelle quips, "And a hell toupee." With the work started, the mood in the studio returns to its prior breezy chattiness. I like Janelle and the other Feral FX artists. Unlike so many other people in Hollywood, they're not constantly on the make, not scheming how they can use me. They don't ask me questions about meeting Actor X or Director Y. They ask me superficial questions about myself that are easy to answer. I ask them questions too. I've become better at small talk. We briefly chat about music and live shows we've seen until it's time to slather me up. They remind me that I won't be able to see or speak for about ninety minutes. They tell me the emergency hand signal to use if I'm having trouble breathing or if I am about to freak out: two held-up "stop" hands. Another artist gives me a palm-sized spiral notebook with the cover torn off and a green marker, in case I want to write messages, like "Hey, my lower back is itchy" or "The void never blinks and is always hungry."

Janelle and two other artists coat my head and chest with a quick layer of Vaseline, which leaves me feeling all squishy. Then they apply the first of three silicone layers. Janelle shaping and sculpting around my nostrils is a strange sensation, and I fight an urge to mash the back of my hand against my nose and rub it. Each moment of discomfort passes reasonably quickly, and the artists distract me with questions I can answer with a grunt or a thumbs-up. They also describe what they are doing and what is coming next. The weight and pressure in and around my eyes as they apply the silicone is disconcerting, though. I hate eye stuff. But I can handle it, I think. The temperature of the silicone is neither as warm nor as cold as I thought it would be. Most of the time I am surprisingly comfortable. Light filters through the applications and my eyelids so I'm not completely in the dark. The second and third layers are applied, and the silicone hardens, tightens around my throat, pushes against my eyes, and the light, or my closed-eyes sensation of light, dims. Concentrating on their chatter helps me remain composed, and so does writing random messages and fake parking tickets on the notebook paper. Janelle compliments my no-look swooping cursive. I write a follow-up joke: "But I don't know how to write cursive." When they add the plaster wraps over the silicone layers, things go full dark. My head, neck, and shoulders ache with the added weight, and I actively concentrate on breathing through my nostrils while not thinking about how small those two breathing holes are. The plaster smells warm and damp, like a living classroom might smell. Not the dead classroom I spent weeks in. What if they leave me inside the cocoon overnight in what could be an added early scene for the new version of *Horror Movie*? I think about scribbling a picture on the notebook; an attempt to replicate the random drawing of the openmouthed bird (I think it was a bird, maybe it was something else) emerging from a cocoon that I made when I was eight. Maybe the artists sense my tension and unease because they increase their chatter, pat my arm, and tell me I'm doing great. I give a thumbs-up, but I don't feel like I'll ever emerge from this cocoon. Maybe that's for the best. I'm a bug in amber, to be kept in stasis for eons. Or I'm safely buried in the ice of a glacier, but it'll melt because everything is melting, and once I'm set free . . . watch out. I try to arch a lip or twitch an eyelid and I can't. I wonder if there is a way to make the cast with eyeholes as well as nostril-holes. Too late now, obviously. If my eyes were open, then this would've been like wearing another mask. I am used to wearing masks. The plaster hardens and the trapped feeling intensifies. I promise myself that when this and the movie are done and finished, I will escape and roam and cross distances and fill spaces. I promise myself that I will be free.

As I'm about to flash my emergency hands, they tell me they're going to start the process of breaking me out of the cast in three minutes. Someone shouts, "Start the timer!" The artists also tell me it's tradition that they draw on the plaster as they wait the final minutes for it to fully harden. Who am I to get in the way of tradition? I don't quite feel their Sharpies and Magic Markers against my skin, but from down below the strata, I hear the felt tips scratch and scritch the craggy surface. I bet you know what I imagine they're drawing. Someone's phone alarm goes off and finally it's time to excavate me. They start cutting in the back, between my shoulder blades. The scissors chew up and through the plaster seam that splits the middle of my head. After some tugging and wrestling, the plaster pops off. I still can't see, but light returns. Next, it's the silicone's turn to be cut, and this part goes quicker, and I move my face and as I wriggle and peel the silicone away it stretches my skin and takes some stray body hairs with it. Leaving pieces of myself behind is part of the bargain, has always been part of the bargain.

I'm given a towel for a cursory wipe-down and there's a shower on the premises that I'll be able to use before I leave. I linger in the chair though.

Janelle peers into the mold and doesn't say anything. Neither do the other artists, one of whom sends a hand inside and quickly retracts it.

I ask, "What is it?"

Janelle says, "It came out great, but, um, the chest part isn't smooth. Your scale tattoos are there, indented, outlined in the mold. That never happens."

They bring the mold over, my newly shed skin. I could say something like, *Well, things changed in the cocoon. What did you expect?* But that would sound goofy. A clunky line from a bad horror movie.

I could make up some bullshit about my fake-named tattoo artist doing some subtle scarification to make those scales bubble up, make them *pop*, as Janelle said earlier.

But I don't.

THEN: VALENTINA'S HOUSE PART 2

18

The trunk closed like a movie slate's black-and-white-striped arm.

Action.

This wasn't the same suburban neighborhood in which we originally filmed, but it looked the same through the mask's eyeholes. I walked, squishing across the mud, to the front door. My body vibrated with the fear that I was not up to this, the fear that this was above and beyond my capability, which was not the same as the fear of failure. Failure meant you should've succeeded but you didn't. I didn't let myself inside until my hands stopped shaking.

Have you ever worn a mask, really worn one for a significant length of time? The best way, the only way, to acclimate to the discomfort of having your head enveloped and the disorientation that accompanies your winnowed field of vision is to learn another way of being. I don't mean that in a multilevel-marketing self-help scam way, though by all means, make your friends and coworkers buy my audiobook to facilitate your ascension to the next plane of self-actualized mindfulness. With the mask layered over your face, allow yourself, what you think of as your *self*, to sink, to recede. Then the mask will step forward and show you a new way to breathe.

I opened the front door and walked through the house, leaving footprints behind that someone would have to wipe away. Valentina's house was not a maze. I already knew my way around. I walked, neither confidently nor sheepishly, into the living room turned hospice. Because Valentina didn't say anything when she saw me, I flowed with the current to the wooden chair, and I sat down across from her.

Her expression was blank, slack, another mask, but her eyes found mine even though they were hidden. One corner of her chapped upper lip was snagged on a tooth. I chose to believe she had been smiling while I was gone, and the lip had stuck.

I wanted to tell her that it was okay, that it was me, not the Thin Kid. But the mask was on, which meant the no-talking rules were in place. The longer we sat in silence, the more I knew this was a mistake, yet another in a series of terrible mistakes. But maybe it wasn't too late. If I took off my mask, I could stop everything else from happening. Choice being real and an illusion at the same time is a horror. It's all a wonderful, sublime horror.

Moments before peeling my mask away—I swear I was going to—Valentina stood up and looked down at me. Her tongue freed her snagged lip, and she said, "Come on. Let's do this."

I stood. She looped a dried twig of an arm around mine. This was not an act of affection or her being desperate for physical contact. Our linked arms were a follow-me command. She pulled and led, and we shuffled to her office. I was afraid again, and I would've pulled away from her if I were stronger. I'm sorry that I wasn't.

Valentina flicked on the ceiling light. The office walls were painted red. I hadn't noticed that before. I don't know if that is an important detail or not. Maybe the walls had been a different color when my mask was off. I followed her to the rolling chair by her desk. She released my arm and sat down. A puff of air escaped, as though she'd been holding her breath.

She said, "Stand behind my chair. Right behind it. Put your hands on the headrest."

I did as she asked. I imagined becoming a statue, a memento, a memory from her brief film life turned artifact, like a projector on a shelf, not exactly forgotten but not exactly remembered, and I would remain in her office for days and nights until the end, her end.

Valentina moved the computer mouse. The dual screens exploded with light and sound. I flinched. She opened her web browser, logged on to her YouTube account, and uploaded a file named "CigaretteCigarette." A swirling colored circle spun while the file uploaded. From somewhere behind the mask, I smiled at her using the same word twice in the file name. It had to be a reference to a Smithereens song. She and I had discussed the band when we were in college during one of those nights at Hugo's. How many nights were there? The number both increases and decreases in my memory. I had liked the band more than she had, because they were too poppy for her, but she had admitted that she liked the one song and the line about a cigarette burning up time. And maybe for the last time, I ached to stop being the Thin Kid, to be who I used to be, as much as I never liked him, so, if nothing else, she and I could talk about the song and everything else and anything else from the burnt-up time of our previous lives.

I stood there silently as she uploaded two more videos. We did not watch them. I would watch the scenes later by myself. The uploads of the screenplay as plain text and as a downloadable PDF and still photos to her blog and website went much quicker. Then she sprinkled links to everything in a slew of horror message boards and fledgling social media accounts. And that was it. The spores were released.

Valentina clambered out of her chair, not without struggle. She again entwined her arm with mine. She said, "We're going upstairs."

We walked out of the office. The staircase to the second floor was adjacent to the front door. The treads weren't wide enough for us to walk side by side. She wouldn't let go of my arm and she turned and slowly side-stepped up the staircase. I had to duck to avoid the first floor's ceiling at the edge of the first of two landings. We rested at the top of the staircase once we reached the second floor so she could catch her breath. Across a narrow hallway was Valentina's bedroom, or what she had used as a bedroom prior to relocating downstairs. The floorboards creaked under my weight as we stepped across the hall and into the room.

The unlit bedroom was compact, low-ceilinged, and Spartanly furnished with a twin-sized bed huddled in the corner to our right. Along the wall across from the entrance and under the eave-slanted plaster ceiling were a dresser and hope chest, their tops frosted with dust.

Valentina pointed at the bed, or the narrow space below the bed, and released my arm. I started bending toward the floor and made it onto my knees when Valentina stopped me, grabbed my arm again. She said, "No, you can't fit under there. Lie on top of the bed. It'll have to do."

I lay face-up atop the covers. Valentina pulled down the window shades. She said, "Pretend you're under the bed," then left the room, and shut the door behind her.

With the door latched closed, the darkness was initially near total but my eyes soon adjusted and I could make out the shapes of things. I chose to stare at the ceiling. Through the wood and plaster I heard Valentina breathing heavily from the hallway.

Valentina knocked twice on the door to ensure I was still paying attention to her. She told me how she was going to help me build more legend and lore into the making of the movie. She told me what we were going to do next. A swell of nausea jellied my legs, and a weak groan bubbled up with my rising bile. To keep from puking, I focused on memorizing her plan's details as though they were the lines I never got to speak on-camera. Then she opened the door.

Valentina didn't have to lead me by the arm anymore. I followed her downstairs and back to the living room. She retrieved one of her prescription bottles from the end table and then we walked to the small kitchen that, with its oak cabinets and white tile counter-tops, seemed to be stuck in the '90s, décor-wise. Pushed up against the wall to our right was a round table with four chairs, one of the chairs pinned between the table and wall. A dark blue tablecloth covered the table's top. Valentina pulled out a chair, the one with its back to the rest of the house, and she told me to sit. I sat.

At the sink, she filled a tall glass with cold water and a squat tea-cup with hot water and set both on the table with the prescription bottle. Viewed through the distorting lens of the orange plastic, the white pills were as fat as cotton balls. Next, Valentina rummaged through drawers until she found a plastic straw. She brought that to the table, along with three kitchen hand towels that had been hanging on the oven's door handle. The towels were red, white, and blue. Then she gathered a cutting board, thick and gray and scarred with slashes, along with a butcher's knife.

When we were upstairs, she'd explained that one of her pre-scriptions was for twelve-hour time-release OxyContin pills. Her prescription was for a whopping 160 mg per dose. She opened the bottle, shook one pill into her hand. "One for good luck," she said, and popped the pill into her mouth. She took a long sip of water from the tall glass, enough water that her deflated cheeks distended, and she threw her head back twice. After finally swallowing, she exhaled and rested her hands on the table, and said, "Those suckers are hard to get down."

She coaxed a second pill onto her palm, closed the bottle with a practiced twist, and placed the pill on the cutting board. The butcher knife's handle was large and ended in a rounded bulge. She ground and pestled the pill under the handle end until the pill gave up its shape and disintegrated into a sandy pile of white dust and jagged crumbles.

Slightly out of breath, she lifted the cutting board with a trembling hand and dumped the powder into the teacup. She stirred the water with the straw, clockwise then counterclockwise.

"Twelve-hour time release, deactivated," she said.

I picked up the teacup, careful to not spill the cloudy water. I didn't need help needling the straw through the mask's mouth slit. I drank, sucking until the cup was empty, until the straw made those silly slurping noises that were always funny when we were kids. My mouth tasted gritty, filmed, and there was a dusty tang that wasn't wholly unpleasant, and I continued to suck at the insides of my mouth after I removed the straw.

Valentina said, "Let me know as soon as you start feeling it. It shouldn't be long. But also, I don't know how much time we have."

Here I pause the retelling to state the obvious, that I dwell on my last visit with Valentina, and sometimes I try to change my memory of what happened. For example, I'll imagine Valentina and I were making another film, a different one, a short one, an obnoxiously arty, pretentious one, where it's just Valentina and me sitting in her kitchen, and sometimes I'm wearing the mask and sometimes I'm not, and when I'm not wearing the mask you still can't see my face because I don't want you to, and Valentina says, "I don't know how much time we have," and she says it repeatedly, theatrically, changing inflection, changing which word is stressed, until we understand.

She drank her glass of water. I watched. My nausea faded and was replaced by a general sense of calm and wellness. Though to say that the feeling built would be wrong. It was more of an anti-building. My fears and anxieties were dismantled, torn down into harmless components and left to drift and then sink into the ocean of me. I was there too, floating, and the distance between me and what was outside, what was beyond the mask's eyeholes, grew.

I don't remember communicating with Valentina that I had started feeling the effects of the drug, but at some point, Valentina left her chair and stood next to me. She lifted my right hand off the table. Her hand was cold and all joints and bones. She folded my fingers into a fist but left my pinky out, extended. The blue kitchen towel was spread over my lap. The cutting board's end lined up with the table's end in front of me. She staged my hand so that my pinky was pressed flat against the cutting board and the rest of my hand was below it, the backs of my fisted fingers pressed against the table's arced outer lip.

Valentina picked up the butcher knife, the blade as long as her forearm, and said, "Don't move. Please."

I was floating but moored.

She pressed her thighs against the table, the table quaked, my inner waters rippled, but my hand remained where it was. I would not move it. It was a stone jetty, able to withstand storms for generations. She leaned over the table with the knife, one hand gripping the chunky handle, the other hand's palm on the back of the blade. She hovered the knife between the two upper knuckles. She expelled three orderly breaths, and as she carefully lowered the knife, she curled her torso over it, behind it, to give it the gift of her weight. Her lips split and showed off her gritted teeth, a stone wall behind which she screamed, and then she pressed down. There was momentary resistance to the gathered forces, and blood blossomed at the blade and skin line. The pain was initially a pressure, one reporting from a distant but approaching front. A single heroic moment was all the pinky could muster, however, as it was weak—others have famously observed the flesh was weak—and I was somewhere else and I couldn't protect that part of me, any part of me. The pinky acquiesced. The blade passed through with an audible *chunk* into the cutting board. The pressure pain quickly became a fire, a conflagration at the end of my finger, a gout of flames and blood. High-pitched squeals came out of the mask. I could pretend it wasn't me making those sounds. Valentina dropped the knife onto the table, gasped, as though surprised. She draped the white kitchen towel over my hand and pressed against the bleeding pinky stump, but she didn't press hard, having already spent her strength. The fire at the end of my finger quickly used most of the oxygen and settled into smoldering coals, hot enough to melt iron. She lifted the towel away to look, to see, which was a mistake, because there was more blood, and the severed bit remained stubbornly attached by a web-thin piece of skin. Valentina convulsed with dry heaves, but to her credit, she finished the job with a quick flick of the knife before pivoting to the sink and retching into its basin. I sloppily wrapped my hand in the wet towel. The blood on the cutting board beaded and shimmied like freed mercury. The blood spreading on the tablecloth was an oil spill, an environmental disaster. I gathered the severed bit of pinky with my left hand, protecting it in a closed fist. It was warm in my palm. My brain tried to make it wiggle. I don't think it did.

Valentina returned from the sink composed, or maybe she had shut herself off. She tightly wrapped my hand in the red kitchen towel and kept it in place with two strips of duct tape. I didn't see where the duct tape had come from. I stood up from the chair, a little unsteady, but confident that I wouldn't fall. I was done falling for now. The safe feeling returned because the pain dimmed, was being held behind a fortified barrier. The worst was over. There would be a worst thing to happen again, but that would be so much later, and I would deal with it then.

Valentina rinsed the knife in the sink. She balled up the cutting board and two other kitchen towels within the tablecloth and threw the blob into the trash. She sprayed and wiped down the kitchen table and just like that, everything was clean. Everything was done.

Valentina placed a hand on my lower back and gave me a gentle push out of the kitchen. I thought she was going to bring me back to the office and store me in a corner so I could be the artifact again, but she went back to the living room, and I didn't follow her because I wasn't supposed to. I assumed she climbed into the pull-out couch bed because the frame's springs creaked and groaned.

If I was telling a story, if I was making this up, I would tell you she said, "Goodbye," or more befitting her humor and personality, "Break a leg." Valentina didn't have any last words for me, and she left me alone.

I floated out of the house and to my car on autopilot, the same autopilot that would bring me to a hospital. I luxuriated in the driver's seat as though I had achieved transcendence by the simple act of sitting. Then I remembered the job wasn't done. It wasn't an anxiety-inducing thought. It was just another task, a harmless item to check off the to-do list, and once completed it would ensure continued inner peace.

My mask was still on, and the severed pinky bit was clutched in my fist. I opened the hand, showing off its ostentatious number of fingers. The pinky bit looked so small but also flawlessly designed, beautiful. Beautiful because it had come from me. I had grown it, like a piece of fruit. The flesh wasn't weak. It was divine.

I lovingly placed the half pinky on a thigh, and I tugged and folded up the base of my mask until my mouth was exposed. The rush of cool air was not a pleasure, but something to be tolerated. I already missed the safety and warmth of the mask. I put the finger piece into my mouth, careful to keep it away from my teeth. My teeth could not be trusted. They were always stupid with want, with the desire to render and chew. With the half pinky on the bed of my tongue, I pressed it up, fitting it into my palate, and it fit like it belonged there instead of at the end of my finger. I tasted copper and salt, and I didn't like it. As a final curiosity, my brain asked the removed half pinky to move again. I don't know if it would've changed anything if it had moved.

I swallowed because it was in the script. My throat was dry, too dry, and rebelling against my wishes, it gripped the half pinky. The mass was stuck, lodged, and I couldn't breathe but there was no panic. I had a solution.

I rolled the mask back down. My mouth fitted into and became the Thin Kid's mouth. My throat instantly expanded and distended not only to accommodate the pinky but wide enough so I could swallow the world.

EXT. SUBURBAN STREET, EVENING - CONTINUOUS

Cleo runs down the street. She is alone.

Her running motion is fluid, confident, as though she could run like that all night if necessary.

EXT. KARSON'S HOUSE - CONTINUOUS

Cleo stops running in front of Karson's house, at the mouth of his driveway.

At the far end is the garage, its wide door flipped fully open. Another mouth, another maw, she can't help but stare into it. It's less a deer-in-headlights stare than maybe one of fascination and longing.

We're afraid for Cleo, but we're also afraid of what she might do, what she might show us.

> CLEO
> (hesitates to call
> out, has seen enough
> horror movies to know
> it would be a mistake,
> but she yells his name
> anyway)
> Karson?

The Thin Kid steps into view, presumably having just exited the house, and he stands in front of the garage.

He holds what's left of Karson's body. He carries it like it was the *practice mannequin* that Karson brought to the abandoned school.

Once fully seen, the Thin Kid casually tosses the body into the garage.

Given a final, brief momentum, Karson loudly smashes into GARBAGE BINS and empty PAINT CANS, his landing unseen within the darkness of the garage.

Cleo tents her hands over her mouth and nose until the noises from inside the garage stop. She is crying but not sobbing uncontrollably.

The Thin Kid remains at the far end of the driveway.

> CLEO
> (whispers)
> Come on. My turn.

The Thin Kid stalks toward Cleo.

She waits a beat, or two, maybe even a third, and it's that third beat that's pushing it, makes us think *What is she doing?* and *Is she just going to stand there and take it like Karson did?*

Then, thankfully, she runs.

EXT. SUBURBAN STREET – CONTINUOUS

Cleo half runs, half walks. Her lack of sprinting speed is not because of exhaustion. She's making sure that the Thin Kid follows her.

The HOUSES they pass distract the Thin Kid. He's drawn to the WINDOW LIGHTS because that means people are home, and he could go into those houses and do what he was made and trained to do.

He slows and eyes both sides of the street. His eyes are no longer focused on Cleo.

She notices.

                         CLEO
                      (patient,
                    encouraging)
                Come on! Stay with me.

The Thin Kid reluctantly obeys.

Cleo breaks into a full run with her back to the Thin Kid,
trying to be like the rabbit lure goading a greyhound into
an angry sprint.

She goes faster, if only to make him go faster.

EXT. SUBURBAN SIDE STREET - CONTINUOUS

Now they're on the street that leads to the wooded path
that leads to the school. Everything is connected.

Cleo passes one house that has all its lights on. Every
window is a boast and a golden invitation.

The Thin Kid slows his pace to a stutter step. He eyes the
house as though he can see into the future, see all the
blood he'll free into the world, and he breaks off from
Cleo's path and wobbles toward the house.

Someone inside, on the first floor, flutters a CURTAIN
closed and shuts off the light.

That action flips a switch in the Thin Kid. His next step is
a long, purposeful, greedy lunge at that house.

                         CLEO
                      (yelling)
                No! Not yet! Not now!

The Thin Kid doesn't listen, is a missile aimed away
from her.

Cleo screams a familiar slasher victim's SCREAM. It's the same scream from the tape recording, but this one isn't a tape recording. It's a guttural, fear-fueled, my-life-is-over scream. But once the scream is over, Cleo's face is composed, determined.

The Thin Kid stops, like Pavlov's monster.

Cleo screams again.

The Thin Kid turns away from the house and breaks into a sprint at Cleo.

Cleo runs.

They are finally in a real chase.

EXT. FOREST PATH - CONTINUOUS

The pursuit continues through the woods. It's a chase we recognize, one we've seen in a hundred other movies. We allow ourselves to take comfort in the familiar and the inevitable: tramping and crashing through branches and brush, the exerted panting sounds, the alternating shots of the Thin Kid and Cleo along with the perspective shots, seeing both characters onscreen at the same time, the Thin Kid looming right behind her, so tall, so close, and we can't help but ask *How can he not have caught her already?* even if we know he can't catch her yet. Not yet. We're a part of the cat-and-mouse game too.

As he's about to grab her, instead of ducking under a BRANCH that reaches across the path, Cleo runs into it with two hands extended, bending the branch, setting a snare trap without the snare. She pauses a beat before releasing the branch. It recoils into the Thin Kid's head, stunning him, slowing him down so she can rebuild her tenuous lead.

They run and they run and they run.

EXT. ABANDONED SCHOOL - CONTINUOUS

Cleo spills out of the woods first, crouching to fit through the hole in the chain-link fence. Her first steps on the cracked, frost-heaved pavement of the empty lot are on rubber legs. She stumbles but does not fall.

The Thin Kid effortlessly slithers through the gap in the fence and is about five paces behind Cleo and gaining.

Cleo sprints up the cement stairs to the school's propped-open side door.

INT. ABANDONED SCHOOL, FIRST FLOOR - CONTINUOUS

Inside the school, Cleo kicks away the cement chunk used to keep the door propped open and tries to slam the door shut behind her.

The Thin Kid catches the door before it closes.

Cleo pulls hard on the door, trying to close it and trap his clawed fingers in the doorframe, but he's too strong now. He rips the door out of her grasp and throws it open.

Cleo stumbles away and runs down the empty, cavernous hall to the stairs.

The Thin Kid is done running. He walks plenty fast enough.

Cleo climbs the stairs two at a time. Some of us -- probably only a few -- notice she has one hand on the railing, and she pumps her other arm while climbing, or in other words, her hands are not in her pockets as she climbs these stairs.

The movie-watching part of our brains might interpret this as a physical manifestation of her desperation to live, an admission that she's not as in control of what's happening as she and we thought. We are more scared for her because of it.

We're also afraid of what Cleo has planned as an endgame.

THEN:
THE END

19

Because we pushed hard in the final weeks, with a few overnighters mixed in, we were going to finish filming on schedule. A minor miracle. Or a medium miracle. Credit to Dan's and Valentina's organizational and leadership skills. The dwindling budgetary reserves were great motivators as well. Having finally completed the night chase scenes we were scheduled to start at 2 P.M. on our last day of filming.

A few days earlier, during a brief meeting after that night's shoot, Cleo insisted that we film the final scene before the penultimate scene. She thought it appropriate we finish filming our movie in the classroom, and then celebrate there. She also pitched the scene flip pragmatically; the staging of the kill effect would take preparation and time, and we wouldn't want to feel rushed to complete that scene to squeeze in the final one. Throughout filming, Cleo had been ever present with her screenplay binder, and usually had offered opinions about the blocking or scheduling only when asked, careful to not step on Valentina's toes. At this meeting, Valentina didn't push back on Cleo's impassioned suggestion that verged on a demand. Valentina trusted her creative partner and best friend implicitly, and she joked that her dream of filming everything in accordance with the story's timeline "had already been killed dead."

Cleo proactively setting the day's schedule was the first of two unusual events leading up to our last day/night on-set. The second was Cleo inviting me to brunch.

I met her at a little diner in North Kingston, which was a thirty-minute drive from the school. It was a Tuesday morning and the place wasn't crowded. The main counter and booths were spotted with gray-haired old-timers having coffee and purposefully burnt toast while reading their newspapers. We were told we could sit anywhere, so we chose the booth in the back.

We'd worked together, closely, for almost five weeks but I'd been safely hidden inside the mask for, essentially, the entirety of that time. I was nervous and didn't know how to act or what to say now that I was supposed to talk. I almost asked her if Valentina had granted us permission to have brunch.

Cleo saved the nonexistent conversation by asking what I was going to order. I said a couple of eggs scrambled, maybe some toast, nothing too heavy. I patted my nonexistent stomach and said that I still had to fit into the suit one last time. I meant it as a joke be-cause it was a joke. Cleo reacted as though she were offended on my behalf.

She said, "Don't take this the wrong way, but you look exhausted, and you've gotten too thin, and to state the obvious, what you've put yourself through physically is too much, way too much." She paused, looked out the window, and shook her head. "I'm sorry."

"Don't be. It's okay." It wasn't okay. The purple bags under my eyes were as big as plums. I'd passed through the previous two weeks in a fog, and I had slept maybe two hours the night before.

Cleo shook her head again. "I don't think it is okay anymore. We're all tired. I'm sure I look like shit too. Not that you look like shit, anyway, forget I said anything. Order whatever you want."

The thing was, she didn't look like shit, didn't look as tired as I felt. Granted, the following is distorted through the lens of mem-ory, as Cleo is doomed to be fixed in my mind. She looked the same as she did when I first met her: impervious and imperial, above (but not thinking she's better than) the proverbial fray, while at the same time, looking like she might get up and run away at any moment.

I ordered the lumberjack breakfast: French toast, eggs, sausage, home fries. She ordered a Greek omelet. The food came out quick and we ate quick too.

I said, "I guess I was hungry."

"Yeah, holy shit, I'm impressed."

Being with Cleo still felt like I was cheating on the movie's rules. I didn't know what to do with my hands now that I couldn't fill them with knife and fork.

Cleo asked, "Do you want something else? We have time, and this is on me, remember."

"You sure? Thank you. Maybe a Coke for the caffeine," I said.

"No coffee, really? Not even tea?"

"No, I hate coffee. I don't like hot beverages. Food is hot and drinks are cold are my eating/drinking rules." I shrugged, admitting I was still a child, the fully grown kind.

"What kind of monster doesn't like coffee?"

The waitress came over and smirked at my Coke request. Cleo and I laughed at the smirk and at me.

I said, "I can't believe this is almost over. I'll never forget this experience."

"I bet."

"And it means I have to find another job again. Ugh."

"You don't have the acting bug now? You aren't going to move to L.A. after this?"

I couldn't tell if she was having fun at my or the movie's expense. "No, probably not," I said. "How about you? What's next?"

Cleo said, "I'm not sure. Every ounce of focus and energy has been on this movie for well over a year now. I haven't allowed myself to think past today, the last day, you know? Maybe I'll sleep for a month and then figure things out."

"Yeah, sleep sounds good. I hardly slept last night after reading the sides. The final one."

Cleo nodded. "The final one."

"Hey, um, can I ask you a question I've been too afraid to ask?"

"Uh-oh. Sure. I think."

"How much of the Cleo in the screenplay is you?"

"She's all me," Cleo said. I saw, more fully, her *I'm going to get up and run away and never be found* look. She added, "And she's not me. *She* played tennis in high school. I was just a nerdy drama kid." Then she laughed loud enough to turn heads in the diner, and she covered her mouth.

I said, "Maybe she needs to hit the Thin Kid with a tennis racquet."

"She totally should. Chekhov's tennis racquet."

"Okay, well, I don't know how to say the rest of it without being blunt," I said, though I couldn't achieve bluntness. I couldn't look at her while I stumbled and fumbled around. "All the stuff about, you know, her hands in her pockets, not actively, what, choosing to die, but, like, welcoming it if it happened. Is, like, that Screenplay Cleo or is that you too?"

"Both." She rubbed her eyes under her glasses, and I tried apologizing, and she cut me off. "No, it's okay, I'm touched you're asking. It's like this: I'm afraid of being someone who could do what the character Cleo does, and I'm afraid of thinking like her, or I'm afraid of thinking like her all the time. I could be wrong, but I think all of us at some point in our lives, especially when we're teenagers, feel like we want to die, and yet, at the same time, we're terrified of it. That's—that's part of the human condition, right?"

The waitress filled a pause with my fizzing soda in a tall, clear plastic cup. I didn't know what to do with her answer, so I got silly. I exaggerated a sip of my drink using the straw, and said, "It's hard to have a serious conversation about the human condition while one of us slurps soda." I belched to punctuate.

"Gross," Cleo said, and rolled her eyes. "She should've put a childproof cap on the top in case you spilled."

"Now I have regrets I didn't ask for one." I sipped again, and then managed some of the bluntness I had promised. "Okay, so, you don't want to die, then?"

"No, not right now."

"Good."

Cleo said, "Look, this movie is not to be taken literally. Valentina and I had an abandoned school and we wanted to make a horror movie using it. I wrote about what scares me, even if I can't fully describe what scares me. What I said a minute ago is only part of what scares me. The screenplay is the full explanation, or exploration. Who was it that said trust your subconscious when writing? That's what I did. There are so many types of horror movies and different ways of approaching them. My favorites are like fever dreams that on the surface defy the logic of our everyday yet, somehow, expose what's really underneath. Those movies are so real—like, too real—and as disturbing as that can be, it feels kind of, I don't know, wonderful."

"Yeah, everyone who sees this movie is going to feel wonderful."

Cleo stuck her tongue out at me. "That's the last time I buy you French toast and a Coke."

"Sorry. I meant that everyone will feel peachy."

"Such a brat," Cleo said, and rummaged through her purse for cash to pay the bill. "I get you're fixated on the Cleo character, but the whole screenplay is me too. Even if Valentina is mostly Valentina and Karson is mostly Karson—his real dad isn't a minotaur, mostly—and the Thin Kid is, well, you get what I'm saying. That's all me too."

"That's what I'm afraid of."

"What?"

"Well, you know Valentina and Karson really well and you used who they are for the story, yeah? You didn't know me at all when you wrote the Thin Kid." I paused because I'd lost the thread already and I wouldn't be able to explain how the weeks in the mask and being in the hotel by myself had changed me. So, I gave her one of my patented jokes/not jokes. "I'm afraid that I'm a figment of your imagination. That you created me."

"Don't blame me. Blame the mask. It's cursed, remember?"

INT. ABANDONED SCHOOL, SECOND FLOOR - CONTINUOUS

Cleo reaches the top of the stairs. Moonlight pours through the large windows behind her. The school could be the ruins of a church or a cathedral. She's out of breath, finally, but has enough left in the tank to sprint down the second-floor hallway.

She doesn't look over her shoulder anymore. She knows he's there.

The Thin Kid crests the stairs next. He's gaining on her.

There's one more door for Cleo to pass through, and as she ducks into the classroom, she doesn't bother closing the door behind her.

INT. ABANDONED SCHOOL, CLASSROOM - CONTINUOUS

We're inside the classroom waiting for her, waiting for them. It feels like we haven't been here for years and it feels like we've never left.

Cleo dashes to the front, to the teacher's desk, atop which is the chainsaw that Karson left behind.

The Thin Kid slowly enters the room, filling it with his new self.

The chainsaw's battered blade reflects the night light filtering through the wall of windows. Cleo lifts the chainsaw from the table, removing the sword from the stone, and yanks the pull cord once, but it doesn't start.

The Thin Kid is closer, and he is bigger and his reach is longer and the expression on his mask is the ageless look of a predator.

He wants Cleo to scream again. He wants her to scream for real.

Cleo fumbles with the chainsaw handle, searching for the
safety to hold down. Finds it, then pulls the cord.

The chainsaw belches a cloud of smoke and ROARS to life.
And it is alive. A dumb, ruinous, ravenous life. Its metal
teeth shout and blur and dance along their ritualistic
loop.

The Thin Kid halts his approach when he's within arm's
reach of Cleo.

They are two points on a circle and they rotate together,
forming their own loop, their own ritual, the bloodied
symbol on the floor between them.

Valentina had us do our little ring-around-the-Rosie take enough
times that we had to refuel the chainsaw.

The room smelled like burnt oil and gasoline. Cracking open
a few windows in the back didn't help any, because it was so hot
and humid despite the late hour. Christ, that chainsaw was so god-
damned loud, we couldn't hear Valentina shouting, "Cut," so she'd
run into our sightline, waving her arms and slashing her throat to
get us to stop.

I grew impatient, and after take nine, I began mimicking her
slashed-throat gesture. Now that the end was near, I wanted it
and I wanted it quickly; a vibe that was shared by most everyone
else. Cleo was the exception, and was her usual helpful, implacable, and kind self. The rest of the cast and crew were short and
snippy with each other. The feeling in the room was not one of
joyous expectancy at the precipice of an improbable goal achieved.
We were on edge, shuddering under the weight of the future we
couldn't see. We sensed calamity and we were about to collectively
lean into it.

For the shots of Cleo and the Thin Kid circling, we left the chain
on despite Dan's safety objections. The first of multiple objections.

Valentina insisted that we needed to see the spinning chain during this initial stand-off, needed to put it in the viewers' minds before the real dance started.

She succeeded in putting the toothy chain in my mind.

> CLEO
> (barely audible, under
> the chainsaw's roar)
> I'm sorry.

She lunges at the Thin Kid and swings the chainsaw horizontally, at his midsection.

He dodges with a nimble step-back, curling his body away from the saw. He rebounds and swipes a clawed hand at Cleo's head, and she ducks.

Their circle broken, they take turns striking, dodging, and parrying.

Their attacks are wild, unpredictable, and their defensive moves are desperate.

One thrust doesn't lead to a counter-swipe or kick. Violence isn't so orderly. Their choreography is chaotic and difficult to follow. It's as though they are tumbling down a hill, entwined as they fight, their movements a blur.

Yet neither makes contact with the other.

There are many close misses, impossibly close.

For as many circle-dance takes as we performed, we did even more for the exhausting fight scene. Maybe if Valentina hadn't insisted on so many takes leading up to the kill, I wouldn't have been as tired, as bleary eyed, as slow to react, or as angry. That's incredibly unfair of me to say, but it's how I want to feel sometimes. No matter how much weight of the blame I can shed, there is always more. I'm being as honest with you as I can be.

Mark removed the chain for the fight scene. The saw sounded different when toothless, and we could tell Valentina hated it without her having to say so. She staged the initial fight takes, directing and detailing our movements for specific shots. She wasn't satisfied with those and then told us to "have at it." She wanted us not to think but act and react.

Between takes, I leaned against a wall because I wasn't supposed to sit while wearing the sweat-filled suit. I didn't drink water through a straw because I didn't want to have to use the bathroom, which was dumb and dangerous because I was most definitely dehydrated. I tried to rest while in my wall-lean and generally ignored the discussion around me. I couldn't tell how it was going, how we were doing.

During our improvised clash, Cleo occasionally brushed one of my arms with the naked blade, got me once in the ribs too, and I imagined the real saw's bite. I aimed my arm swipes at her shoulder's height or lower in case I accidentally hit her. She ducked into one blow, a direct head shot that sent her glasses flying. She kept her feet and her hold on the saw, laughed it off, and with my guard down, she pretend-disemboweled me, stabbing the chainsaw into my stomach.

About halfway through shooting the fight scene, someone, maybe Dan, I don't remember, asked if we had enough footage. It was the kind of question that wasn't rhetorical but asked as if the question was its own answer.

Valentina said, "I need as many shots as you"—she pointed at Cleo and me—"will allow." A funny word, as "allow" implied we had a choice. She added, "The blade looks obviously chainless when it's not being swung around or whenever, you know, you look at it." If we didn't know better, it was almost like she was passive-aggressively asking to put the chain back on. She wasn't asking

that of us, I don't think. For one, Valentina had no problem being direct with what she wanted or what she thought would work
best. Though, I will *allow* that she was speaking for the movie, or
the movie was speaking through her, communicating its desires
and requirements. Maybe that doesn't make sense if you've never
participated in a large collaborative project, and the project's out-
sized, greedy need overtakes any concern for what might be best
for the individual cogs. It's not as farfetched as it sounds, when
you consider, oh, I don't know, patriotism, organized religion, or
corporations-are-people-too capitalism.

Valentina added, "I'll need all the footage I can get to cut something together that looks real."

Before the next take (or was it the next one, or the next?), Cleo
set the chainsaw on the desk and shook out her arms. She whisper-
asked me how I was doing.

I wiggled my clawed hand, meaning *so-so*.

She said, "My arms are going to fall off."

Finally, at a stalemate, Cleo and the Thin Kid unclinch and
step back, rejoining their circle with the symbol on the
floor as the center between them.

Cleo is clearly tiring: her body is hunched, her breaths
are as loud as the chainsaw, which flags lower in her grasp.

The Thin Kid stands as still as a statue, arms slack and at
his side.

Cleo suddenly vaults forward and raises the chainsaw over
her head.

The assault surprises the Thin Kid. He doesn't dodge or
step back. All he can do is reach out and grab her wrists,
bracketing the chainsaw in place, the blade pointed to the
ceiling. The chainsaw is now another sword with a name,

the one that could fall on either of their heads, on any of our heads.

The saw won't choose sides. The saw is neither picky nor discerning.

Cleo screams a new scream, one from the hell of a battlefield, one of our many hells, and the whirring saw falls closer to the Thin Kid's head.

We can't read or know anything from the etched expression of his masked, gargoyled face, but there's something there in his almost shy or embarrassed forward head tilt.

Some of us believe he would be okay with Cleo winning. Whether he is rooting for her or against himself doesn't matter. Some of us don't think about the horror of the reluctant monster and we get mad at the Thin Kid for showing this weakness, for not being the indifferent force of nature we assume evil to be. Some of us think the truth of what kind of monster the Thin Kid has become is somewhere in the vast middle.

With the chainsaw drawbridging toward the Thin Kid's crown, he removes one buttressing hand from Cleo's arms and he backhands her in the right shoulder.

Cleo falls to her left and drops the chainsaw. She slides across the floor and slams into the wall below the chalkboard. Her glasses are gone.

At the same time, the chainsaw clatters to the floor, engine stilled.

The silence in the room is a new character.

The Thin Kid picks up the chainsaw.

Cleo scrambles into a crouch, a runner in the starting blocks.

We know the masked killer, the monster, never speaks. But some of us want him to. Some of us want him to say, "I'm sorry," to mirror what Cleo said when she first started up the saw. Some of us don't know what it is he could possibly say.

They hold their positions for a beat: the Thin Kid standing with the chainsaw, Cleo ready to spring.

Cleo's face without her glasses has become a different mask, or maybe she's been unmasked, finally. Monsters can reveal who we are.

The Thin Kid rips the pull cord and brings the chainsaw back to life. He raises it to a dizzying height over his head. He is not mocking Cleo by parroting how she most recently held the saw; he is honoring her.

Cleo shoots forward, becomes a blur, and maybe on her face, for a moment, we see a snarl. A snarl is a different kind of smile.

It's Cleo's turn to lock arms with the Thin Kid, to hold and prop the chainsaw in the air between them.

Her colliding momentum forces them away from the symbolled floor spot, and they list until they are in front of the teacher's desk.

The Thin Kid, as inevitable as gravity, pushes back.

Cleo's sneakers slide over the warped linoleum until the backs of her legs bump into the desk.

The Thin Kid keeps pushing, and he bends Cleo backward until she's on her back, pressed against the desktop.

The teacher's desk is a sacrificial altar; it always has been.

Spotlighted in an ethereal glow, Cleo's and the Thin Kid's arms remain locked together on the chainsaw.

———

The decision to reattach the chain onto the saw for the climax of the kill scene had been made the week before, a decision made without my input. I'm not saying that I would've voted against the real thing, but I like to think that I would've. They also had agreed that if after the rig was set up and I did a practice run or two with the mannequin in Cleo's place, and Cleo didn't feel safe, we wouldn't go through with it.

The shot was inspired by the notorious kitchen scene in the original 1974 *The Texas Chain Saw Massacre*, which was Cleo's favorite horror movie. The camera was to be positioned behind me and slightly below the height of the desk so the viewer could see some of the length of Cleo's body, but not her head and face. My body would obscure what the camera angle did not hide.

Mark and Dan bolted a steel plate, almost but not quite a foot tall, into the desktop. It was to act as a crude face shield for Cleo. Attached to the plate on the other side was a six-inch-thick block of wood about a foot long. Cleo was to lie on the desk with the right side of her head a few inches away from the plate. She would also wear eye goggles to protect against the flying sawdust and spraying chain oil the shield didn't block. The camera wouldn't see the plate as I leaned over her body and cut the wood on the other side of the plate. To viewers it would appear that I was cutting into Cleo, the effect heightened by the chainsaw's change in pitch as it ate through the wood.

The attached hunk of lumber was longer than necessary for the shot, so I could get in some practice cuts. I'd used a chainsaw one time in my life prior to that night. I'm going to tell that story because it is short, and it'll delay my having to tell you the rest.

A winter nor'easter had knocked down a mostly-dead-already pine tree in our backyard when I was fourteen. We didn't own a chainsaw, so my dad borrowed one from a guy he worked with at the factory. Dad told me the guy's name was Lefty. I asked why he was named Lefty. Dad held up the chainsaw and waggled his eyebrows. I thought it was a funny joke; my mother did not. Given that my father's real nickname was Whoops because of his proclivity to spill, knock into, and drop things, my mother was having mini heart attacks as he too-gleefully hacked at the tree. She and I stood by the back stoop, about twenty feet away, and she wouldn't let me get any closer. Mom wore a winter coat over her pajamas and burned through half a pack of cigarettes. I waited her out though. She went into the house to use the bathroom and I rushed over and begged Dad to let me have a try. The snow around the tree was peppered with holes made by wood shrapnel and stained brown in spots from the chainsaw's exhaust. I slipped my skinny hands into his too-big and warm work gloves, and lifted the idling saw. It felt heavier than me, young Thin Kid that I was. Dad stood behind me and he levered the saw into gear. My arms vibrated and the power was too much, but I giggled because there was joy in the this-could-go-wrong feeling. In thrall and compelled by the saw (remember, in Cleo's screenplay, she described it as being alive) I obeyed and lowered it into the thick trunk, but too quickly and at a bad angle. Once the blade made contact, the saw kicked right back up, like the tree had spit the saw and me out. I probably would've fallen if Dad wasn't standing behind me. Blinking away terror tears, Dad redirected me over to a thin branch so I could make a successful cut. And I did.

The saw we had on-set was smaller and I was now bigger. The costume gloves fit better than my dad's work gloves had. I could work the safety and the pull cord myself despite the claws at the ends of my fingertips. I knew better how to use my weight and where to aim saw entry so there wouldn't be kickback or to lessen the chance of kickback. Seeing was another matter, however. The occluded-eyehole field of vision meant I had to hold my head a certain way to fully see what I was cutting. I didn't let on about the sight issues because . . . well, I don't know. It wasn't that my fear of disappointing everyone was greater than my fear of hurting Cleo. I honestly didn't believe her getting injured was a real possibility once they bolted that steel plate into place. Like everyone else in their early-to-mid-twenties on-set, I believed we were invincible, despite our making a film about vincibility.

My first practice cut took two inches off the end of the wood block. A warm knife through butter, as they say.

Dan asked, "Why is he holding his head like that?" He knew that I wasn't seeing much in this lighting, but even then, he followed the rules. He didn't ask me the question directly. He asked it in that general way so that someone else, probably Valentina, would answer.

And she did, saying, "Let's worry about the acting after he practices."

Mark stepped in and positioned the mannequin on the desk so I could better practice my bend over Cleo's body while making the cut. I made two more cuts, and I took my time. I'd be fine if I took my time; a measure-twice-cut-once approach to horror-movie slashing. I shut the saw down and gave the room a thumbs-up.

A quick and hot conversation bounced around. Dan opened by saying it'd look great on-camera but he didn't like it, and if we went through with the stunt, there would be only one take. Valentina said of course there'd only be one take. Mark seemed spooked, but he had a big, obvious crush on Valentina and would trip over himself backing her whenever he could. He said the shield did its job and ran a hand over the mannequin's face, then rubbed his fingers together, and he never did say if he felt anything. Karson and Mel chimed in, expressing unease and doubts, too, but none of the doubts were posited as lines in the sand. They were the just-to-be-on-record kind of statements. Cleo said she felt safe, felt confident and ready to do this. Dan again asked what I could and couldn't see. Someone suggested cutting out larger eyeholes, since this was going to be our last shot, and we wouldn't need the mask anymore.

Valentina and Cleo balked at cutting the mask. They said I could see fine.

I would've balked at damaging the mask too if I could've. Which I know is a chickenshit thing to say. At that point, what did the rules of my talking/not talking when in the mask mean? Of course I could've said something or done something or refused. But I didn't.

There was more discussion, and I don't remember who said what but none of us admitted we were concerned or scared enough to cancel or alter the shot. We had already jumped and were in the free fall of about a week's worth of cumulative bad decisions. We weren't able to pull the parachute's rip cord because we were mesmerized by the earth rushing up to meet us.

No one believes me when I tell them that the rig and stunt were less dangerous than our collective drive. Dammit, we wanted to finish the movie. All we wanted was that one shot. Cleo included. She wanted that shot more than any of us.

Valentina runs into the classroom and is out of breath.

She does not have a weapon of any kind. We don't know how she is going to stop this. Maybe she can't. Maybe she won't.

Valentina doesn't scramble to the table and grab the Thin Kid and attempt to pull him away.

She wanders into the middle of the classroom, then stops and floats down onto her knees.

Her face is a mask too. Everyone's face is a mask.

Cleo's and the Thin Kid's arms remain locked together on the chainsaw handle.

———

Cleo wasn't pressing the saw away from her body, wasn't holding me away. Her touch was so light I didn't notice it was there.

I focused on the wood side of the steel plate, the plate painted black in case it decided to sneak into the camera's view. And I focused on the blurring chainsaw blade, which, if it dropped or fell now, would plunge into Cleo's chest. The staging of her body on the desk was different than it had been with the mannequin. Her body filled more desktop space and I was more bent over and would have to reach out farther when it came time to make the cut. I didn't want to linger in this position. I would go fast but would not be in a hurry.

Valentina shouted, "Action!"

> VALENTINA
> (shouts, plaintively,
> and after the events of
> this scene, we'll reevaluate
> how this shout
> sounded, what it meant,
> what it means)
> Cleo?!

We don't get lingering close-ups of the Thin Kid's or Cleo's face. We don't get to see her final expression. That's between the Thin Kid and Cleo.

It happens quickly.

Cleo's arms drop. Whether she conceded the battle or gave in to exhaustion will be left up to the viewer.

On film—and I was forced to watch this scene over and over in courtrooms—Cleo initially let go of the chainsaw with one hand, her left hand, and she hid it inside her jeans pocket. That was not in the script.

I hesitated, didn't cut the wood. I couldn't see the movement, but some part of me sensed Cleo working her hand into her pocket. I knew something was off, something was wrong. Then she pulled lightly on the chainsaw, a fish nibbling bait at the end of a line, and the tug was just enough to make the saw waver. I turned my head and looked at her face because she wanted me to.

All I could see through the mask's eyeholes was her face, the face of a talented, kind, strange, eerily intelligent young person, one of two people who had taken over my life for the past five weeks of filming. I barely knew her, and yet, through reading the majority of her screenplay and watching as she acted on-set—when she was, in theory, being someone else—I knew too much about her.

Bent over the table, holding the growling saw, I was me, but I was the Thin Kid too. My character saw the character Cleo, and she had inexplicably done terrible things to me, and I would cut that wood like I was cutting her neck.

I didn't look at Cleo very long, perhaps two seconds of film time, which is very different from two seconds of real time.

The Thin Kid plunges the chainsaw into Cleo's neck and drags it into her upper chest.

The Thin Kid makes one long, deep cut. The saw changes pitch as it bites into a lower, guttural register we feel in our stomachs.

Cleo twitches and vibrates with the saw, and when the Thin Kid wrenches it free, she stops moving.

The Thin Kid does not succumb to a frenzied urge to continue cutting and slashing, to share all her blood with the classroom.

He throws the saw to the floor behind the desk. There's a clattering CLANG, and a pained WHINE from the unsated, dying chainsaw engine.

The Thin Kid stands over Cleo's body. He's weary, tired, perhaps regretful, but not in the way we would be regretful.

He nudges Cleo's leg with a hand.

Some of us see the nudge as warped affection, as though the Thin Kid is a child asking if they're finally done playing the game. Because of the POV, some of us register that we didn't actually *see* the blade penetrate her flesh, and some of us are disappointed by the lack of gore and don't think about anything or anyone else outside ourselves. Some of us think and hope Cleo might pop up, scrabble off the table to grab the chainsaw again, become the slasher for the next movie or the next or the next . . .

Cleo does not move.

She is dead.

I've lived and died, over and over, in those two seconds. Know that I am in no way equating what I went through with Cleo's death. I would not devalue the unfathomable loss of her life. I use the word to describe my experience because there are many ways to die.

How could I possibly explain or communicate what I saw in her expression? I could write something pithy and cheeseball for this fucking audiobook, something that calls back what I wrote before, like the look on Cleo's face was her falling and staring at the earth rushing up to meet her and, in that moment, I became the monster or maybe I always was one.

But I won't. I refuse to describe or detail or decipher or extrapolate meaning from the look on her face. I can't. I don't trust my memory. I don't trust what happened and what has happened since.

It is always there waiting for me, in quiet moments and in loud ones, framed in the eyeholes, because I've been wearing a mask ever since.

Cleo said, "I'm sorry." I heard it, and despite the growling saw, there was a heartbreaking hitch in her voice, the despairing hitch of regret for a future act and its ramifications.

She didn't say it loudly enough for the boom mic Mark held above the desk. Mark was the closest crew member to Cleo and me, and he later testified that he saw Cleo say something quick, something that could've been *I'm sorry* but he couldn't hear it. Maybe technology now exists that could take the audio, erase the chainsaw roar, and pull her words out of the aural abyss, but that tech wasn't available in the mid-'90s.

But I heard it. She said it.

Then Cleo pulled on the saw again. She pulled more forcefully, yanking the chainsaw down, and at the same time, she sat up. Her pulling on the chainsaw and sitting up is clearly visible in the film.

I instinctively bent lower with the levering chainsaw to maintain my balance before I could process what was happening and lift myself and the saw back into position. I was so careful to avoid sudden movements, I didn't lift with enough force. I didn't have time to step back and away or release the safety button. All those instantaneous decisions are not instantaneous; they still take time, they consume time, the kind of time one can only define in a meticulous, frame-by-frame autopsy.

I didn't know or see that Cleo sat up. In my jumbled and confused field of vision, her face grew bigger as it closed the distance between us. What I saw made no sense and was disorienting because it seemed like I was falling into her.

It wouldn't be until however many chaotic minutes later, as Mel peeled the blood-spattered suit off me (and it stuck to me, like it didn't want to come off) and we waited for police to arrive and I was crying and kept saying, "She pulled the saw down," that Mel would tell me Cleo sat up on the desk. Mel said, "She just sat right up."

The chainsaw bit into the right side of Cleo's neck. I don't want to linger here, either. Saying this is not making anything better, not absolving anybody or anyone, including you, the audio reader. My hands, my real ones inside the gloves, felt the chainsaw bite into her skin. I'm no longer afraid of anything except the memory of that saw meeting her neck. Now, listen, there's no question Cleo died by suicide, by forcing the saw into herself—it's all on film and the screenplay is full of suicidal ideation—and her family and the courts begrudgingly agreed. Of course, as I'm sure you're well aware, Valentina and I were still legally and civilly punished for negligence in regard to on-set safety. Anyway, what I am afraid of is remembering or discovering there was a part of me that, for a microsecond, pressed the chainsaw deeper, just a little deeper.

The saw severed Cleo's jugular vein. Blood sprayed my face and arms, and she fell back onto the desk. Before bleeding out she placed her other hand, her right hand, into her jeans pocket. I threw the chainsaw on the floor, behind the desk. There was a terrible, awful silence, and I could see out of only one eye because blood had splashed into the other, and I tried applying pressure to her spurting neck wound, to stanch the blood, which spurted with each weakening heartbeat, and I felt that as well, and her eyelids fluttered, already more than half-closed. Dan caught this part on film too, and in the final frames before he dropped the camera and the film cuts out, I'm the monster and my clawed hands are around her neck.

Others rushed to Cleo, calling her name, and they pushed me away. Dan pressed a towel against her neck, and everyone yelled, argued, was crying, and somehow a decision got made and Valentina, Dan, Karson, and Mark carried Cleo's limp, probably already-dead body away to the van and then to the hospital.

The steel plate and block of wood were stubbornly still attached to the desktop. We had once believed in the make-believe infallibility of that contraption, and that it would keep someone safe from the other thing we were making.

I stood next to the desk, dripping blood, staring at the spot where Cleo's body had been, until Mel grabbed my arm and pulled me away.

The Thin Kid does not nudge Cleo's leg again. He waits and watches her. He would stand there watching forever, if necessary, but Valentina takes him by the arm.

The Thin Kid does a double and triple take. He doesn't know who to look at.

> VALENTINA
> (gentle)
> Come on. Let's go.

Valentina loops one arm through his and slowly leads him away from the desk, from Cleo.

The Thin Kid is reluctant. He stops, turns, and stares at a spot on the floor. Valentina looks too.

The painted and blood-crusted symbol is gone, as though it were never there.

Valentina tugs gently at his elbow, and the Thin Kid obeys. They progress through the classroom, and the Thin Kid looks back at Cleo again, to make sure she's still there, that she'll always be there.

They leave the classroom.

We linger for a moment, long enough to hope for a different ending. But the end has already happened, so we must leave too.

CUT TO:

EXT. SUBURBAN STREET, NIGHT - MINUTES LATER

The Thin Kid and Valentina walk arm in arm down the middle of the street. A funerary march.

We follow to honor who and what has passed.

FADE TO:

INT. VALENTINA'S BEDROOM, NIGHT - MINUTES LATER

While Valentina's bedroom is bigger and cleaner than Cleo's bedroom was, it's a stereotypical teen space.

There are some band and movie POSTERS on the walls, as well as a few of her DRAWINGS and illustrations. One large painting depicts the cross-section of a cut lime, exposing its green inner flesh.

A large CALENDAR hangs on the back of her closed door. All the month's days are neatly x'd out. Maybe today's the last day of the month. Maybe she was supposed to tear off this sheet and move on to the next month and she forgot, or she didn't care anymore, couldn't face x'ing out all the days to come.

Next to her BED is a NIGHTSTAND with a small, shaded LAMP. The lamp is on. It's the only light on in the room.

The door opens and Valentina leads the Thin Kid inside.

Valentina closes the door behind them, releases his arm, and points to her bed.

                    VALENTINA
                 (cool, calm,
                 instructive,
                 as though
                 punctuating a
                 conversation we
                 weren't privy
                 to)
          Under there.

The Thin Kid knows what to do. He crouches to the hardwood
floor on all fours, and crawls to the bed.

The evening's blood has yet to dry on him.

He goes onto his stomach and shimmies into the dark space
under Valentina's bed, slithers until we can no longer see
any part of him.

A bloodstain is left behind on the floor. The random loops
and swirls don't appear to be so random, and while not a
perfect replica, it has enough in common with the SYMBOL
Cleo drew in the classroom that we recognize it. Or is it
that we see what we want to?

Valentina, displaying no signs of our shared recognition,
wipes up the blood with a BATH TOWEL, then pushes the towel
under the bed.

If the towel is a gift, it is accepted.

Valentina climbs into her bed, slides under the covers, and
turns off the light.

We hear her breathing, which quickly falls into a deep
rhythm.

We listen, but we don't watch Valentina as she goes to
sleep.

We look under the bed.

We search, but we can't see the Thin Kid in the darkness even if we know he's there and he'll always be there.

FADE TO BLACK

20

I probably should end the audiobook here, at Cleo's death. The rest of this will likely feel anticlimactic. Or will it? Muahahahaha!

Eh, we'll see. But if we call this the denouement, then artistically speaking, we'll have an excuse.

I wish I had another revelation for you, something like the origin of the mask. I could make something up, like I had somehow gotten wind of Valentina's plan to make a horror movie, I made the mask using goat's blood and an occult-informed mask-making-for-dummies book, and I sent it to her, but that would be a lie. I'm not here to lie to you. Yes, I'm aware that's something a liar would say.

So, you don't get any more info on the mask. You know as much as I know, which is how it should be, frankly. What I have for you here, at the end, is the reboot.

Filming is almost finished. Almost. Shooting the reboot has been a big letdown. Not at all what I imagined it would be. Part of the problem is that I built up in my mind how the filming would go and what the reboot would be and mean, and it was impossible to meet those expectations. To tell the truth, I'm more than a little depressed about the whole thing.

Don't get me wrong, it's going to be a great movie. You're all going to see it. Most of you are really going to like it. You'll thrill to the transgression and spectacle and then you'll participate in the buzz and the Letterboxd and social-media conversation. (I use the word "conversation" as snarkily as possible.) Will the movie be something you take with you, that stays with you, burrows into and lives in a corner inside you? That, I don't know.

The production has been beyond professional and everyone involved is immensely talented and is giving their all. The DP is cool and hardworking but aloof. There's no Mark equivalent here. The actors playing Cleo, Karson, and Valentina are nice. I mean "nice" in the way someone is friendly to you and smiles and manages eye contact for the full two-minute breezy chat about nothing, and then you declare them as being *nice*, as though you really know who they are. So, yeah, they're nice people, but they're not Cleo, Karson, and Valentina. What a dumb, obvious thing to point out. I thought (and maybe hoped) being in the company of the young actors, especially during our scenes, would be like interacting with ghosts and I would be awkward around the new Cleo and new Valentina and at the wrap party I'd get drunk and say to them all the things I didn't and couldn't say to the real Cleo and real Valentina. The new actors are not ghosts—they're barely avatars. They are reminders that this is not the same movie. And Jesus, these actors are so damned young. My heart weeps at the thought that we were ever that young. Instead of sharing in their holy-shit-we're-making-a-big-movie, it-doesn't-get-better-than-this excitement and enthusiasm, I want to tell them that it in fact won't get better than this, that this too will end and maybe even before it's finished. I didn't think I would be such an Eeyore on-set. I miss everyone from the original, and I miss them hard.

At least the new Thin Kid looks the part of a scared rabbit, and he is replicating my acting method. I haven't asked Marlee if she required that he approach my character that way or if he's doing it on his own. The new Thin Kid doesn't speak much or at all when on-set and when we're on location, he spends his downtime in his trailer. Oh, I've made note of when he arrives and leaves his trailer.

I don't know what I was expecting from the reboot. Well, that's not entirely true. I was expecting a sense of fulfillment from having helped shepherd Valentina's and Cleo's vision to completion, finally, after thirty years of disaster, tragedies, sacrifice, disappointments, pain, and some dumb, stubborn hope, perhaps the poisonous kind, growing in the cracks of my heart like grass tendrils sprouting through the pavement. Hell, after thirty fucking years, man, I was expecting an emotional catharsis, an apotheosis. I was expecting meaning-of-life-level kind of stuff, you know? I wasn't expecting boredom and cynicism and vanity (my own, most disappointingly) and hours alone in the commissary or wandering the sets like a B-grade Phantom of the Opera. Maybe there's a chance for apotheosis still.

So, here's the deal. I am not being used very much in the reboot. You'll see. Eventually.

Talk about a resource being wasted!

I have had much less screen time than what Marlee had proposed to me. I don't think she's solely to blame. I don't think she was lying to me about how much she would use me. Would the joke *Don't worry, you'll always be used in Hollywood* be too cheap, too easy a shot?

Maybe when the high ideas and ideals and the screenplay met with the realities of filming and budget and market and studio involvement, adjustments had to be made. I am an adjustment that had to be made.

Maybe I am too differently shaped in comparison to their Thin Kid. He's at least two inches shorter than me. Plus, I'm the Thin Old Kid now and despite my ill-advised crash diet, I still probably outweigh him by twenty or thirty pounds, though it doesn't seem possible I have any more weight to sacrifice for the film. Maybe if I lopped off an arm. With all that in mind, it doesn't make continuity sense for me to swap in and out with him as much as was originally planned.

Maybe Marlee and the producers are turned off by my insistence upon wearing the original mask and not their expensive redesign. I promised them I was not a difficult actor to work with, but maybe I am a little difficult. I can admit that. But it's not like I'm throwing fits over my trailer size (I don't have nor do I want a trailer) or the font on the back of my character chair. I calmly explained my position regarding the original mask and how it would help me help the movie. It isn't that the new mask doesn't look good or isn't designed well. Not at all. The new mask is gorgeous and malleable, able to walk the line between being a mask and looking like a living creature, and you're going to love it when you see it onscreen. But when I wear it, it doesn't work. The new mask doesn't have the soul of the original. I can't be *me* in the new mask.

Maybe after the FX crew discovered my torso scales and the rough plate at the end of my finger nub, the word of my body modifications (for lack of a better term) leaked and spooked the movie's decision-makers, motivated them "to lessen the burden of his on-screen responsibilities," to quote one producer I overheard. I can't help what I've become. I am what I am, I gotta be me, blah blah blah.

The only scene in which I have appeared, so far, is Karson's death scene. It's an important scene, I grant you.

The set for Karson's house, the first floor, anyway, was built on a soundstage on the studio lot. After staging and chatting with the DP about the shot and giving me direction, Marlee ducked into an adjoining room that had a portable monitor. She preferred to watch the action as it unfolded on a screen to better experience how it will look for the viewers. A bell trilled for quiet on the set, then Marlee shouted, "Action." I waited a few extra beats to replicate in miniature the suspense and long build of the screenplay. I stepped into the doorway, to be viewed in silhouette and from across the filmic desert. I menace-walked across the dining room to Karson. At the end of the take, Karson, from behind the camera, was all smiles and told me I was great, so scary. Didn't he know I was going to kill him? Marlee shot the scene again four more times. Five takes. I spent the full morning in the makeup chair for five lousy takes. I mean, Christ, I was just warming up, crawling back into the Thin Kid's headspace. Five takes is a perfect metaphor for the reboot experience thus far. In the last take I walked backward from Karson to the opposite archway, which is an oft-used technique in horror movies: have the actor go backward and then play that bit of film in reverse to make for a creepy, unnatural walk. Like the professional I am, I did the take, but my heart wasn't in it, because the Thin Kid wasn't a specter, he was real, so why would he move like that? The Thin Kid wasn't ethereal and dreamlike, he was unblinking, remorseless inevitability. Eh, what do I know? Anyway, at some point during one of my ambles, they'll cut away and replace me with the other Thin Kid for the kill. They did film the kill as the Thin Kid taking a large bite out of Karson. Kudos to them for the effort. Watching the practical effect in real time was a bit too behind-the-curtain for me. I have a hard time believing the big chomp will look real on film, but everyone on-set seemed pleased with what they shot.

For my part in the scene, Marlee acquiesced to my request, and I wore my original mask, not the new design. You won't be able to see a difference when you watch the movie because of the lighting, but I know you'll be able to tell it's there. You'll be able to feel it.

I'm going to volunteer myself to be in one other scene, the one they're shooting later today. Today, they're filming Cleo's death scene.

I arrived at our main on-location set early. There have been other on-location shoots, but most of them have been handled by the second unit. Today I'm at an elementary school destined for the wrecking ball, north of L.A., up near Bakersfield. Thanks to a controversial budget-override vote, a shiny new academic building has been built in the lot adjacent to the venerable fifty-year-old building. The town will knock down the old school as soon as filming ends and use its footprint for the new school's green space and playground area. Kudos to the location scouts, as the production won't have to worry about cleanup and Humpty-Dumptying things back to the way they were.

When I say I arrived at the location early, what I mean is I didn't leave, or I didn't leave when everyone else did. I was here yesterday, and after the shoot I stayed overnight in the new Thin Kid's trailer. The locked door wasn't locked for me.

The trailer, from what I understand, is a big one. One enters into a small kitchen and sitting area with a wall-mounted flat-screen television and video game console on the dining table. Between the front and the back, the trailer narrows into a hallway with cabinets/storage on one side and a bathroom on the other. The bedroom is in the rear. The bed is a trundle, fold-down type, with a twin-sized mattress.

The bed was just right. Not that I slept much. Don't worry, I didn't mess up his sheets and blankets, I lay on top of them wearing my mask, underwear, and sundry body scales. I wasn't cold and I wasn't warm. My skin itched, but not unpleasantly, so I didn't scratch. Besides, my fingernails were too long, too sharp.

Morning came and went and now it's midafternoon and there are the unmistakable sounds of people stirring outside. The machine of the movie winding up one more time. I crawl and shimmy under the bed. Despite my age and cranky joints and tendons, I can still make myself small enough to fit into the dark spaces.

Right on schedule, the new Thin Kid enters the trailer. He carries sides and a canteen of water. He settles in the front sitting area, and from my vantage, I see parts of one shoulder and the back of his head. He doesn't hum or whistle or read aloud, not that he has any lines, and he doesn't play music on his phone even though he's by himself. The only sounds are the cushion creak when he adjusts his sitting position and the script pages turning. I admire that he doesn't need to fill the empty space with his noise, and it gives me pause. Maybe I could show him. Maybe he could learn.

Eventually he walks into the bedroom, toward me. Christ, he looks like he's thirteen years old, looks like he hasn't ever shaved yet, but in a certain light, his head turned a certain way, he does bear an uncanny resemblance to the young me. Spaghetti legs dangle out from orange shorts, and a baggy plain white T-shirt billows over his narrow chest. Has he been wearing white T-shirts, *my* white T-shirts to set all along and I haven't noticed? Is this shirt a special choice for today? Does he know all I wear are white T-shirts, that it's part of my post–*Horror Movie* uniform? I don't want to sound like an egomaniac, but given his attention to the character details, attention to my original approach to the character, he must know. It doesn't take very long to find online discussion threads about how I wear nothing but white tees to conventions and what it means. Is he wearing it in honor of me, or is this him usurping, engaging in a metaphorical coup of my character? Or is it a total coincidence? The problem when you foolishly think one thing has meaning: you then think everything has meaning. I've yet to say the following in the slew of recent interviews when asked what makes *Horror Movie* so scary: in a movie chock-full of symbol and portent, it all amounts to nothing, to the horror of void. Most of you can't handle that. I don't blame you.

Anyway, I decide to be flattered by the white T-shirt, but ultimately the why of his wearing it doesn't matter. It won't change what is going to happen.

He clambers onto the bed and sits with his legs folded. I can tell he's sitting by how the weight is distributed through the mattress above me. He does deep-breathing exercises and I pattern my own breaths to match his. I match them perfectly.

There's a knock on the trailer door and a call of his name. I won't remember his name and that is how I will choose to honor him.

He leaves, heading for the makeup chair. He'll be back in roughly two and a half hours. Plenty of time for me to get to work.

I crawl out from under the bed and walk to the cramped mini hallway, that thin space between the two larger spaces of the trailer. I place small cameras in odd, unexpected places—in a ceiling panel, a corner of the room, perched below the windowsill—so they can record jarring POV shots, ones that walk the line between pulling you out of the movie, of letting your lizard brain know that you are watching a movie, and making you frightened of what you'll see next and how you'll see it.

I dowse a patch of unmarked, unscaled skin stretched over one of my ribs. At the end of my pinky, the one that had a missing piece and a scale plate, the one that grew back overnight, is a sharpened nail. All my fingers are tipped with these razors, but the one at the end of the pinky is the sharpest. I flick and slash the skin on my left side and invite the blood. I set to painting the movie's unaccountable symbol, the one that means everything and means nothing, on the floor in my blood. I'm no artist, but I have been practicing. Once it's completed, I stand with the symbol between my feet and I wait. I wait for the end that I am rewriting.

As a part of his routine, the new Thin Kid returns to the trailer in full costume. Someone holds the door open for him. He struggles inside and whoever holds the door says, "Ten minutes." The new Thin Kid does not acknowledge the time delineation, displaying wisdom beyond his years. He's already in character.

The trailer door shuts and he doesn't see me in the little hallway because I don't want him to yet. He won't see the symbol, either, unless I decide to show it to him. I briefly imagine pressing his severed head against it as his eyelids flutter their last.

I wonder if he'll attempt to return to the bed and continue his breathing exercises or remain in the trailer's front and look at the sides or stand quiet and still like that totem he wants to become.

He reaches for something on the table, and it's the TV remote. He awkwardly paws at the buttons and turns on the screen. It streams some obnoxious gamer's Twitch channel.

An unexpected cue, but a cue nonetheless.

I emerge from the hallway, fully formed. My skin is entirely scaled and plated. There is no mask. The mask is me.

I spin him around so he can see me, and I grab him by the neck, squeeze, and lift him off the floor. His legs kick and his feet flipper briefly, until he passes out or dies. I'm not sure which. The latter would be a mercy. I drop him onto the sitting-area table. He's nothing but a young man, a child, in a rubber-and-latex suit. How could he possibly scare anyone?

I try out my new razor claws and cut and gouge trenches, digging into the dirt, digging through the layers until I find his blood. He stirs, moans, and I wrap a hand around his throat again to silence him. Aware of the ticking clock (fucking hell, I can't tell you how much I hate film people when they use the phrase "ticking clock" as a general, default guideline to plot, but when in Caligula's Rome . . .), I have to rush things a bit. I squeeze hard enough to crush the little cardboard box of his larynx. He can't call out to anyone now. There are choking sounds but they're not significantly louder than the yammering Twitch streamer on the TV.

I grab a shoulder and fold him into a sitting position. His head lolls loose, untracked. He swipes at me with weakening arms, and his rubber claws are no match for my real armor.

My mouth twitches. It wants to open. I strike, burying myself into his throat. The first bites are small ones, teeth-clicking and ratlike. I gnaw through latex. The taste is chemical and powdery until I reach skin and blood, and I bite so quickly I nip my own tongue, but I don't stop. I bite and I root into a different kind of rubber, vein and ligament, and the tough, apple-bite of cartilage. The new Thin Kid's last breath whistles through the new hole I made and into my own throat because I'm swallowing everything. That deliciously warm breath triggers a waterfall of saliva that lubricates my new machinery; elongating teeth, gumline receding to expose even more teeth, my jaw bones popping and releasing from their tracks, and if there's pain it's a different kind of pain that sharpens my focus and resolve, and my mouth drips with want and it unhinges, expands, engulfing his neck and collarbone and upper back, and I fill my mouth and I bite and my teeth click when they meet again.

I want nothing more than to linger and to finish consuming him, but I have to finish something else first. I carry what's left of his body to the bedroom and stuff it under the bed.

My blood-slicked skin is clay under my hands and tongue. I shape and re-form myself to look like the new Thin Kid, or enough like him that no one will see or know the difference. Well, they'll know in an animal-sense kind of way. They'll keep their distance and side-eye me. They'll be afraid of me, afraid of what I've done and who I am without knowing who I am, but they won't say anything. You can always count on people to not have the courage to say anything.

Even if someone recognizes me as not being the new Thin Kid, I don't think it'll matter. I'll convince them that we need to finish the movie. Monsters can be very persuasive.

I finish my pre-scene preparations by licking myself and the table clean of blood. They haven't called for me to come to set yet. I've finished with time to spare. I think it's rather considerate of me to not hold up production.

We'll film the chainsaw scene, which is really where the original movie ended, in my mind. Something has always felt off about Valentina leading the Thin Kid home to her bedroom and hiding him under the bed. I don't think she or Cleo would be upset if I changed the end in keeping with the spirit of the original movie, in the spirit of self-destruction.

After the chainsaw scene, I will go back to the trailer and you will watch me finish consuming the new Thin Kid. I think folks would have loads of fun picking through that carcass for metaphorical and psychological meaning.

Or after the chainsaw scene, I will go on an old-fashioned monster rampage, the kind where no one and nothing is spared. A rampage that will come to your town.

Or after the chainsaw scene, I'll go for a more subtle ending and more postmodern. Something like this: Marlee yells, "That's a wrap," and there's applause on-set, and the applause is for me, and as the crew share hugs and high fives, I slink away, but a camera follows me, and another camera follows the camera following me as I walk out of the school and I walk until I disappear into the woods or submerge myself into the Kern River.

Or, no, I'll walk the streets, and the streets will become more streets, and I'll walk and walk and the cameras will go with me as I walk the earth. The movie won't end. Either sitting at home or in the theater you'll be given a QR code or a link so you can go online and continue to watch me walking the earth, and maybe you'll watch for another ten minutes, or even an hour, and you'll get bored or tired of the gimmick (but it's not a gimmick) and shut it off. Some of you will come back to watch, and watch obsessively, and I'll be there on the screen, walking away, walking toward, walking in the movie that won't end until the end of everything.

Here's the knock on the trailer door and the call for me to come to set.

I haven't decided on the new ending.

I guess you'll have to watch the movie to find out.

ACKNOWLEDGMENTS

Thank you, Lisa, Cole, and Emma, and friends and family, for the support and encouragement that makes this, any of this, possible.

Thank you, Stephen Graham Jones, for randomly suggesting I watch a YouTube video of Walter Chaw and John Darnielle discussing *The Texas Chain Saw Massacre,* which led me down a rabbit hole and at the bottom was this book. So, yeah, thank you, Walter and John.

Thank you, John Langan, for listening to me whinge and whine on our weekly phone calls, and for always offering ideas and *Simpsons* references/jokes, including "No, comma."

Thank you, David Slade, Natasha Kermani, Brea Grant, and Alejandro Brugués, for the calls and emails helping with research and answering my film/set questions.

Thank you, invaluable first readers Natasha, Brea, Alejandro, Josh Winning (go read his creepy, fun take on the horror film, *Burn the Negative*), Stephen Barbara, and Sidney Boker.

Thank you, Jennifer Brehl, for the edits that make me read smarter, and for everything else that you do. Big thanks to everyone at William Morrow and Titan Books, as well.

I fear I am forgetting someone important, and if so, I'm writing this toward the end of my concussion summer (don't ask), so I have an excuse.

Thank you, for reading!